"Wells has a g
and dangerou
flair, and the 1
me up reading
—Dan Stump_, _.._y_ucry "r ue_

"…a seemingly ruthless rancher who protects an extremely small town against a gang of outlaws, and nearly makes the extreme-sacrifice in the process."
—John A. Driscoll

"A heavily holstered tale of the renegade reign of terror over a small town in Wyoming which is taken over by an outlaw gang... Prairie pogrom and most combative."
—*Kirkus Reviews*

DAY OF THE OUTLAW

Lee E. Wells

Black Gat Books • Eureka California

Dedication:
To Jess and Bee Freeman—Friends

DAY OF THE OUTLAW

Published by Black Gat Books
A division of Stark House Press
1315 H Street
Eureka, CA 95501, USA
griffinskye3@sbcglobal.net
www.starkhousepress.com

DAY OF THE OUTLAW
Originally published by Rinehart & Company, Inc., New York,
and copyright © 1955 by Lee E. Wells. Reprinted in paperback
by Dell Books, New York.

ISBN: 979-8-88601-135-7

Cover design by Jeff Vorzimmer, ¡caliente!design, Austin, Texas
Cover art by Robert Crofut
Text design by Mark Shepard, shepgraphics.com
Proofreading by Bill Kelly

First Stark House Press/Black Gat Edition: January 2025

ONE

Winter held the land but its grip was gentle rather than fierce, unusual in the normal run of Wyoming weather. The snows had come, endless days of drifting white, but the storms had not swept out of the Canadian Arctic with their usual deadly fury. The clouds and winds came with an air of apology, as though asking the inhabitants of the scattered ranches and isolated villages to understand that the season had a certain amount of appearance to maintain.

Only once had one of the dreaded "blue northers" appeared over the Snowtip Range, whipping down off the jagged ramparts and sweeping with destructive force upon this wide and almost empty valley. Ranches were buried in deeply drifting snow. The main road and back trails that led to the single community serving this land were all but obliterated. For three days the wind howled, beat itself futilely against the adamant ramparts of the Bitter Peaks Range, then whipped south down the valley, seeking easier conquest elsewhere.

For a few days the valley was paralyzed. Gradually riders bucked the drifts, paths were beaten across the range from ranches to the village of Bitter, and along the main north-south road leading up from Colorado into the lonesome grazing lands stretching eastward from the Green River, life began to move.

The areas about the few ranches were gradually extended in crisscrossed trails until they resembled trenches in the otherwise smooth expanse of white. The main road to the few stores of Bitter was widened by travel, beaten flat and packed hard by hooves. Thin ice glinted on Squaw and Winter Creeks but the Picket

River flowed like a dark snake, its waters a chilled, steel gray.

Travel was never heavy in this valley, even in the best weather. But now that the storm had passed and the sun glistened with blinding brightness on the snow, two riders headed toward Bitter. They rode from the north, two black dots, alien against the walls of snow drifted along the edge of the road. The horses moved as though glad to be released from stable and snowbound corral, eager now to stretch muscles on an easy ride rather than to pit their strength against the huge drifts.

The riders themselves felt this sense of release. They rode erect, swaying easily in the saddle. The great bowl of the sky was a clear washed blue and the sun was a rinsed yellow, warming, but too weak to melt the hard crust of snow that crumbled in a thousand small fragments at each touch of the hooves.

The men wore wide-brimmed hats pulled low to shield their eyes from the million-faceted glitter of the snow. Heavy, fleece-lined coats were unbuttoned but their hands were gloved and they both wore woolly chaps that came down over their high-heeled work boots.

The two men were almost identical in size, both deep-chested, broad-shouldered men who had met the challenge of this grim land and were quietly conquering it. Dan Murdock was the shorter of the two by a scant inch. The tan of summer had faded but his long, flat-planed face was dark and, although he was clean-shaven, the jaws still held a bluish cast. His chin was mallet square and stubborn, offset by wide lips that quirked slightly as though he inwardly smiled at some secret joke. His nose was long and straight, bisecting high cheekbones and brown eyes. He glanced at his companion and spoke in a deep, level voice.

"A new year, a new ambition, Blaise?"

The other man laughed, the sound brittle and empty against the desolate land. Blaise Starrett's pale eyes held hard splinters of light as they swept the white world. He had that way of looking at a man, a horse or a mountain, his lids almost closed as though he hid an inner cynicism, an unbending facet of his personality best kept to himself.

He glanced at the close-looming Bitter Peaks, the distant purple-blue veil of the Snowtips far to the west. He turned to Dan, his head moving in a swift, restless motion. His lips were a tight line and he made a wide sweep with his arm.

"No, Dan, still the old dream." He smiled and some of the hardness left his face so that he became a friendly man. "I'm not like you, wearing out a dream like a pair of jeans. I've learned how to make one last."

Dan shrugged. "Jeans? Or a dream?"

Blaise Starrett gave Dan Murdock a quick, intolerant glance. "Is life always a joke to you?"

"Time to get serious when I'm old," Dan said and pulled off his gloves to fashion a smoke. He shook out tobacco and papers, working fast for the air had a bite to it despite the warming sun. He finished the cigarette and scratched a match against his spur rowel. After he took a deep drag, he added, "You're too serious, Blaise. No man's arms are long enough to go around this valley."

"They are if you squeeze hard enough," Starrett said. He twisted in the saddle and looked once again at the land. "Dan, sometimes you remind me of a hound dog, lean and running but not sure where the hell you're heading."

"You know where you're heading?"

Starrett's horse shied at its shadow and jumped

sideways. The tall man controlled the animal with a quick pressure of his knees, then fell in beside Murdock. His glance was long and searching and it was a moment before he spoke.

"You've been my foreman for five years, but you still don't give much of a damn, do you?"

"Any complaints?" Dan flicked ashes carefully off his smoke. He was a big, lazy-moving man who seemed eternally relaxed.

"You know what I mean," Starrett said, the vague stirrings of a temper beneath his tone. "You ramrod a dozen men and you've done your job. But I still feel you're not behind Star, that's all."

"I'm an easy man to fire," Dan said and dropped his cigarette in the snow. "Is that what you want, Blaise?"

"Damn it, no!" His voice softened. "I want to grow, Dan. I want Star to grow. I want to know if you plan on growing with Star."

"Never make plans," Dan said dryly. "That's why I take time for fun." He laughed, a soft, easy sound that carried in the stillness. "You don't want HC range, Blaise. Hal Crane won't sell. He's told you that before."

Starrett snorted. "He'll sell. Don't forget, Dan, every man has a price."

"You don't want to buy," Dan said bluntly. "You want to steal it for half its worth."

Wheeling his horse, Starrett pulled ahead and blocked Dan. His face was set and angry. "Damn it, that's what I mean! You're either with Star all the way, or against it . . . which?"

Dan crossed his gloved hands on the saddle horn and watched his boss. Finally he sighed.

"You're getting jumpy, Blaise. We've pulled some hard hills together and likely we'll pull a few more. But greed is never pretty in a man."

"So now I'm greedy," Starrett snapped. "I'm greedy

because I want to build up a big spread instead of loaf in the sun and tell windies. That's the difference between us, Dan. It don't take much to make you content."

"Sure," Dan said. "Once you were content with four sections and sixty head. Then it had to be twelve sections and two hundred head. You want the whole valley, Blaise?"

"Maybe I'll get it," Starrett said flatly. "I mean it, Dan . . . make up your mind. Either quit . . . or stand behind me."

Dan's lips pursed. Momentarily he toyed with the idea of quitting, then dismissed it. He had the long past to think about, and a man like Starrett was not easily put aside. Too many things entered into a man's thoughts. Starrett and he had ridden a thousand hills together, seen the wheeligo girls in a dozen trail's end towns, but Starrett was the ambitious one and Dan did not envy him. A man came and went pretty much as he pleased: Dan had done this. Starrett, for old time's sake, had made him foreman five years ago and in his own peculiar way Dan Murdock had appreciated it. He would do this for a friend, because he was a friend . . . and for no other reason.

If he stayed now, he would do so because he liked Starrett, not because he shared the man's ambitions. Dan also knew that he stayed on the Star payroll because of Paula Preston. A man had a chance with a woman when he was a foreman and not a thirty-a-month puncher. He felt even with Starrett, who had also taken a sudden interest in Paula.

Starrett said, "I'm waiting."

Dan's attention came around quickly. "Can't you give a man a little time?" He smiled and Starrett's edginess vanished. "What the hell are we squabbling about?"

"Damned if I know, Dan. I'm jumpy." Starrett racked

his horse around and they moved on. "I don't want a fight with Crane. But I won't duck one, either."

"Then either let Crane alone or pay him a fair price."

"Not a penny more," Starrett said with quiet determination.

"You're talking trouble."

Starrett's lips slowly curled in and pressed. "All right, so it's trouble. It's up to Crane. But I've got to be sure of my own men, every one of them . . . including you. You have to wear my brand all the way."

"I never drew gun wages, Blaise."

Starrett pulled his head about and his pale eyes glittered, then slid away. His voice softened but it did not entirely hide the steel. "There's always a first time. You'll have to decide when."

Dan felt a stirring of irritation, more a feeling of hurt, a sense that Starrett had devalued a friendship, using it as a lever to force a decision. After all these years Starrett knew how Dan thought, what he valued. Dan bit at his lip and blankly watched his horse's ears swivel forward and back. He heard Starrett move impatiently and Dan sighed.

"I'll think it over."

"Don't take too long," Starrett warned. He laughed, suddenly changing the subject but still subtly exerting the pressure of a man's own feelings against himself. "Remember the time you spotted a marked deck they were using against me, Dan? It took both of us to whip the crowd."

He talked on. Dan listened for a moment and then heard only the rhythm of the voice as his thoughts drifted off. Dan sighed, a soft sound that Starrett did not hear. Starrett did not look far down the trail he rode, blinded by this new change that had come over him the last few years. He'd push, he'd pressure, and there'd be resentment, anger. There would eventually be gunsmoke and good men whom Dan knew and liked might die from Star bullets, maybe his own. Dan's eyes clouded. There must be some way to bring Starrett to his senses, some way out of this if he had time to find it. But Starrett would press for a decision and Dan knew it could not long be put off.

They rode the remaining miles in silence, each deep in his own thoughts. Now and then, each would covertly study the other. At last they saw Bitter ahead. Snow camouflaged the village and it was revealed only by the dark, exposed walls of the buildings or the glint of sunlight on glass. Dan looked ahead with a feeling of disappointment, a surprising contrast to the eagerness with which he had started this trip for supplies. Now it was only a dull routine of the workday and even the town looked drab, its buildings crouching half-buried in the snow, fearful of the immensity of valley, mountains and sky that made it insignificant.

They passed Larry Teter's house to the right and Dan rode more erect as they approached Phil Preston's lumberyard. He threw a searching glance at the narrow office window, hopeful of a glimpse of Paula. But he didn't see her.

To the right was Larry's barbershop and undertaking parlor, next the Wyoming Bar, its hitchrack empty, the long pole inches deep in undisturbed snow. He turned his horse with Starrett's toward Frazin's General Store to the left. They reined in and Starrett immediately swung out of the saddle.

Dan remained for a moment, looking back beyond George Gorton's blacksmith shop to the lumberyard, now almost wholly hidden. He had the half-formed hope that Paula might step out into the street. Instead, Clay Majors called and Dan half turned to wave a greeting toward the livery stable across the street.

"Snowed in at Star?" Clay called in his bluff, rich

voice.

"Not much," Dan replied. "Got empty stalls for these crow-baits?"

"What else but empty in this weather?" Clay demanded. "Bring 'em over any time."

Dan nodded and circled the rack, stepped up on the plank sidewalk, the packed snow and thin scum of ice crunching under his boots. He followed Starrett into the store and, once inside, the heat from the pot-bellied stove midway of the big room struck him like a palpable thing. He hastily pulled off his gloves and opened his jacket wider, watching Vic Frazin and his son, Bob, listening to Starrett and nodding. There was always something fawning in the manner of these two men that bothered Dan so that he could never talk to them for long without wanting to walk off. Then he saw Ernine standing behind the notions counter.

"What brings you to town?" she asked. Her voice was low, impersonal. She was but half a head shorter than Dan, a statuesque woman in her middle twenties, made vivid by the shining black hair that framed her olive face. A really beautiful woman, Dan thought, if you could get beyond that wall of ice about her. He tipped back his hat with his thumb.

"Nothing like bucking thirty miles of snow to see the big town." Her smile in reply was a faint lift of the lips, a moment of warmth.

"You took a bad bargain. Dad could warn you about that." She glanced at her father. Her smile remained but with a faint hint of bitterness. She started to speak, but Vic came hurrying down the aisle. Dan could see her withdraw behind the barrier again, as she casually turned away to measure some cloth.

"Well, Dan," Vic said in a hearty voice, "I didn't think you or Blaise would get out in this weather."

"Oh, we made it," Dan's voice clipped. Vic Frazin was short and rotund, his belly accented by his black work apron. His head was round, balding, leaving a fringe of wiry black hair, streaked with white, over each batlike ear. His face was heavily scored, the lines deep in the putty-colored skin. His smile, gold-toothed, was wide and friendly, but the eyes were shrewd and weighing and a man could make his choice as to which he would believe.

Nor was his son, Bob, much better—just younger and less ugly. He too had the putty nose and his eyes shifted or narrowed as though he scented a bargain or a close deal downwind. Both their voices were high-pitched, filled with friendship as false as a hair brand on a dogie. Dan was glad when Starrett joined them and gave the supply order.

Suddenly Dan needed to escape. The Frazins irritated him and, strangely, so did Starrett. His voice filled the room, dominating all of them. He stood tall, sure and confident. He always had, but now Dan saw in it the man's attitude toward the whole valley. His very presence was a pressure and Dan suddenly wanted to escape it. He mumbled something about stabling the horses.

"Better, Dan," Starrett agreed: "We'll stay over 'til morning. No use bucking the snow at night."

Dan stepped outside, buttoning his coat. He paused at the hitchrail and looked toward the lumberyard again but there was no sign of Paula. He turned and looked south beyond the bridge across Winter Creek, his eyes following the dark, empty line of the road into the white distance. Just this side of the bridge stood the old stage station, now used as a community house of sorts whenever an itinerant preacher came through. He and Starrett would probably stay the night there. He heard the muffled clang of Gorton's

sledge on the anvil from behind the closed doors of
the smithy. Dan glanced again toward the lumberyard
and, with a shrug, untied the horses and led them
across the street.

The stable had the good smell of hay and horseflesh,
of old leather and comfortable dust. Clay closed the
doors behind Dan as he led the horses to empty stalls
at the rear. He was stocky and broad with a face like
the animals he kept, brown eyes watery and bulging,
teeth large and yellow.

He walked toward the office with Dan and his deep
voice filled the narrow space between the rows of
stalls. His black vest hung open, revealing a collarless,
smudged shirt. His hands were big and thick, the
fingers stubby and powerful.

"Funny weather we're having. There's a warm wind
coming up. It'll sure make the roads belly deep in
mud." He frowned and shook his head. "A bad winter
. . . can't remember one like it. No good, Dan. Little
snow means little water next summer."

Dan grinned. "Clay, you always hang crepe."

"No," Clay protested. "This chinook wind keeps up
and the snow melts, we'll all be tied down until it
freezes again. You'll see."

"We'll see," Dan agreed and turned to the door. Clay
talked on.

"You'n Blaise come just in time before the mud holed
you up. So did Hal Crane and a couple of his riders."

"Hal's in town?"

"Over at the Wyoming Bar, last I seen. I reckon you'n
Blaise will run into 'em."

"Yes," Dan said slowly. "I guess we will." He smiled
to hide his sudden worry and stepped outside. The
building cast a blue shadow on the snow and he had
to squint his eyes against the reflected glare. A warm
wind touched his face and he saw the slow drip of

water from an icicle at the corner of the building.

He looked at the closed, silent door of the Wyoming Bar, noting idly how the wide verandah made a deep, contrasting shadow on the porch. He shoved his hands in his pockets and pushed away from the building to return to the store. He glimpsed the girl a split second before his shoulder struck her. Her smile changed to a startled O as she staggered, her foot sliding on a patch of packed snow, and she fell toward Dan.

He caught her and her hands gripped his sleeves. Her fingers sank into his arms, held for a long second. She pushed herself away and, with a laugh, adjusted the pert little bonnet on her corn-silk hair. She wore a long, gray coat, trimmed at neck and hem with thin, cheap fur. It and the black, buttoned shoes were marked by snow.

"Dan Murdock," she accused in a throaty voice, "do you always run into people?"

"Looks that way, Vivian." He smiled and took off his hat. Again he felt the impact of Vivian McLear, a strange quality like a powerful magnet, something other men had felt, too. She was not tall, really, but she gave the impression, an effect of the slender, well-developed body that even the coarse, shapeless coat could not conceal. Her face was delicate, the cheeks long and planed, the short nose pert, the lips small but perfectly formed, the upper protruding slightly over the lower.

"In town for long, Dan?" She bent to brush the snow from her coat and her laugh was clear in the winter air.

"Until tomorrow, maybe."

"It's good to see you. You're always in and out, Dan. The town doesn't see much of you."

"Maybe after spring roundup I'll loaf a week."

"Spring." She said it as though she thoughtfully

measured the spread of time. Then she smiled. "Good day, Dan."

Dan watched her go. He suddenly felt the impact of unseen eyes and his head lifted, startled. George Gorton stood in the door of the smithy. He filled the dark recess, his big bullet head thrust forward on his thick neck, solid arms akimbo, powerful hands on his hips. Broad shoulders and deep chest pulled at the cloth of his soiled shirt. He scowled at Dan, low forehead deeply creased, and his short, black hair bristled upward like a stiff, wire brush. His eyes cut away from Dan and followed Vivian.

His scowl vanished as he watched the woman. He nodded eagerly to her friendly wave and continued to stare after her. Dan started across the street to the Frazin store. Instantly Gorton's bullet head swiveled and again Dan saw the angry scowl.

He's in love with her, Dan thought. He had never before given the bear of a man credit for finer human emotions. Not that Dan blamed Gorton, for she was a striking, alluring woman. Dan honestly admitted that he might himself have taken a greater interest had it not been for Paula. No one knew where Vivian had come from, although there were rumors and whispers among the women, for gossip played a major role in the narrow life of the valley.

At this moment, several miles to the south, nine riders pushed doggedly toward Bitter. They rode as a group, bunched, held not only by the narrow channel of the road through the world of deep snow, but also by a common effort and something of a common fear. This fear had steadily lessened, easing off in direct ratio to the miles they put between themselves and the Colorado border.

Even so the fear had not wholly vanished, nor would

it ever in the life of any one of the nine. They were a hard-bitten lot, all but one seemingly cut from a pattern, though there was no real resemblance between them. They all had something of violence held thinly in check, something feral in the eyes squinted against the snow glare. Each man wore belt and gun outside his heavy coat and a rifle rode ready to hand in its scabbard at each saddle. Their broad-brimmed hats were pulled low to minimize the dazzling light.

Now and then one would look back over his shoulder, eyes sweeping the deserted white wilderness, swinging in a wide arc from the silent pinnacles of the Bitter Peaks to the distant, cold and violet line of the Snowtips. Then he would straighten and there would be a momentary softening of the tense, pinched face or stubbed jaw. But alert suspicion never left, as though phantom pursuers lurked just behind, ready to strike when least expected.

A giant of a man rode at the head of the loose cavalcade. Despite his size, his movements were quick and sure. Like the rest, a Colt rode at his hip, clear of the mackinaw. His mount carried four thick pouches, two before and two behind the saddle. Now and then one of his companions would glance at the pouches and his eyes would light in swift pleasure, or he would lick his lips in anticipation.

The man's hat shaded his square face, stone-blocked and thinly covered with skin that stretched tight along the temples, around the corners of the jaws, along the nose and about the rugged chin. His eyes were gray, steady and chill as the winter world about him, just as cruel and merciless.

One of the horsemen spoke and Jack Bruhn slightly turned his head, catching Tex Darrow's long and searching look. Bruhn straightened, his eyes casting

far ahead, face impassive. But, he thought coldly, it's
coming. It was in the cards before we hit that bank
and now, with fifty thousand dollars in the pouches,
Tex will bring it to a head. He wondered, without
emotion, how he would handle it. He had no doubt
that he would. Tex, maybe one or two others would
die, but Jack Bruhn would still ramrod this outfit
when the gunsmoke cleared away.

But Bruhn never crossed bridges until he reached
the river. Right now he cast ahead for a place where
they could hole up. The men rode with more ease now
that the immediate pressure of pursuit was well
behind them. This was the first day they had not
ridden hell-for-leather and Bruhn was grateful for it.
Five years ago, he thought wryly, he would have made
the ride with little thought and few after effects. Now
he was tired and sore. Maybe he was getting too old.
He dismissed the thought and glanced back toward
Shorty Ratner.

Shorty rode slouched in the saddle, twisted to favor
the side that had taken the bullet. Bruhn noticed his
set, bloodless lips, the draw of the jaw and nose to the
pain that must be flooding his body, the feverish glaze
in the watery, blue eyes. Just one lucky shot, Bruhn
thought heavily, and a man's cards run out, his string
breaks. None of them thought the wound too bad at
first, but now Bruhn knew it was serious. They'd have
to hole up soon or leave Shorty stretched out along
the trail somewhere.

Tex had hinted that the wounded man was a threat
to their escape. Bruhn had vetoed the idea of leaving
Shorty, and he knew that he played into Darrow's
hands by doing it. The way Tex argued made sense,
but Bruhn could simply not force himself to give the
final orders that would leave Shorty to face freezing
or a hangnoose. It wasn't Bruhn's way, never had been

. . . and he saw no reason to change now.

A laugh sounded and Bruhn eased his weight in the saddle, glancing back. He caught Denver's whiskery grin and saw the answering smile of the young stripling beside him. Bruhn faced front again, frowning, thinking of Gene Hiatt and wondering if he had been wise in taking on the kid.

Gene Hiatt thought much the same thing, only half listening to Denver Gorce's long, drawn-out joke, hearing the creak of saddle leather, the shuffling whisper of hooves in the snow. None of it seemed real. He rode in a fantasy, and sooner or later he'd wake up and find himself home again.

He saw again the sharp, acid-etched picture of himself holding these very horses while the men robbed the bank. He heard the smash of the shot that got Shorty, heard the roaring reply of the bandit guns as they whipped through the town like a raging tornado and then out into the snow-swept range.

Up to that moment Gene might have cleared himself of the false rustling charges back home. But now he could never remove the outlaw stain. Bitter, angered, feeling he might as well truly wear the owlhoot brand since it had already been slapped on him, he had thrown in with this band. Maybe some youthful idea of adventure had remained when he heard Jack Bruhn and his gang were close at hand and he had ridden to find them.

Now he knew them for what they were . . . nothing glamorous here. Bruhn was cold and adamant, a man who demanded obedience, who thought and planned crookedly. Tex Darrow and Juarez Smith were twisted men with no sense of loyalty or decency. Pace Odlum would smile as he put a bullet between your eyes. Vause and Egan were rat-faced men who reminded Gene of slinking coyotes. Shorty Ratner was not much better. Denver Gorce was the best of the lot but the outlaw strain touched him, making his humor subtly macabre, giving his philosophy a sinister twist, his remarks a distorted value.

The dark thoughts roiled in Gene's brain. He had damned himself. He was beyond the pale, beyond that invisible point where a man could return with hope for life and the future. Now he would always be on the run, feeling that inner core of fear that never leaves the outlaw. Where would it end? A gun-blasting finale that would fling him lifeless in some dark and noisome alley? Long years in jail that would take his youth and his strength? He thought of a rope and a gallows, and could not help the twisting pain in his chest and had to close his eyes tightly against the sharp, torturing thrust of it.

"Hey," Denver said with surprise. Gene hastily looked around. Denver's bearded face was lifted to the sky and he had cuffed back his hat. "Feel that wind?" he demanded. "Warm . . . chinook, sure as hell."

Gene shrugged. "What of it?"

"What of it!" Denver exclaimed, and waved his arm about. "The snow'll melt . . . mud. Roads without a bottom. We'll have to hole up somewhere."

Charley Vause spoke carelessly over his shoulder. "High time, too. One thing for it, no lawman can travel, either."

Denver chuckled. "Ain't it so! If there was a town around, we could sure licker up and raise a little hell after all this running. How'd you like that, Gene?"

Gene forced his smile. "I could rest," he admitted.

"Rest? You crazy! With all the money we got to divvy and you want to rest!"

Denver's laugh sounded flat over the expanse of silent snow and Jack Bruhn looked stolidly around, then straightened and spoke quietly to his horse.

TWO

Starrett was not in the store when Dan returned nor did Vic Frazin know where he had gone. Dan felt certain he was at the Wyoming Bar across the street and he knew that Hal Crane and his riders were also there. He felt a touch of alarm, started to the door, then stopped.

He doubted if Starrett would start anything now, particularly with the odds against him. Starrett never jumped blind. Dan took a handful of crackers from a barrel, bought some cheese from Bob Frazin. He poured a mug of coffee from the pot on the stove and sat down to a makeshift lunch.

He idly watched Vic work with frowning intensity on a ledger at his rolltop desk. Dan wondered lazily if business and the making of a dollar encompassed the whole of Vic's life, its metes and bounds. Ernine counted bolts of cloth behind the dry goods counter.

Dan took a long swig of coffee. He had heard that years ago Ernine had been quite different. Some said she had lost a love, and it was never quite clear whether the man had died or had simply dropped out of her life. Since then she had been courted by a few bold enough to face the challenge of her frozen beauty, but none had lasted long. She was like a sleeper, and some day the right man would come along and wake her up. It would be interesting to see the change, Dan thought, but there was the chance he wouldn't be around.

He arose impatiently and Ernine looked curiously at him, no warmth in the deep brown eyes, one dark brow arched in an unspoken question.

"Not much weight to an ordinary puncher, is there?"

Dan asked impulsively. She showed surprise, then shrugged.

"Depends on who . . . and how you mean it, Dan."

"Take it any way, I guess."

She studied him a moment and he could not be sure but that a faint warmth came to her eyes. "Depends on the man . . . and the girl."

Now Dan blinked in surprise and his gaze sharpened. "You, Ernine? Would you?"

Her shoulders stiffened and he could sense the hardening of her reserve. "I'm particular anyhow, Dan, and no part of the question. Ask someone else."

Dan smiled and walked to the door, buttoning his coat. Ernine studied his broad back, her eyes enigmatic. When he had finally stepped out on the porch and closed the door behind him, she folded her arms, her fingers tightly pressed into her flesh, and looked broodingly at the far wall. Finally she sighed and turned again to the bolts of cloth, checking them with renewed concentration.

Dan paused out on the porch. The snow looked even more watery and the chinook wind seemed stronger. Give it twelve more hours and the valley would be a lake and the land would have no bottom. He glanced to the northwest, knowing that often a heavy storm followed these thawing winds, but the sky was clear and the sun shone as though it never expected to dip below the purple haze of the western peaks.

He considered going to the lumberyard. Not that he could tell Paula his problem, for he had not even hinted yet that he considered marrying her. True, he saw her every time he came to town and he had the hunch that she knew he was close to serious about her. Until now he had been content to let the future shape and build this thing between them. By spring he had hoped to openly court her, but now he could plan on nothing. But maybe seeing her might crystallize his own decision.

He pulled his hat low against the glare of snow and started down the steps to the street. He saw Starrett come out of the Wyoming Bar and Dan stood poised, expecting Blaise to come across the street toward him. But Starrett angled away to the lumberyard. Dan descended the steps, still watching, and he saw Starrett enter the office.

Dan halted, feeling a surge of anger and disappointment. He could not talk to Paula with Starrett in the office. He stood a moment and then, with an impatient turn, slogged across the street to the Wyoming Bar. He saw Phil Preston leave the lumberyard, cross the street. Phil saw Dan and hurried up.

"Well, Dan, glad to see you." Phil was a man in his late fifties, his face almost untouched by wrinkles, his brown eyes alive and sparkling. He extended his hand, nodding back over his shoulder. "Just saw Blaise."

"I know," Dan said and his tone made Phil look sharply at him. He made no other sign but looked up at the sky and removed his hat to let the warm wind touch the thick shock of brown hair, salted at the temples.

"Early thaw, I reckon. Going to be in town the night?"

Dan shrugged, his irritation still spurring him. "I guess so. Depends on Blaise."

"Good." Phil looked back at his office. "Why don't you come to the house for supper? I get lonesome for man talk of an evening."

Dan was pleased but a glance at the blank windows of the office dispelled it. His lips pursed. "Sure I'd be welcome?"

Phil laughed and replaced his hat. "I'd bet on it. The minute I tell Paula, she'll want to cook something special. You'll come?"

Dan smiled, relieved. "I'll be there. Just didn't want to—butt in."

"Six then," Phil nodded.

Dan indicated the Wyoming Bar. "A drink?"

"Not now, Dan, thanks. Want to see Clay Majors about lumber for some stalls. See you tonight."

He nodded and walked on. Dan remained, still smiling. He looked at the lumber office again but could see nothing through the windows. Now it didn't worry him and he felt a minor triumph. Let Blaise talk to her for a few minutes. Then he sobered. How could you draw a man's pay, take his orders, be loyal and still be his rival for the prettiest girl in the Territory?

He stepped up on the porch of the Wyoming Bar, glanced again across the street, sighed, and pushed open the door. The Wyoming Bar was far from magnificent but it served the purpose of drinking place, news emporium, political forum and unofficial men's club. The bar extended along the back wall, the mahogany dully reflecting the light from windows covered by a checkered oil paper. The brass rail was bright in spots, dull green in others. Sawdust covered the floor. Round tables were spaced about the rest of the room, their tops covered in a green cloth, empty and strangely forlorn.

Two men stood in almost the exact center of the bar, their backs to Dan, but there was something familiar in the set of their shoulders. Tommy Rikes polished a glass behind the bar and he looked up as Dan entered.

"Well, Murdock! What brings you to town?"

"Blaise, mostly," Dan answered. He saw Ava Rikes at a table in the corner, touched his hat and nodded pleasantly. Her red lips broke in a smile. Then she returned to her solitaire game.

The men at the bar did not turn but their shoulders

stiffened as Dan approached. Dan glanced in the mirror and recognized two of Hal Crane's riders, Lewis and Claggett. They were nondescript men with thin faces and level, questioning eyes. Dan ordered, then turned to the men.

"Howdy," he said gravely. "Snow bad up your way?"

They were quiet a moment, suspiciously weighing his words, fingering their shot glasses, their distrust a tangible thing. Then Lewis shifted slightly and shrugged.

"Not too bad," he said distantly and the tension eased. Claggett craned beyond Lewis to catch Dan's attention.

"Melting now," he said to show that he, too, would meet Dan's courtesy. Then he straightened and the room was silent except for the clink of glass as Tommy Rikes poured a drink. He placed it before Dan and leaned against the bar.

"Anything new your way, Dan?"

Dan told him the news of the range, Tommy nodding now and then. The HC hands listened but did not join in the conversation. Tommy refilled the HC riders' glasses and Dan morosely watched him, his mind busy with Starrett. Tommy was short and inclined to be pudgy, a basically cheerful man perfectly fitted for his job, dispensing drinks, jokes and gossip. His thin, dark hair was oiled and neatly combed, brushed flat to the crown of his head. He wore a checked vest with a heavy gold watch chain above the white bar apron. A ring flashed on one finger and he laughed in open pleasure at some remark of Lewis'.

Dan looked down at his glass. This wasn't making a decision. He had put a great part of himself into the building of Star, many of his dreams, much of his labor and his thought. Now he must see a good ranch transformed into a gunsmoke spread.

He angrily tossed down the drink, signaled Tommy
for a refill. On the other hand, he could refuse any
part of Starrett's plans. So he would leave Star . . .
and a part of himself for others to use or misuse as
they saw fit. A hell of a thing! His hand dropped to his
gunbelt and he touched some of the looped cartridges.
He jerked his hand away as if already those leaden
slugs sped toward someone he knew. How would it be
to go to Paula marked as the gun-fighting leader of a
gunsmoke crew?

He glanced beyond the far end of the bar and saw
that Ava watched him. She gave him a long, searching
look and then, with a slight move of the head, invited
him to join her. She swept up the solitaire layout as
he sat down.

"Did you lose your best friend?" she asked in her
husky voice. Dan smiled.

"That bad? Just thinking over something."

Ava leaned back. It was said that Tommy met her in
Denver where she sang and danced in a big saloon,
and she carried obvious marks of her past. Her lips
were painted and her cheeks rouged, but even without
these she was a striking woman. Her hair was piled
high in a profusion of small curls and ringlets.

She wore a wine-purple dress, cut low at the neck,
exposing the white shoulders and the slight shadow
where the cleft between her full breasts started. She
dressed boldly and yet it was a part of her. The only
flaws were a slight pout to the lips and a discontent
in the eyes.

"Thinking," she said. She studied her hands and the
emerald she wore on a slim finger beside the broad
gold band of a wedding ring. "I do too much of it."

"Too much?" Dan said in slight surprise. Discontent
showed in the swift cut of her eyes, the slight fold in
the corners of the mouth.

"What else is there to do?" she asked in a weary tone. "Same people, same buildings, same road." Her shoulders lifted, fell. "Same damn' mountains, same valley. You get so you talk to yourself."

Dan looked at Ava and her deep eyes asked for sympathy or an answer. He had no answer. So he only shrugged and she sighed.

"You like it, Dan." It sounded like an accusation.

"It could be better, but give it time. The town will grow as the ranches grow. You'll see."

"At sixty?" she asked without rancor. "You're no help, Dan."

She picked up the cards and shuffled them. Dan watched her moody face with its bold beauty. Tommy had no business bringing her here. She's used to crowds and excitement. She'll blow up someday and leave him.

The door opened and Dan heard a man stomp the snow off his boots. Lewis and Claggett turned, expectant. Dan looked over his shoulder and saw Hal Crane walk to a table and lift a finger to Tommy. Lewis and Claggett joined Crane at the table and Dan could hear the low murmur of their talk. Three men sat at their ease behind him whom he might face with gun and bullet within a few weeks. The thought twisted his lips and Ava saw it.

"It must be bad," she said, card held poised over the table. "I thought I was the only one."

Dan shrugged and Tommy came to the table, hovering over Ava. His face softened as he looked at her.

"Can I get you something, honey?"

"Nothing," she answered shortly. Tommy straightened, hurt and showing it. He realized Dan watched and his perpetual smile returned. The door opened again and Tommy looked up.

"Well! Here's your boss, Dan."

Dan hastily turned. He saw Starrett but his glance quickly moved to Hal Crane and his two riders. They sat very still, watching Starrett with level eyes, their faces suddenly expressionless.

Crane was not a large man but he had a dynamic quality that dominated the larger men beside him. He sat straight, narrow shoulders well back. He had a thin face, accented by a long and pointed nose. His eyes were dark, quick, and now they watched Starrett with a challenge.

Starrett's stride broke when he saw Crane and the two HC men. Dan grew tense. Then Starrett gave them the briefest of nods, his eyes veiling. It was enough. Crane eased slightly in his chair and Dan, too, felt relief. Starrett walked to the bar, grinned at Dan and waved him over.

"Have a drink," Starrett said. "I'd set it up to the house but HC's here."

Dan accepted the glass that Tommy shoved before him. "You sound damn' happy."

Starrett laughed softly. "So I am." He lifted his glass. "Here's to the prettiest girl in Bitter Valley."

Dan lifted his glass, paused. "Mind saying who?"

Starrett considered and then shook his head. "She's too good to be mentioned in a place like this. But you know who I mean."

Dan studied the amber liquid in the glass. Starrett had it bad, but then so did Dan and who was he to blame any man for looking twice at Paula? He knew that Starrett wanted to rowel him about her. It was a part of the man's need to feel important. Dan didn't like it but he calmly lifted his glass.

"To her."

He downed the drink and, without a word, returned to Ava's table. She glanced up, looked sidelong at

Starrett still at the bar and showing his surprise. Ava's eyes cut back to Dan.

"Some drinks don't set well," she said and then gave full attention to her game.

Starrett stood with fingers drumming uncertainly on the bar. Then he glanced at Hal Crane. He hitched at the gunbelt under his coat and walked to the table. The three men looked up, startled. Lewis became suddenly alert and deadly. Claggett sank back so that he could easily reach his gun. Crane stiffened slightly but he remained seated, unmoving, only his eyes glittering. Starrett halted a few feet from the table.

"I want to talk to you." His voice was flat and harsh. Dan started to ease out of his chair and Ava had forgotten her game, sensing the tension in the room. Crane folded his hands on the table.

"Nothing to stop you, Starrett. I'm listening."

"Alone," Starrett snapped and his arrogant glance cut to the two riders. Crane studied Starrett, taking his time.

"Talk?" he asked finally, "or quarrel? There's a difference. I'll listen to one but have no time for the other."

Starrett's lips thinned but he shrugged. "Talk, Crane. A business deal—between you and me."

Crane studied him a moment, then glanced at his men and gave a slight nod toward the bar. Lewis and Claggett walked to the bar, making an elaborate business of eyeing Starrett.

But he paid no attention. He pulled out a chair and sat down across the table from Crane. He leaned forward and spoke in a low tone, quickly and earnestly. Crane listened and then slowly leaned forward himself.

Dan realized he had mistaken the motive for Starrett's action His right hand dropped from the holster and he caught Ava's slight smile. With a muttered apology, he swept up his hat and walked to the door.

The sun behind the building sent long, golden shafts onto the street, casting the shadow of the saloon ahead onto the slushy snow that had a strange, steely look though it was soft and melting. Water stood everywhere.

Dan glanced toward the lumberyard and his eyes lighted in surprise. Paula Preston came out the, door, his first glimpse of her since he had ridden into town. He hastily stepped down from the saloon porch and his boots sprayed gouts of water and slush as he crossed the street.

She saw Dan, stopped. Even some distance away he could see her warm smile. It made his heart beat faster. He came up and removed his hat.

"I'd hoped to see you before this, Dan," she said with a smile that took the sting from her words. He could only look at her for a moment, eyes level and filled with something that caused hers to deepen as she looked away.

She was not tall, the crown of her head coming to Dan's chin. A gray, fur-lined cap framed the oval face and heightened the clear color of her skin. Her forehead was high and Dan had a glimpse of the dark brown hair that looked bronze when the sun caught it just right. Her nose was short, straight, with just a delightful hint of snub. Her lips were full and her smile could warm a man at the sight of it. Her eyes were a soft green, changeable, sometimes sea colored, again as clear and blue as the sky.

Her coat was tightly buttoned and her slender, gloved hand grasped it close at the neck. Her high-buttoned shoes snugged to trim, small feet. The hem of the dark skirt beneath the coat had picked up some of the clinging snow. Dan suddenly realized that he stared. He caught himself.

"I'm sure sorry, Paula. I started over and then I saw Blaise go in. I didn't know . . . that is . . . I thought maybe...." He floundered badly. She smiled and rescued him.

"Oh, Blaise. Yes, he called. But I looked for you." She smiled again. "Dad says you're coming for supper. That will make up for it."

"I wouldn't miss it," he said quietly. "It makes the trip worthwhile."

"We'll expect you—my father and I."

He nodded and she walked away, following the narrow track beaten in the snow that led to the woodshed beyond the lumberyard, curved about that small structure and led directly to the kitchen door of the Preston home. Dan remained where she had left him, hat still in his hand, watching the slender figure silhouetted against the snow, noting the grace of her walk, the set of the small, proud shoulders.

He finally sighed, content, and put on his hat. A glance at the lengthening shadows told him it was about four, and even this early there was a sense of the waning of the short winter day. He turned to the Wyoming Bar.

He stepped inside, his glance sweeping the room. Ava still played solitaire. Lewis and Claggett stood at the bar, talking quietly to Tommy Rikes.

Starrett and Crane sat at the table, both leaning over it, deep in low conversation. Dan saw that Starrett's jaw was set. Dan walked to the bar.

"One for the weather?" Tommy asked. Dan nodded.

He toyed with the glass, drank half of it, then turned to rest his elbows on the bar, one heel hooked in the rail below. Lewis ordered another drink and Dan heard Tommy stir busily behind him. Suddenly Starrett jumped up and his chair teetered back, caught against the one behind it. His voice filled the room, harsh and angry.

"You're a damned fool, Crane. You think you can force me to raise the price."

Crane's voice cut like a whip. "Who's a fool? I'm not! You think you can drive me out if I don't take your sniveling offer."

He stood up, finger tips resting lightly on the table, leaning toward Starrett, his lips thin, eyes hard. His voice was low, even, yet filled with a savage fury.

"Get this straight, Starrett. HC can take care of itself. We don't need your money, we can use that range ourselves. Don't think you can force us out. Star's not big enough and never will be. If you want to prove it, just start any time you're ready. We can handle anything you can throw at us and send it back with interest. Want to try it?"

Dan froze. Ava's head jerked up and for once her eyes were alight. Tommy stood quite still behind the bar and Dan could hear the quick, ragged suck of his breath.

Starrett stood rigid, his handsome face a dull red, his pale eyes ablaze. Dan knew Starrett would take the challenge here and now and he forgot everything but his ingrained loyalty to Star. He looked from the corners of his eyes at the two HC men. He came slowly up on the balls of his feet, tensed and poised. He could drop his glass, slash down for his gun and cover the two men at the first move from Starrett.

Silence held, built up. Starrett's hand clenched, opened, clenched again. Crane's hands hung lightly at his side, the right just below his holstered Colt. HC or Star would be without a boss, one or the other, in a matter of seconds.

The front door opened and men crowded in. Dan's

eyes cut to them, recognized none. One was a granite, square-faced man with an air of quiet authority. The rest crowded in behind him, a motley, hardcase crew. One of them, with the bland face of a teenage kid, recognized the signs of an incipient fight and his pale eyes lighted in a strange, unholy pleasure. Another man, pinch-eyed and stubble-cheeked, glanced at the big man with a twisted grin. His voice carried clearly.

"Looks like we stepped into something, Jack. Maybe we can see how amateurs sling a Colt. Me, I'll bet on the gent behind the table."

Dan heard Tommy Rikes' frightened gasp, the explosive gust of his breath, and then his voice sounded, filled with awe and fear.

"Jack Bruhn and his gang! God! We're in for it!"

THREE

Starrett and Crane were held by surprise at this unexpected threat that had materialized from nowhere. Tommy Rikes' voice carried clearly, and now the nine strangers had an aura of evil and danger. They eased into the big room, forming a crude half circle with their leader in the center. They offered no threat and yet they placed themselves so that they commanded every man, every move. They watched, keen-eyed and alert, like a pack of wolves.

The man who had spoken so easily walked to a table, sat on its edge, one leg swinging free. His hand remained close to his gun. The smooth-faced, handsome kid looked at Starrett and Crane with pale, avid eyes, his red lips slightly parted. That man, Dan knew, would like to see a killing.

A third edged up to the table and this one was swarthy of skin, his black hair coarse and untrimmed, and his smoky blue eyes betrayed his mixed nationality. Dan looked at the leader, who showed no expression on the square, commanding face. Dan saw the man just beyond him sway slightly. His face was drawn, the squinted eyes filled with pain and slightly glazed. His coat parted and Dan saw the bloodstain along the left side near the hip. Wounded! They're on the run, maybe ugly.

The man perched on the edge of the table looked from Crane to Starrett, back to Crane again. His lips were thin, cynical, a lifetime of hard and evil living revealed in the crooked smile, the black eyes that held a cold fire.

"Well," he said with a chuckle, "go to it."

The big man spoke, his deep voice level. "Leave it alone, Tex. This is none of our business. That goes for the rest of you."

"Why, Jack," Tex spread his hands in an elaborate gesture, "no harm in watching."

"Let's get a drink," Jack said tonelessly. Ava suddenly arose and left the room by a door just behind the bar. Jack Bruhn halted in mid-stride and his voice was suddenly sharp.

"Where'd she go?"

"Why . . . why, just into the storeroom," Tommy answered. Jack eyed him levelly, then signaled a bearded man just behind him.

"Check it, Denver." As the man started past, Jack gripped his arm. "Leave the woman alone . . . no passes."

"Why, Jack!" Denver chuckled. "At my age?"

He circled the bar and opened the door. Tommy half turned, little sweat beads on his forehead and upper lip. Denver opened the door and looked inside.

"Your pardon, ma'am," he said, closed the door and turned. "Storeroom, Jack."

Bruhn nodded, leaned against the bar. The HC men edged away. Starrett and Crane had forgotten one another and they slowly wheeled about as the outlaws joined Bruhn. Two of the outlaws, however, remained by the door. Dan noticed it.

Dan leaned against the bar, keeping his hand well away from his holster, and watched the outlaws through the back mirror. Tommy Rikes stood uncertain as though for the first time in his life he feared to see his bar lined with customers. Bruhn flipped a coin on the bar. His faint smile was tight when he looked at Tommy.

"Drinks, friend, all around. Don't worry about your cash till. We've got enough of our own."

Tommy suddenly sprang at the row of whiskey bottles as though serving the drinks offered reassurance and protection. He lined shot glasses on the bar and filled them, now and then spilling some of the whiskey. He came to Dan, looked up, surprised that this was not another outlaw. Dan smiled and nodded, and Tommy showed a spark of new courage as he poured the drink.

Dan caught a movement in the mirror and he looked up. Crane signaled his two men and they left the bar. Bruhn's heavy voice filled the room, easy, level, and yet carrying a threat.

"Where you rannies headed?"

Two of the outlaws turned with an easy, fluid motion and impassively watched the two riders who halted dead in their tracks, their faces blank with a kind of fearful surprise. Crane took a deep breath.

"Out . . . and about our business."

"Better stick around, friends," Bruhn said. "We might not stay long and we like your company."

Crane's lips thinned. "Suppose we don't?" he snapped. Bruhn's wide shoulders lifted, fell.

"You might try it . . . but you never know."

Dan eased up from the bar. He could see quick anger touch Crane, then indecision, followed by anger again. Lewis and Claggett stood unmoving. If Crane took the challenge, then there was nothing for it but to take a hand. Dan watched the man called Tex and the breed beside him. Take them first, he thought, then hope you're alive to get another one.

Crane breathed deeply, then looked at his men and slightly shook his head. He sat down at the table and once more tension left the room. Dan softly exhaled and leaned his elbows on the bar. He noticed that the storeroom door stood slightly ajar and he could not remember if the bearded outlaw had left it that way or not.

Dan continued to watch the mirror, studying each man reflected there. Nine of them and, right now, six of us . . . make it five since you couldn't count on Tommy Rikes. Odds two to one, maybe more, for these nine men are used to violence. Dan frowned, feeling trapped.

The man with the bloody shirt leaned heavily on the bar, head hanging slightly. Now he convulsively picked up his glass and downed the drink. He stood a moment, then passed his hand over his face, turned and staggered to the nearest table. He fell heavily into a chair and pillowed his head in his arms. His decrepit black hat fell to the floor.

Jack Bruhn slapped his glass on the bar, walked to the table as his men turned to watch, two of them following him. The leader shook the wounded man, who only mumbled incoherently.

"How is it, Shorty?" Bruhn asked and there was a strange, gentle note to his voice. Shorty turned his head and Dan saw the pallor on his cheeks beneath the stubble.

"I . . . I'll be all right, Jack. Don't worry about me . . . I'll keep up."

"Sure, Shorty."

Bruhn glanced up, caught the questioning look of the man called Tex and the stripling with the pale face and strange eyes. Bruhn shrugged and frowned, looked around to the bar.

"Is there a doctor in this damned town?" His harsh eyes rested on Tommy, who licked his lips and hastily nodded.

"Sure, sure! Doc Langer. Back of the blacksmith shop."

Bruhn looked down at Shorty and wearily rubbed his hand along his jaw. He looked toward the door, signaled to one of the outlaws who lolled against the wall.

"Charley." The man straightened but Bruhn now looked at the others, weighing. He pointed his finger at Claggett. "You . . . you go with Charley and get the doctor. Leave your gun here."

"Me!" Claggett demanded.

"Show Charley the way," Bruhn said shortly. Dan stirred and Bruhn caught the movement, his head coming around sharply. "Any argument, friend?"

Dan looked at Shorty, back to Bruhn. "Most times walking patients go to the doctor."

"We'll change the rules," Bruhn said. "Maybe a lot of 'em. You! Shuck that Colt and get along."

Claggett lifted his hands to his belt buckle. Tex and the half-breed watched him narrowly, their fingers splayed over their own guns. Claggett looked to Crane in appeal. A dull red suffused Crane's face.

"It's one thing to ask a favor," he said in a choked voice. "Another thing to spur a man. You stand hitched. That's an order."

Tex looked over his shoulder at Crane, eyes cold and

narrow. His thin lips pursed as though he considered a strange new species of creature and couldn't quite make up his mind about it. He rubbed his knuckles along his jaw, the rasp of the stubble loud.

Without warning or change of expression, he swung on the ball of his foot and his arm lashed out, the clenched fist travelling in a short piston stroke that cracked loudly off Crane's chin. Crane's head snapped back, he hung suspended for a long second, then spilled backward, arms swinging wide, his feet turning at the ankles. He struck the bar with a dull thud, his body lurching forward with the impact, then settling back against the mahogany and sliding slowly down it. His rump struck the brass rail and he sat there, like a sodden drunk, then bumped to the floor and fell to one side.

Dan lunged forward. But a gun barrel jabbed in his side and the bearded Denver smiled a warning through his whiskers, his eyes slitted and waiting. Dan settled back on his heels.

Silence held the room. The eight outlaws calmly looked at Crane stretched in the sawdust, slack and unmoving. The others stared with a growing sense of horror. Lewis made a strangled noise in his throat and jumped away from the bar.

His hand whipped to his gun and his fingers touched the walnut butt. The Colt had always been a tool for Lewis, never a weapon. He was slow, pitifully slow.

The kid with the handsome, pale face did not seem to move. Yet something flashed in the light and a blast of flame jumped from his hand, a spear of fire that lanced toward Lewis. Smoke billowed and, through it, Dan saw the pale eyes alight, dancing, filled with a glee that made something twist and crawl within him.

Lewis jerked half around and his gun, only half out of the holster, caught on its lip, gave a half spin and dropped to the sawdust. His right arm hung limp as he catapulted against the bar, caught himself. He hung there, face slack with surprise, eyes rounded. It would be minutes yet before the shocked nerves would begin to register pain. The kid stood waiting, legs spread, Colt held uptilted, ready to drop and fire again. His red lips held an angelic smile and his brows arched high in twin questions. The flicker in his eye showed his anticipation.

"Pace," Bruhn growled, "you can be too damned quick with a Colt."

Pace didn't move, his eyes fixed on Lewis. He spoke softly with a note of regret. "Why, Jack, he wanted to play gunhawk. I . . . like that game."

A snap came in Bruhn's heavy voice. "Put it up, Odlum. You've dehorned him. You don't notch your gun on an unarmed man."

Pace stood poised for another long moment and, slowly, the flame died in his eyes. He settled back and a shadow of disappointment flicked across his face. He stepped to the bar and with a quick, deft move of his fingers ejected the spent shell. It made a glittering arc that held them all a moment and then dropped soundlessly into the sawdust. His soft voice was startling after the deep silence.

"All right, Jack. But now the sawbones will have two customers. He'll like that."

Crane moaned and stirred. His eyes slowly opened and he stared glassily along the level of the floor. He suddenly lifted his head, surprised. He jerked upright and then froze when he saw Bruhn, solid and dominating, a few feet away. Crane's glance shifted to Tex, who grinned and blew suggestively on his knuckles.

"Still giving orders?" he asked silkily. Crane's glance shifted, swung to the others. He saw Lewis at the bar, now clutching his shoulder, the shirt and his fingers slowly staining. Crane pulled himself up, looked down at the clinging sawdust on his shirt and trousers. He refused to look at Claggett.

"Do as they say," he choked. "Nothing else for it."

Claggett very carefully lifted his gun from the holster and gingerly placed it on the nearest table. Bruhn watched impassively.

"All right, Charley. He'll take you to the doc."

The outlaw frowned at Claggett, who moved slowly to the door, held in a stunned world of unreality. As Charley swung open the door, Bruhn spoke again.

"If the doc argues, Charley, persuade him. He'll listen."

Charley grinned, then scowled at Claggett, jerked his thumb toward the open door. They went out and the door slammed behind them. Crane rubbed his hands along his trousers, then nodded toward Lewis. "I'd better see about him," he suggested.

Bruhn shrugged. "Sure. But he'll hold until the sawbones comes."

Dan started to help Crane but the bearded outlaw beside him shook his head. "Don't get so restless, friend. I'll buy you a drink."

Dan hesitated, noticed again that Denver still held his gun. Now Odlum, Tex and the half-breed watched, hoping he would disobey. Dan swallowed his mounting anger and turned to the bar.

"I'll take the drink, but I'll pay for my own."

Denver's shaggy brows rose under the brown, dirty hat. "Uppity," he said but he made no issue of it, holstering his gun and swinging in beside Dan at the bar. Dan edged away from the brush of the man's body. Tommy Rikes, his forehead again beaded with sweat, hastily filled the empty glasses. He dredged up a ghastly smile and his voice squeaked as he urged the men to have another drink. They all responded, even Bruhn after a searching glance at Shorty's pale face.

Dan wondered why the outlaws had not bothered to take his gun and those of Crane, Starrett and the others. Tommy must have some sort of weapon hidden behind the bar, standard equipment for any saloon, no matter how peaceful. So far the outlaws had been well able to take care of themselves.

The thought angered Dan even more. He couldn't tell if Hal Crane had the nerve knocked out of him, but there was still Starrett and himself. If some sort of concerted action could be made, there was a chance—though maybe a slim one.

He tried to get Starrett's eyes in the mirror, make some signal to show that he was ready. Then Dan had another shock. He had a clear view of Starrett's face for a moment. He watched Bruhn with something akin to wonder. As Dan watched, Starrett's eyes grew thoughtful, actually pleased, and then he sat down so that Dan could no longer see his image in the mirror.

Dan lowered his eyes to his glass and he slowly moved it around on the bar between thumb and fingers. Blaise was no ally and Dan was at a loss to explain it. That left him Crane, and Crane had already tasted outlaw treatment. Dan eased slowly about and watched Hal, working over Lewis.

Hal ripped open the man's shirt and tried to stop the bleeding. From the sag of the shoulder and the useless hang of the arm, Dan judged Lewis had a splintered shoulder. Hal looked angry but Dan knew that, right now, he dared not bank on the man's help. Seven men lined against him, and Dan knew each was a killer. He would have to wait for the breaks.

Suddenly Bruhn, who had been staring into the bar mirror, turned and walked to the door. He opened it and looked out, studied the street in every direction. He looked thoughtful, and then his craggy jaw set. He turned, closing the door behind him.

"We'll stay here, boys." The outlaws turned, surprised but pleased. Bruhn looked at Dan. "Shuck your gun on the bar. That goes for you, mister," he added to Crane. He looked at Starrett, his glance an order. Starrett shrugged.

"You're the boss, Jack."

Bruhn looked sharply at Starrett as though trying to understand a slight friendliness where he had expected only distrust and hatred. He grunted and gestured toward the bar.

Dan hesitated. Tex, Pace and the half-breed watched him as though silently counting off the seconds they allowed him in which to comply. His lips flattened but he slowly moved his hand to his Colt, lifted it out of the holster between thumb and two fingers and placed it on the bar. Starrett came forward readily enough, placed his gun beside Dan's and stepped back with a smile that said he didn't mind this at all. Dan stifled an impulse to hit him. Hal Crane reluctantly left Lewis, surlily placed his gun on the bar and returned.

Bruhn walked ponderously around the bar. Tommy hastily backed to the far end. The big man crouched, looked under the bar and, with a grunt of satisfaction, pulled out a sawed-off shotgun. He broke the barrels, ejected the shells and placed the weapon beside the three Colts. He looked to the outlaw who still loafed by the door.

"Egan, it's pretty muddy outside."

"Sure is, Jack."

Bruhn stabbed a finger at the weapons. "Take these out and pitch 'em in the street. Grind 'em down in the mud while you're at it."

Dan started and Bruhn's cold eyes swiveled instantly

to him. Dan settled against the bar but he felt a churning anger. No need to ruin a good Colt, he thought, and then realized that Bruhn had made exactly the right move from his point of view.

Egan swept up the weapons and went outside. The door closed behind him with a sound of finality and, for the first time, Dan felt helpless. But there are others . . . they're bound to learn what's going on. There's the Frazins, Gorton, Larry Teter, even Phil Preston. His eyes glinted and his fingers balled slowly into a fist, then relaxed as he threw a hasty glance at Denver. The man had not noticed.

The storeroom door opened abruptly. Ava came out and Tommy tried vainly to signal her back out of sight. She didn't look at him. She stood framed in the dark aperture and Dan had the crazy idea that she deliberately put herself in the middle of this situation. He couldn't understand why. Any woman would run a risk around this gang, but Ava was striking. The dress fitted, her full figure, accenting each curve, suggesting each line.

Tex straightened, eyes wide, and he gave a low, long whistle. Ava slowly turned and looked at him. She did not smile, nothing about her face softened, her eyes remained level. Tex circled the bar and stopped a few feet away. His eyes moved boldly over her and then he swept off his rakish, battered Stetson and made her an elaborate bow.

"Ma'am, my apologies. I sure didn't see you real good before. You make this damn' town look beautiful."

Dan's fingers tightened on the edge of the bar. A shadow of fright passed over Ava's face as though she suddenly recognized her danger. Then she seemed to deliberately shrug it off. A ghost of a smile touched her lips and she lowered her eyes. Tommy stood frozen and stricken.

Shorty groaned, a long and horrible sound. All of them whipped about. Shorty had flung out his arm and now he rolled to the edge of the table and off. He lay face up on the floor, eyes closed, his breath coming in tortured rasps and his nostrils pinched even as Dan looked at him.

Bruhn growled an oath and jumped to the man's side, bent down, tearing at Shorty's shirt and feeling for the heartbeat. Tex hitched at his gunbelt and slowly approached. He stopped a foot away, thumbs hooked in the ornate buckle, looking impassively down.

"Gone?" he asked finally. Bruhn looked up over his shoulder. "No, but the damn' doctor had better get here."

Tex shrugged. "Hell, it makes no difference. Shorty's near the end of the trail anyhow. Leave him for the undertaker. This way, he just holds us up."

Bruhn looked up at Tex. For a moment Dan had an impression that a powerful beast crouched, ready to spring. Then the cold light in Bruhn's eyes was masked.

"Shorty ain't holding us up, Tex. We're stuck here by the mud. No one will move across the country until the roads and trails have a bottom again. So we might as well get Shorty patched up while we're waiting. It's a chance to rest up, too."

Tex's eyes locked with Bruhn, challenging but still not quite sure of himself. He rocked forward on his toes, back on his heels, glanced toward the men at the bar and apparently found no real support there.

"How about the local lawman, Jack? Are you forgetting him?"

Ava spoke from beyond the bar, hastily, as though she had not given her words a thought. "But Bitter has no lawman!"

They all looked about, surprised. Dan wondered if she had lost her mind. Then he noticed the way she glanced at Tex, something new and alive in her eyes. It worried him and he shot a quick look at Tex. The man's slowly widening smile confirmed Dan's fears.

"Well!" Tex breathed softly. "Maybe this is a good place. No lawman . . . no one can trail us . . . and the town sure has promise."

A slow flush touched Ava's cheeks. She didn't look at Tex, nor would she meet the stricken, puzzled eyes of her husband.

FOUR

Bruhn stood up with a growl. He looked at Tex, though he spoke to all of his men. "We'll stay here. Let's get Shorty off the floor."

They pulled tables together, lifted Shorty and placed him on them. The man moaned, but his eyes did not open. Bruhn straightened and tugged at his lower lip.

"Egan, you and Gene take the horses to the livery stable. See that they're cared for."

Egan nodded and Gene Hiatt looked down at Shorty, swallowed with an effort. He felt that in some strange way he had changed places, that the wounded man was himself in some not-too-distant future. When Gene looked up, his face was tight and the eyes deep with murky shadows. Bruhn smiled cynically.

"Does a little blood bother you, kid?"

Gene spoke with a confidence that didn't quite come off. "No, I . . . don't mind."

"Better not. You'll see a lot before they hang you. We all do." Bruhn's voice dropped, slowed. Then he shook himself out of the mood, his words clipped.

"If you find anyone at the livery stable, bring 'em

here. Lock up the place and bring the keys." He turned to Egan, his face tight. "You handle it. Gene'll go along to help."

Egan hitched at his gunbelt. "Hell, Jack, we'll take care of things."

Bruhn lifted his hand in warning. "See that you do. But do it quiet, understand? Don't get the whole town buzzing. Just pick up whoever you find and bring 'em here, pronto."

Egan glanced at Hiatt and jerked his head toward the door. Dan fought down a rising feeling of entrapment and panic. He had an impulse to grab Egan and Hiatt, hold them here, but his better sense prevailed.

He rubbed his hand along his empty holster as he watched the two outlaws go out the door. Then he turned slowly to the bar. Ava remained standing in the doorway and Tommy had not moved. Tex boldly stared at Ava.

"A whiskey, Tommy," Dan said sharply. Tommy moved like an automaton, his face troubled. He placed the glass before Dan and then half turned so that he could again study his wife. Ava's chin lifted and she steadfastly kept her eyes on the far wall.

Dan glanced covertly in the mirror at the outlaws. His mind worked fast but it could find no satisfactory answer to the problem. Now Dan's gun was gone, along with all the rest. At this moment, perhaps, two renegades securely locked his horse in the stable. Dan's lips pressed tight a moment. If he could only slip out of town, get word to one of the ranches, this bunch of ridge-runners would find Bitter damn' unhealthy.

Bruhn came up to the bar. His heavy voice snapped at Tommy. Dan saw how pitifully small the village was, how easily it could be held by a few hardcases, such as the nine who had ridden in from nowhere. It was even worse now that the mud and slush completed the town's isolation.

Bruhn swung around when the door opened. Claggett and the doctor came in ahead of the outlaw, Vause. Doc Langer was a slender man in his late forties. His nose was long and his lips thin, the mouth circled by deep creases that long hours of work had placed there. His sandy hair had thinned to a few wisps and his shoulders were rounded. He looked ugly and awkward . . . except for his eyes. They were deep, filled with an understanding gained from his constant battle against disease and death. Now he was angry and he smacked his black bag down on a table and glared about the room.

"What is the meaning of this outrage?" he demanded. He glared at Bruhn, recognizing the big man as the obvious leader. "I've never turned down a call yet, and I've never needed a gun at my back."

Bruhn's granite face softened into something like contrition.

"Sorry, Doc. I guess Charley got out of line." He jerked his thumb toward the man on the table. "He's bad hit . . . so's that gent over there."

Doc Langer saw Shorty for the first time and the anger instantly left him. He looked quickly at Lewis, eyes sharp, missing nothing. His fingers worked at the strap of the black bag as he talked.

"Busted shoulder, Lewis? Bleeding bad?"

"I stopped it," Hal said shortly. Langer pulled instruments and bandages from the bag.

"You'll live a while then. I'll look at this one first."

The doctor looked at Shorty's face, took his pulse. He deftly cut away the shirt, exposing the bandage, now stained and dirty. Langer glowered at Bruhn.

"Want to kill this man? Ever heard of changing

bandages? What the bullet won't do, the dirt will." He removed the bandage and bent to his task, working swiftly. He straightened, a thin and frail man but with no real fear in him.

"He's not far from dead and maybe the world would be better off." Tex whipped upright but Bruhn made a swift, warning signal. Langer didn't notice. "He won't live unless he's given the best of care . . . maybe not then. You'd better decide what you intend to do."

Tex gave Bruhn a quizzical glance, looked at Pace Odlum, then the half-breed. Bruhn's jaw set and he studied Shorty and the doctor. He suddenly lifted his head, his hard eyes on Vause.

"Who was at the doc's house?" he asked abruptly. Charley looked blank, then shrugged.

"Just an old woman—his wife." He nodded toward the doctor.

"How large a house?" Bruhn snapped. Charley shrugged, puzzled.

"There's an upstairs. Hell, Jack, I don't know. Maybe three bedrooms up there—parlor, a kind of office, a dining room and kitchen downstairs."

Langer looked up from Shorty's wound. "What has my house to do with this?"

Bruhn smiled, "Why, Doc, that's easy. Shorty will stay there and get that good care you talked about."

Langer straightened, his eyes flashing, his thin face tight. Dan saw the fury mount in Langer's eyes and jaw and he straightened, with a cold chill of fear for the little man. Langer looked sharply from one man to the other, recognized the quiet deadliness of each. His lips pressed tight as he fought for control. He looked at Bruhn and then away, over at Lewis.

"I'd better look at this one," he said and Dan eased against the bar again, recognizing the unspoken surrender.

What next? Dan wondered grimly. Now they've taken the only doctor in town. No chance of getting to his horse in the small stable back of the house. Dan helplessly watched a prison being built about him and the town. They're bound to make a mistake—overlook something. Watch for it.

Bruhn's ability to command showed in his swift, decisive orders. Under his direction Shorty's gun and belt were removed. Vause went outside and Dan heard the protesting wrench of wood. The man returned, lugging a long, narrow shutter that would serve as litter.

Ava moved back against the wall, apparently unnoticed. Bruhn waited patiently for Langer to finish his work with Lewis. He joined Tex, the breed and Pace Odlum at the bar, and the four men kept Tommy busy pouring drinks.

Dan noticed that Tex moved grudgingly to let Bruhn stand beside him. The breed gave the big man a quick flick with dark eyes that gleamed balefully and then were hooded. There was strain here of some sort, Dan sensed, and he wondered if he could make use of it.

Pace Odlum fascinated Dan. There was such utter evil in the smooth and handsome face, the pale eyes. Tex and the breed drank heavily and Dan knew that they were dangerous men. But the boy, Pace, quiet and smiling, was the man to watch. He would be like a sidewinder, striking without warning, a man whom death delighted, as drink or love delighted more normal men.

The door suddenly opened and Dan wheeled about. There was a scuffle outside, an oath, and then a figure catapulted into the room. Egan, angry and ruffled, strode in and Dan glimpsed the troubled face of the man called Gene, who remained a moment in the door, then entered and closed it.

Clay Majors skidded to a halt, lunging against a table. He straightened and Dan saw the trickle of blood from his puffed lip, the beginning of a bruise high on one cheekbone. Good for Clay, Dan thought, he gave them an argument. Egan strode to Majors, grabbed his arm and whirled him about. Majors tried to wrest free but Egan cursed, shoved him toward the bar. Bruhn impassively watched as Majors came to a rocking halt before him.

"What the hell is this?" Majors demanded. His swollen lips were pulled back from his yellow teeth and his fists were clenched. Bruhn looked inquiringly at Egan and Hiatt.

"He gave you trouble?"

"Some," Egan grinned. He handed a big key to Bruhn. "But we finally persuaded him."

Bruhn looked again at Majors. "We've taken over for a while. We won't stay long and we don't figure anyone will get hurt or lose anything unless they rowel us. Just do as we say and everything will be fine."

"But, no damned—"

"Clay," Dan said quickly. "This is the Bruhn gang. Take a look at Lewis."

Majors blinked and, for the first time, saw Doc Langer working on Lewis' shoulder. He realized the man stretched out on the table was wounded. Majors' eyes widened and his skin took on a pasty pallor. He swallowed and the fight left him. Bruhn weighed the key in his hand, looking thoughtful. Tex Darrow shoved his hat back and grinned at Bruhn.

"Well, Jack, what next?"

Bruhn looked up, heavy brows lifting. He shrugged. "We've got the saloon and the livery stable corralled. The sawbones will do as we say."

"How about the rest?" Tex demanded.

"What's left?" Bruhn snapped. "The barbershop, the store and the lumberyard. There's a few houses. Any problem there?" Dan stiffened when Bruhn mentioned the lumberyard. He looked sidelong at Tex, saw Pace's pale eyes, the pinched, ratty faces of Egan and Vause, the breed's swarthy countenance. They had already noticed Ava, Tex especially. What would they do when they saw Paula?

Bruhn pitched the key again and grabbed it with an air of finality. He turned to Doc Langer.

"How long will you be?"

Langer snapped without looking up. "As long as it takes—no more, no less."

Bruhn smiled and Dan read admiration for the doctor in it. Bruhn paced to the front door, back, thinking, and all of them watched him. Hiatt cleared his throat and Bruhn's cold eyes cut in a quick question to him. Hiatt pointed to his muddy boots.

"It's getting worse and worse, Jack. Give it two more hours and a horse'll sink belly deep in that gumbo."

Bruhn nodded. A strange warmth came into his eyes and for once his smile softened the rock-hard structure of the jaw and chin. He swung to the bar.

"Tex, you and Denver pay a visit to the store. Make sure there's no horse stabled over there. If there is," he pitched the key to Tex, who deftly caught it, "lock 'em in the stable. Just make sure there's none loose in case someone decides to ride despite the gumbo."

Tex showed a grudging admiration for Bruhn. He glanced toward the breed. "Maybe I'd better take Juarez in case we run into trouble. Bound to meet someone."

"No," Bruhn said shortly. "Juarez gets too excited and you can be gun hasty, Tex. That's why I'm sending Denver along. Get the job done and come back."

Tex frowned and his fingers tightened about the key.

Bruhn watched him impassively and again Dan felt the electric flow of distrust and hatred between the two. He waited, hopeful, but the moment passed. Tex nodded.

"All right, Jack. If we meet anyone, bring 'em here?"

Bruhn chuckled dryly. "We're getting too crowded now." He tugged at his ear lobe. "The store will have guns—and ammunition. We'd better round it up and make sure there's no extra Colt or scattergun hiding under a counter or in a desk drawer."

"That could be a lot of hardware," Denver said uncertainly. "what do we do with it?"

Bruhn wheeled about and his cold eyes speared at Tommy. "Is there a vacant building in town?"

Tommy spoke grudgingly. "There's the old stage station by the bridge. It ain't used unless a preacher comes along."

Bruhn smiled. "Well, we're not sky pilots, but I guess we can send a man to heaven in our own way just as quick as a preacher." His smile vanished. "The place is livable?"

Tommy nodded and Bruhn, satisfied, swung around to Tex and Denver.

"That'll be the place. We can watch the road and we can keep an eye on this damn' town. We'll take the guns and ammunition there and bunk right beside 'em. That way, we'll all sleep peaceful."

Dan fished in his pocket for tobacco and paper. He kept his eyes lowered, knowing that they must show his feeling of angry despair. He wondered what kind of man Bruhn must be, for he thought of everything. Now the main source of weapons would be barred. Step by step, Bruhn cut off all avenues of escape, closing the trap so tightly that there was no hope for a man to work out of it.

He reached for a match and cut his thumbnail across

it. Bruhn glanced at him when the sulphur flared but Dan bent his head to the flame, his eyes hidden. Breaks, Dan thought. Maybe this thing between Tex and Bruhn, whatever it was, would flare into the open. Dan remembered an old saying, something about dividing and conquering, and he desperately prayed that it would hold true here.

He looked again at Starrett, remembering the tight places they had worked out of in the past. He had a shock. Starrett watched Bruhn, fascinated. Surprise and admiration for the bandit leader showed openly in Starrett's eyes. Bruhn was shrewd and smart and Dan gave him credit, but he was an enemy to be overcome. None of this showed in Starrett's expression. Dan's jaw tightened. What in hell was wrong with Blaise! What's on his mind?

Bruhn continued to pace, snapping his orders. "Make sure no one in the store has a gun. Denver, you report when you've got the place corralled. We'll make arrangements to move the hardware to our new home."

Tex looked over the bar at Ava and ran his tongue around the inside of his cheek. One brow lifted as he smiled and a wicked glint came in his eyes. He walked to the end of the bar, disregarding the rest, and now he had an unrestricted view of the woman. His eyes moved up and down and his smile widened. He spoke carelessly over his shoulder.

"Now, Jack, let's think this over a minute. Me, I'd like to board out with some of the folks around here. It could be cozy. You thought of that, Jack?"

Ava's eyes widened and a fiery color raced up her neck and into her face. Tommy's jaw dropped and his eyes rounded. He caught the full implication and his face went paper white, the color of killing anger, not fear. He made a strangled sound deep in his throat. Dan sensed what was coming and he threw himself athwart the bar, arm reaching for Tommy.

But Tommy moved too fast. His arm whipped beneath the bar, reappeared, a heavy bung starter held like a club in his hand. His eyes turned glassy and wild, blazed at Tex in a venomous fury. Dan's fingers touched Tommy's shirt but he could not hold him as Tommy lunged toward Tex.

"Stand hitched," Bruhn roared. Tex took a hasty step backward, his slack lips and pinched eyes showing sudden, stunning fright at this little man who advanced with murderous determination. Tex forgot his holstered gun in this split second of panic.

Dan clawed himself erect, intending to whip around the bar between Tommy and Tex. Pace Odlum stood a few feet away, a faint color touching his lean face, lips pulled back over even teeth in a delightful smile.

Dan caught only a blur as the man's hand whipped down and up. The room blasted with a single shot that rocked off the walls, bounced back and forth in roaring echoes. Tommy didn't hear them. The slug caught him full in the chest and slapped him against the back bar.

Bottles tipped over and others wobbled. Tommy, face abruptly slack and blank, eyes still staring, dropped the bung starter and fell forward on his face. His head struck the edge of the bar, bounced limply up and then thudded onto the floor.

There was no sound in the room. Burned black powder made an acrid smell.

FIVE

Ava screamed. The sound wrenched out of her corded throat, cut into the nerves. It broke the stunned silence that held all of them.

Dan suddenly whipped about, facing Pace, who still held the Colt, muzzle up. His pale eyes glittered as he looked at the limp form on the floor. With a choked curse Dan lunged toward the man, hands reaching for him.

Pace didn't notice for a fraction of a second and then his head whipped about. Dan had almost reached him. He saw the stripling's eyes light with a twisted, inward joy. The Colt whipped down and Dan slammed into the man, his fingers instinctively grabbing the gun wrist and twisting the arm to one side. Pace did not lose his grip on the weapon. It roared again and Dan felt the heat of the muzzle blast, but the bullet smashed into the wall above the open storeroom door.

Pace's lips writhed and he made peculiar animal growls as he tried to wrench his gun free. Dan felt heavy hands claw at him from the rear. He had a blurred glimpse of Bruhn at Pace's side. Then they were wrenched apart.

Bruhn held Pace easily, while the breed, Juarez, and Denver clung to Dan as he tried to break loose. Pace sought to free his gun but Bruhn pressed on the thin wrist, twisted. Pace's fingers opened spasmodically and the gun thudded to the sawdust. Bruhn gave him a shove and Pace stumbled back against the tables. He caught his balance but lunged forward again, pulled up short when he found himself looking down the black muzzle of his own gun.

"Hold it, Pace," Bruhn snapped. He kept the gun leveled. "I don't want to give you a slug."

"He hit me!" Pace said in a choked voice. His lips were bloodless. Bruhn slowly straightened, nodded, his eyes wary and the gun steady.

"Sure, Pace. He won't do it again. Besides, you killed his friend." His voice was soothing as though he carefully explained something to a child. "You shouldn't have done it, Pace. I've told you time and again you're too quick with a Colt."

Dan tried to free himself again but the two outlaws held him. Juarez cursed in Spanish and Denver grunted as he held grimly on.

"Take it easy, you fool! . . . want a gun barrel . . . over your head? . . . Maybe . . . better for you anyway."

Dan made one or two more ineffectual attempts to free himself and then gave up. He stood quite still, feeling weak with the backwash of the hate and wish to kill that had swept over him. Juarez and Denver still held him, but the bearded outlaw eyed him suspiciously and then cautiously released him.

"That's better," he growled. "You want to get yourself killed damn' quick?"

Bruhn momentarily turned his head to look at Dan. "You getting some sense?"

Dan took a deep breath but could not keep the angry quiver out of his voice. "Why'd he have to do that? What in hell was the use?"

Bruhn looked at Pace, searching the thin, tight face as though he again sought an answer that had long eluded him.

"I don't know why. I reckon Pace don't either." His voice tightened. "How about it, Pace? It's over?"

"I'll kill him," Pace snapped.

"Not until I tell you, Pace," Bruhn said like a parent giving an order. "If you do, you won't live a minute afterward."

Pace jerked as though he had been slapped. His eyes blazed. Then he looked away, swallowed, and some color came back to his face. He shot Dan a venomous glance.

"All right, Jack," he said evenly. "If you say so."

Bruhn studied him closely, doubting his sincerity. Doc Langer spoke from the end of the bar. He had turned Tommy over and now he looked up, still crouched. His pointed face was tight with anger and the brown eyes no longer held sympathy and understanding.

"He's dead . . . before he hit the floor."

Pace's head jerked around. His lips moved, twisted and then broke into a wide smile.

"Of course," he said with a touch of pride. "I always place a slug where I intend to."

Perhaps it was the smile and then the crowing little laugh. Ava suddenly broke the paralysis that had held her. Her eyes focused on Pace, the impact of his deed striking her full force. Her neck corded and suddenly she leaped for him.

Pace involuntarily stepped back. Tex wheeled, lunged toward Ava and his arms circled her. She tried to break loose and almost succeeded. Her hair came loose and streamed down her back and she clawed toward Pace. Tex held her, slowly forcing down her arms, placing his weight against her. As swiftly as she had moved, she collapsed, sobs shaking her. Tex held her close and looked over her shoulder to Bruhn, signaled with his eyes toward the body on the floor. He glared at Pace.

"Get a drink, Pace. For God's sake, don't show your face to her."

Bruhn assumed command again. His heavy voice snapped.

"Put him behind the bar . . . out of sight. Move, damn' you!"

Dan felt suddenly sick at this useless killing. Claggett, moving like a man in a bad dream, walked to the end of the bar and looked dully at Dan, waiting for his help. Doc Langer arose and brushed the sawdust from his knees. He looked at Tex, holding Ava, her head buried in his chest. He stood a moment, striving to regain self-control.

"Get her a drink, a good strong one. She needs it." His glance fell on Bruhn's broad face and hard jaw. He took a deep breath. "Haven't you done enough damage? Why don't you go away and leave us alone? We haven't done you any harm."

Bruhn's deep chest lifted and a shadow passed over his eyes, was gone. He disregarded the doctor and glared at Dan.

"Get moving, friend. Get him out of sight."

Dan slowly turned and walked to the bar. He had never known hatred like this before. It was a fire in his chest, a talon in his brain. He saw Pace Odlum through a red haze and the sight of the rest of them was a goad that made him fight to control himself. He dimly heard Tex as he bent to help pick up Tommy and carry him behind the bar.

"Denver, bring a slug for the lady. Where does she live?" There was no answer and Tex's voice lifted dangerously. "Damn it, answer me! Where does she live?"

Hal Crane spoke, voice muffled. "Take the street between the smithy and the store. There's a little street off of it just before you reach the Spade Road. Her house is the last on the right."

"I'll take her home," Tex said. Dan straightened as Denver brought a whiskey glass to Tex. He took it and made Ava lift her head. He spoke to her in a low and gentle tone. The man's face softened and his hand soothed Ava's shoulder. It struck Dan as a miracle until he had a glimpse of the narrow eyes. They were alight and glittering, and the cynicism negated the apparent sorrow and understanding of the whispered words.

But she listened. Her sobbing eased. Tex held the whiskey glass out to the still weeping girl. He spoke insistently, and Ava took the glass and drank, her eyes wide on the man's face. The whiskey choked her and her face convulsed as she dropped the glass. Tex instantly had his arm around her and turned her toward the door, his voice still whispering.

"Tex," Bruhn snapped.

Tex looked up over the girl's bowed head. "I'm taking her home."

"Not alone. You've got another job to do."

Tex smiled and met Bruhn's commanding stare. He realized he held the key and he pitched it to Vause.

"You take it, Charley. Jack, I can go anywhere alone. Who would stop me?"

Bruhn's gray eyes narrowed angrily. Tex still smiled, his arm around Ava's shoulder. One brow rose and then he walked calmly to the door and out. He closed it very quietly behind him. A silence held the room until Pace spoke irritably.

"Jack, I want my gun."

Bruhn started, swung about. He lifted his hand as though surprised that he still held the weapon. He looked up under his brows at Pace and then, without a word, reversed the gun and gave it a toss. Pace deftly caught it, whirled it about so that he again held it half poised. His pale eyes lighted, sparked and he threw a sharp look at Dan. Then he licked his lips and slowly put the Colt in the holster and started to the bar.

He whipped about when the door burst open. The gun again blurred up from the holster and lined on the two men who plunged into the room. A streak of fear cut through Dan when he recognized Phil Preston and Larry Teter. They came to an abrupt halt, staring at the gun, then wonderingly around the room.

Larry Teter was at one time a lean and powerful man. Now his muscles had slackened and a once flat stomach had slowly taken on fat so that he puffed after the short run to the bar. His face was square, freckled, his bristling hair a fiery red, his eyes a mild blue with little laugh crinkles at the corner. He stood now with his jaw hanging.

Phil Preston sensed the situation far more quickly than Larry. He still did not understand, but the leveled gun, the hard-featured strangers who mingled with his friends, the strained attitude of Dan, Hal Crane and Doc Langer told him something of the story before he saw Lewis, pale and wan with bandaged shoulder, and Shorty Ratner's still form stretched out on the table. His face went pale but he kept his voice even.

"We've heard some shots. What's this all about?"

"Keep 'em covered, Pace," Bruhn said. He circled them, coming up from behind, patted their bodies in search of weapons. Finding none, he stepped back. Phil and Larry turned to face him. Phil spoke again.

"A holdup?"

Bruhn disregarded the question, looking sharply at the two men. "Who are you?"

Larry swallowed. "I . . . I'm the barber, next door. Me'n . . . Phil was in the store. We didn't think much about the first shot . . . but this last one . . ."

"Barber," Bruhn cut in and faced Phil. "What's your business?"

"The lumberyard. I asked if this was a holdup."

Bruhn smiled frostily. "In a manner of speaking, maybe it is. We don't want your money, though. We just aim to use your town for a few days."

Phil's eyes narrowed, then grew round, and a subtle pallor came to his skin. Dan knew that Phil now faced the fear that had gnawed at him. These renegades were a threat to everyone in the town. Dan looked at Juarez with the swarthy face, Pace Odlum, the handsome killer who still held his gun on the two men, at Vause and Egan who appeared to have the ethics of wounded rattlers. It shook Dan and he moved around the bar and up to Bruhn.

"Just what do you figure on doing?" he demanded. Bruhn read something of the fear that Dan felt. His voice carried no real threat, but a note of quiet reasonableness.

"Like I said, we intend to use your town. It's a good hideout. No lawman can reach us and," he glanced toward Shorty, "we got a man to doctor. We need to rest and we got some business of our own to talk over. So long as we're safe here, we'll take over the place." He smiled. "You people ain't very hospitable."

Dan ignored the thrust. He jerked his thumb toward Lewis and the bar, behind which Tommy lay. "Is this a sample of the treatment we can expect?"

Pace spoke, still watching Phil and Larry. "Don't waste your time with him, Jack. A forty-four slug answers every damn' question I can think of."

Jack sighed. "Leave it be, Pace." He faced Dan and he spoke without anger. "Things got out of hand . . . and it was no fault of ours. One gent pulled a gun and he's lucky to be alive. The other tried to brain Tex. I'm sorry he's dead, but it was his own fault."

Dan's face flushed. "Because your man, Tex, made—"

Jack's harsh voice cut in. "Both of 'em started trouble, no matter what the reason. Keep that in mind, and that goes for the whole town. We'll get along peaceful with you, so long, as you let us."

"You mean so long as you can saddle and spur us," Dan snapped.

"Name it how you like, friend. We settle things in our own way, and we make our own rules. We want no trouble and no more killing. There won't be none so long as you people treat us right."

Dan's tone held a wide sarcasm. "And how do we do

that?"

"Leave us alone. Don't, argue with us. If anyone—man, woman or child—tries to slip out of the town or pull a double-cross then he'll find himself dead or in so damn' much trouble he won't be able to claw out of it. Does that satisfy you?"

Their eyes met and locked. Dan breathed deeply, feeling the angry constriction in his chest. He heard the faint stir of Pace behind him, grew aware of Denver, Juarez and Vause watching him, knew that Hiatt and Egan were off to one side. Dan expelled his breath in a long, soft sigh, but his eyes flashed.

"It sounds fair enough," he said grudgingly. "But can you hold your killers in line enough to keep your promise?"

Dan heard a step behind him and a hand gripped his shoulder, whirled him around. Pace Odlum glared at him, an insane, flaming light in his pale eyes. He rammed his gun muzzle against Dan's buckle. Bruhn forced Pace back, stood between him and Dan.

"Pace, I've warned you. Put up that damn' Colt. Put it up, I say!"

Now Bruhn and Pace entered a battle of eyes and Dan saw the slight quiver in Pace's slender body. His flaming anger died slowly and he holstered the Colt, turning nonchalantly to the bar. Bruhn faced Dan. His voice was calm but Dan thought he saw a faint trace of sweat above the shaggy brows.

"Don't you or the town worry about what I can do with my men, friend. I can handle every one of them."

Pace's chin lifted sharply but he did not turn from the bar. Dan saw Juarez's startling blue eyes narrow and his hand clench slightly. But no one said a word.

SIX

Bruhn abruptly squared his shoulders and stepped around Dan. He walked to the tables, studied Shorty Ratner, then looked over at Doc Langer.

"He can be moved?"

"Suit yourself," Langer said shortly. Bruhn deliberately walked to the smaller man and his big fingers taloned into Langer's coat front. He jerked the man forward and half lifted him off his feet. Langer tried ineffectually to break the grip but Bruhn held on with ease.

"Doc, you'd better get things straight in your mind," Bruhn said, his tone low and deadly. "Don't get the idea you can just let Shorty die. You're going to give him the best you got or they'll plant you in boothill beside him. That's a promise." He released Langer so suddenly that the doctor almost fell. "Now, can he be moved?"

Langer swallowed and answered reluctantly. "He shouldn't be, but he can't stay here."

Bruhn nodded. "We'll take care of our other business first, then. Oh, and remember to tell your wife to nurse Shorty good. One of my boys will be around to see that she does."

Bruhn looked at Denver. "Better take care of the store. Take Charley with you."

Denver walked to the door, Vause joining him. They went out and again a silence held the big room. Bruhn's harsh eyes swept over them all and he smiled, trying to ease the tension and hatred that was almost a palpable thing.

"All right, nothing else we can do." He gestured toward the bar and looked significantly at Dan, Crane and the others. "You might as well have a drink. We all need it and none of you will be going far for a while. Egan, you serve the boys."

"Me?" Egan demanded.

"You've had enough snakebite poured for you, so even it up." Bruhn smiled again. "Besides, maybe we ought to be polite since we've got such a nice invite to stay. You can watch for tricks on that side of the bar. Doc, join me?"

Langer snapped, "No, thanks. Whiskey and bullet surgery don't mix."

Bran caught the implication and flushed. "Suit yourself. Belly to the bar, friends, while you got a chance."

The outlaws moved to the bar, Egan going behind it and looking over the whiskey bottles with the air of a connoisseur, face alight. He poured the whiskey, lifted his own glass high.

"There's nothing like a good drink among friends, and nothing like having it on the house."

Dan did not touch his glass. Crane stood beside him and Lewis on the other side, hoping that the impact of the raw whiskey would lessen the pain that seared through his shoulder. Claggett stood beyond Crane and, next to him, Starrett leaned against the bar and looked thoughtfully into the mirror.

Dan patiently waited until he caught Starrett's glance. He looked significantly at Bruhn's reflection, back to Starrett, silently asking what they could do. Starrett looked shocked, as though Dan had forcefully called him out of a train of thought. He too glanced at Bruhn, and his lips pursed and again that peculiar look came into his eyes. He slightly shook his head, his frown a warning to do nothing.

Dan moved impatiently with a touch of anger. He wished he knew what Starrett had in mind and he wondered if they would have a chance to talk very soon. The outlaws took their ease at the bar but Dan could see all too well that they were still alert and dangerous. No one could leave without their knowing it and even silent signals must be given swiftly, covertly.

The street door swung open and Dan, hearing the noise, looked up in the mirror. Bruhn, Pace and Juarez wheeled about as Vic and Bob Frazin came fearfully into the room, followed by Denver and Vause, who prodded Vic ahead with the barrel of his Colt.

The overhead lamps gave a peculiar sheen to Vic's face, pasty, fearful and without color. He licked his lips and moved nervously into the room. Bob walked stiffly, arms straight at his side, face frozen, his eyes mirroring the same fear that held his father. He was unaware of everything but the outlaws at his back, and moved in a strange, walking paralysis. Denver's single word halted the Frazins and they stood frozen, unmoving.

Denver stepped around them and walked to Bruhn, jangling a ring of keys in his hand. He gave them to Jack, half turned and grinned at Vic and his son.

"Have you ever seen such scared rabbits, Jack? Made me feel kind of mean herding them over here."

"That's something new for you," Jack replied dryly. He hefted the keys. "Everything's all right? No trouble?"

"None at all. We walked in and that jasper," he pointed to Vic, "came hurrying up, showing his gold teeth and right anxious to take our money. Damn' near had to pick his jaw up off the floor when I pulled my gun on him."

"This'n," Vause prodded Bob with his gun, "turned plumb green and then white. Never knowed a man could have so many colors. These people sure ain't much used to guns."

"No one else?" Bruhn demanded.

"Just these two. They said their family was home fixing supper. We locked the place up and made 'em take their horse over to the stable."

"How about the gun and ammunition stock?"

"Whole rack of rifles, another of scatterguns," Denver answered, "a showcase of Colts. Some ammunition on the shelves back of the showcase and some boxes of it in the back storeroom. But no one's going to get to it. You got the keys."

The break! Dan thought in sudden exultation. Give him, and one or two more, just fifteen minutes and no locks would keep them from the Colts. It would be easy to break in silently and get the weapons under the cover of night.

"Locked," Bruhn said and shook his head. "Not good enough. We'll move it tonight."

Denver looked shocked. "Tonight! Jack, it's a man-size job just slugging through that mud out there, let alone toting ammunition boxes. We've done a heap of riding—"

"You're forgetting we got friends." Bruhn's glance swept along the bar. "They'll be mighty pleased to do the job for us. Of course, we'll kind of keep an eye on 'em."

"Why, sure!" Denver said.

"Charley," Bruhn ordered, "check the stage station. See if it's locked. If it is, use a slug on the door. Get back here pronto."

Vause left. Bruhn looked at the Frazins and Dan saw the slow curl of contempt move his firm mouth. He spoke harshly and Vic cringed.

"We don't figure on gunning you down. Get yourselves a drink. You need it."

He sat down at one of the tables, placing the store

keys on the green cloth. He rubbed his hand thoughtfully along his jaw, glanced again at Shorty. Bob remained stiff and unmoving, but Vic swayed and then he shivered, suddenly swung to Phil Preston in frightened appeal.

"Phil, what has happened? What will they do to us?" His voice held a high-pitched quaver. He came to Phil, hands reaching out for support. Sudden dislike showed in Phil's eyes, to be instantly replaced by an understanding of the man's fears. But he edged away, avoiding the reaching hands.

"Have a drink, Vic." He pushed his full glass into Frazin's hands and watched the man gulp it down, his shaking hands spilling a few drops. Phil sketched briefly what had happened, then looked at Bruhn, immobile and massive at the table. "Keep your head and do as they say, Vic. We won't be hurt."

"But we'll be robbed!" Vic wailed. Phil bit his lip, annoyed.

"Maybe. But worse things could happen. Keep that in mind. You'd better take care of Bob."

Vic caught Phil's implication. His face paled and he turned, walked back to Bob. After a fearful glance at Bruhn, he forced his son to sit at a table, pulled up a chair beside him. Father and son sat quietly, fearful, their eyes darting here and there. Vause came in, soft mud making a brown layer over his boots.

"All unlocked, Jack," he reported. "Plenty of room to spread our blankets—even lamps and a big stove. It'll make the best spot any of us have seen in a hell of a time."

"Good." Bruhn wheeled about, facing the bar. His blunt finger speared in turn at Dan, Starrett, Preston, Larry Teter, Hal Crane, Claggett and then the Frazins.

"All of you will help us. Charley, you and Egan stay here and watch the doctor and that wounded rannie.

If Tex comes, tell him where we are." He glanced at the rest of his men. "Let's get ourselves camped. Keep a close eye on our . . . friends."

All of them were herded outside, Bruhn and Denver leading the way, Pace, Juarez and Egan in the rear, their hands resting in easy suggestion on their holsters. Gene Hiatt moved out with them and, just as they left the saloon, Dan caught a glimpse of the young man's face. He saw strain and trouble in the eyes for that brief moment and he realized that this one was different.

Then they were outside and Dan was surprised that it was pitch dark. He realized that he had been inside the saloon for a long time and that the short, winter day had ended. He saw the lights from the store and, looking between the smithy and the lumberyard, he saw the glow of lamplight from the Rikes' place, Doc Langer's and the Preston home. He thought of Paula and hoped desperately that she would stay in the house.

He moved down the steps with the rest. The outlaws, pressed in closer so that there was no chance of making a break. And, once Dan's feet touched the street, he gave up even this slim hope.

His feet sank to the ankles in mud and there was an evil, sucking sound each time he took a step. The whole valley would be like this, he knew, and now it might be days before any outside help could possibly come.

They reached the store and there was a long delay while Bruhn fumbled with the key and lock and finally threw open the door. He strode in, the rest straggling after. Bruhn strode down the aisle to the rear, stepped through the warehouse door and disappeared. He bellowed for a lamp, his voice muffled. Egan took one from a wall bracket and carried it into the storeroom.

Dan looked longingly at the rifles in the wall racks, the blue shine of Colts in the glass case. He only tortured himself. Pace, Juarez and Hiatt watched from the end of the aisle and, even if Dan could have reached the weapons, he knew they were empty.

Bruhn reappeared, Egan following him with the lamp. Pace looked inquiringly at him. "Big job?"

"Enough. But we got the men to do it."

His hard eyes swung to the door as it suddenly opened. For the first time, Dan saw Bruhn's gun speed. The massive hand dropped, snapped up, and held the muzzle of his gun trained on the doorway. A soft gasp swung Dan around in sudden panic.

Ernine stood just within the door. Surprise held her immobile, tall and stately, and it put a tinge of delicate red in her cheeks. Her brown eyes had widened and deepened. Her lips were a deep red against the sudden pallor of her skin.

"Who are you?" Bruhn demanded, slowly coming out of his crouch. Denver whistled.

"Hey, that's something I missed!"

Vic quickly stepped toward Ernine, but Juarez caught him, flung him back and his gun lifted in a menacing gesture. "You want a bullet, eh?"

Vic wheeled toward Bruhn, his hands spread out and up in appeal. "That's my daughter. She won't harm nobody. She didn't know . . . don't hurt her."

Bruhn shot a scathing glance at Vic and then holstered his gun. He looked at Ernine and then pointed to one side. "Get behind that counter and stay there. Do as you're told and you won't be hurt."

Ernine stared, then her eyes slowly moved to her father, who desperately signaled her to obey. Something of her usual composure returned and she swept the outlaws with a haughty glance, walked slowly to her place behind the counter. Dan wished that her father and brother had some of her courage.

Bruhn walked about the store, looked at the gun racks and turned to the men in the aisle. He ordered Phil and Claggett to take the rifles out of the racks, Larry Teter and Bob Frazin to take the shotguns. They were to be tied through the trigger guards into loose bundles. Vic was to take the Colts out of the case.

Crane was set to taking the small paper boxes of shells out of the shelves and stacking them on a counter. Bruhn beckoned Dan down the aisle and, with Egan still carrying the lamp, led him to the storeroom.

"Take those cases and stack 'em outside on the floor. Egan, you watch him." He walked into the main room and Dan heard him order Juarez and Pace to look around for supplies the outlaws would need. Denver took a stand at the front door, and Hiatt came to the rear of the store. Egan placed the lamp on a barrel and made a gesture toward the ammunition boxes.

"You heard Jack," he said with a crooked grin. "Get to it. We want to be settled cozy by morning."

Dan glared, roweled by the man's tone, but he started to work. He took the boxed ammunition out in the main room and gradually a respectable stack of boxes grew at one end of the aisle. Dan finally took the last box outside, thudded it down on the floor and straightened, stretched.

Hiatt stood a few feet away, but the man obviously didn't know anyone was about. He looked beyond Dan, bemused, a new light and wonder in his eyes. It struck Dan how young he was. There was nothing harsh and evil in the eyes, no deep lines of dissipation about the mouth or in the cheeks. A kid, Dan thought, not like Pace Odlum, young in years but older than the world in repellent, evil knowledge.

Dan stole a glance in the direction in which Hiatt gazed so earnestly. He saw Ernine, still erect and proud. She had pulled herself even deeper behind her strange reserve and it was almost as though nothing that happened about her was real or had meaning.

Dan's eyes cut to the door when it opened. Denver swung around, ready for trouble, but grinned when Tex Darrow entered and tried to kick some of the gumbo mud off his boots. Bruhn walked toward him and Tex looked up with a catlike grin.

"I took her home," he said. "She come close to hysterics but I poured whiskey down her. She passed out . . . maybe the whiskey, maybe her husband. Anyhow, she won't be no bother until morning."

"Can she get a gun?" Bruhn demanded. Tex chuckled and opened his coat, pulling a Colt from his waistband. "I went over the house from top to bottom. This was all."

Bruhn nodded and turned away. Now the real labor of the night began. It was not far from the store, across Spade Road to the building beside Winter Creek. Dan had walked it many a time in a few minutes. But tonight it was different.

Deep mud sucked and clung to Dan's boots at each step. He worked grimly with the others, carrying the heavy wooden cases of ammunition out of the store, along the quagmire of chilling water and mud that had once been a street, into the old stage station. The cases were stacked in a far corner, the rifles and revolvers placed beside them.

There were many trips and it seemed to Dan that the work would never end. He had worked longer and harder, but never at gun point.

The outlaws took no chances. There was always one or more of them close at hand, watching closely, ready for trouble. Despite the chill of the night wind, Dan soon found himself sweating.

The older men, Vic, Phil and Clay really suffered after a few trips. They puffed and panted, and sweat stood out on their foreheads in the lights of the store or the stage station.

Dan returned with the rest to the store for the last load. All of them were tight-lipped, cold with the indignity of this forced labor. Bruhn was not blind to the signs and he watched them all more closely.

They had just picked up the last cases when the front door swung open and Paula stepped swiftly inside. She halted abruptly when she saw the crowd of men and, like Ernine, her face went blank in momentary surprise. Her eyes widened, catching reflections of the lamp in golden flecks. Bruhn was instantly at her side.

"Who are you, ma'am?"

Phil spoke up. "She's my daughter, sir."

"Dad! What's happened?" Paula took a step toward him but Bruhn placed his hand on her arm.

"Ma'am, your paw will be busy for a time." He pointed to the counter where Ernine stood. "Join the lady over there. She'll tell you what it's about. Your paw will be back in about ten minutes."

Paula looked at Bruhn, then at Ernine, who made a slight signal for Paula to join her, and her level glance was also a silent warning. Dan stood with a case on his shoulder, and he felt himself grow cold with sudden fear. Paula, mystified but sensing some real danger here, walked over to Ernine's side. Bruhn smiled.

"That's reasonable, ma'am." He glanced at Hiatt. "Now you got two of 'em to watch, Gene. Not a bad job." He turned and his heavy voice grew grim. "All right, let's get this load over."

Dan caught Paula's searching, puzzled look and he, too, tried to send her a silent message of warning and encouragement. Then he started toward the door.

Pace stood there, but the young outlaw saw nothing but Paula. His pale eyes were fixed on her and, in the lamplight, his lips looked a deep crimson. Dan felt his nerves knot in his stomach.

Now he must find some way out of this trap, some means of besting these killers. Sure as day would come, Pace Odlum would make trouble for Paula. Dan read that in the narrowed pale eyes as he passed.

SEVEN

The yellow-faced clock on the kitchen wall between the two windows ticked noisily in the discouraged silence that had come on the three men seated at the table. Paula, working at the big range to warm up a meal long since cold, nervously rubbed her hands along her apron, started to speak, then changed her mind.

Dan, seated across from Starrett, leaned on one elbow and watched Paula's reflection in the dark kitchen window. He was very much aware of Phil just to his left and Starrett across the table. Now and then he caught a partial reflection of Starrett's harsh profile in the window.

A strange and uneasy peace had come to Bitter, like the enforced quiet of a penitentiary, Dan thought, with the silent guards prowling the walls and armed to the teeth.

He watched Paula's trim figure at the range. He remembered the look in Odlum's pale eyes and again he felt the writhing knot in the pit of his stomach. Suddenly Phil's fist banged down on the table and Paula gave a soft, startled exclamation. Dan looked around.

"Damn it, it makes me boil every time I think of the high-handed way they took over the town!" His fist lifted again, then the fingers opened slowly in a gesture of futility. "But what can we do?"

"I've run myself in circles trying to figure that one out," Dan said wearily. "They've got all the guns and ammunition."

"Searched every house from top to bottom," Phil added bitterly. "We'll be a week straightening up the mess those two jaspers left here. Nothing to defend ourselves with."

Paula came to the table with a steaming bowl of potatoes. Dan watched her, struck anew by her beauty. Then he noticed Starrett also watching Paula with a new, soft light in his eyes.

Starrett felt Dan's gaze and he looked hastily around. Their eyes met and locked. There was challenge and then a slight narrowing of Starrett's eyes, a tightening of his jaw. So this, Dan thought with a sudden shock, is how friendship dies . . . quietly, in the way Starrett slowly sat back in his chair.

Paula sat down to the table and Dan looked from her to Starrett and the thought struck him that they would make a handsome couple. But so would Paula and me, he thought angrily. He looked down at his plate, confused, wanting her and knowing that this desire had put a barrier between himself and Starrett.

"How easy they did it!" Phil said abruptly. "You'd never believe it. Just lock up all the horses, corner all the guns. Put a couple of boys to bunking in the stable to keep an eye on the horses, and you can stay in the town as long as you please."

"The mud helps," Dan said. "As soon as the roads get a bottom, they'll have a problem. Too easy for someone to ride in, or for one of us to get out."

"But how long will it last?" Phil demanded. Starrett

moved restlessly and made a gesture of easy confidence.

"So they've taken over for a while. It won't be long. They haven't done any looting."

Phil whipped around, angry. "But they killed Tommy Rikes, and Lewis won't do any roping or real work with that smashed shoulder of his. I suppose that was all right?"

"Well, no," Starrett said uncomfortably. Paula placed her hand on her father's balled fist.

"Dad! After all, what can we do about it? I'm sure Blaise . . . or Dan hates this as much as you."

Phil managed an embarrassed smile. "You're right, of course. I just get so damn' mad." He lifted a gaunt finger in warning. "But don't be so sure what they'll do. You can't predict that kind."

"Odlum kills for the love of it," Dan said soberly. "Tex Darrow is a man who takes what he wants. Juarez Smith is sneaky and dangerous. Egan and Vause are coyotes. Denver has a sense of humor but I figure he could crack a joke while he robbed his grandmother."

"You're forgetting Shorty Ratner," Starrett said in dry sarcasm.

"Good chance he'll die. That's one less sidewinder with a gun in our backs." Dan toyed with a crumb of bread. "There's the kid, Hiatt. I don't know about him."

"The nice-looking boy?" Paula asked. "He kept watching Ernine."

"An outlaw and renegade," Phil snapped.

"Maybe," Dan said slowly. "He's with 'em, all right, but his brand's not real clear."

"Arguments aside." Phil pushed back from the table. "We're so damned helpless that I'm worried."

"So am I," Dan said. Starrett chuckled dryly.

"Worry never yet roped a steer. Leave 'em alone and

Bruhn will keep his promise."

"If he can keep the rest in line," Dan added. "Something's bothering that bunch of renegades. I don't know what it is, but they could be clawing at one another at the drop of a hat."

Phil twisted about, a new hope in his eyes. "You reckon so?"

Dan shrugged. "Just a guess. Might mean something. But one way or the other, we got to keep our eyes open for the first little slip. They're bound to make one sooner or later."

"What would you do?" Starrett demanded. "They still got eight guns ready for us."

"We could see someone slips out for help," Dan replied soberly, "or we can play for the chance of getting the upper hand."

"Like drawing to an inside straight," Starrett sneered. Dan's head snapped up.

"What's wrong with you, Blaise? You act like you want these renegades in town!"

"You're crazy," Starrett growled. "I'm saying play along with 'em until they leave." He gestured toward the dark window. "That mud gumbo won't last long. Once they can travel, this gang will leave in a hurry. They're on the run, anyhow."

"So we wait—" Dan started.

Paula hastily arose. "Now that's enough. You men clear out of the kitchen until I rid it up. Into the parlor, all of you—and talk of something else for a change."

It was after eleven by the time Starrett and Dan climbed the stairs, Phil leading the way with a lamp. The hour had been strained. Talk was erratic and tentative, for they mentioned things like weather and the cattle market when their thoughts were on the outlaws. There was also a silent but intense rivalry between Starrett and Dan for Paula's attention. She sensed it, too, and divided her words and brief smiles equally between the two.

Now it was actually a relief to follow Phil into one of the cold upper bedrooms. Phil placed the lamp on a marble-topped table and went to the windows bent to peer out. He straightened.

"No light at the Rikes'. I guess Ava's gone to sleep. Hope she has."

"Be hard," Dan sighed, "with Tommy laid out in Larry's back room."

"Damn' useless murder!" Phil growled and walked to another window. He peered out again. "Someone stirring at Doc Langer's."

"Nursing Shorty," Dan said shortly.

"A hell of a thing." Phil went to the door, paused. "First time in my life I ever wished a man would die.... Good night."

"Good night," Dan and Starrett echoed and Phil softly closed the door.

They heard his steps move slowly down the hall and then another door closed. There was silence in the house and an even more ominous silence in the dark night beyond the windows. Dan jerked down the blinds. Starrett sank on the edge of the bed, leaned back, hooking his knee with his clasped hands.

"Dan, you keep watching Paula all the time and you acted like I had no right to talk to her. Why?"

Dan saw a chair against the wall and sat down. "I could ask you the same question."

Starrett rocked slowly back and forth, watching Dan narrowly. Finally he lifted his shoulders in a faint shrug and grinned.

"I'll answer it, Dan. I intend to marry her. What's your answer?"

"The same."

Dan expected anger but the only sign was a faint

coloring on Starrett's lean cheeks, a glitter in the eyes that swiftly disappeared. Starrett stopped rocking.

"I figured as much. But you haven't a chance."

Dan sighed. "Blaise, you've changed. Don't know why, but you're not the man I knew even a year ago. If this had come up then, you wouldn't have said that."

"What would I have said?" Starrett asked sharply.

"You'd figure I'd have just as good a chance as you and you'd have probably said something about making a fair and square fight of it. Now, it's just 'no chance.' You figure you're that good."

Starrett dropped his knee and bit at his lower lip as he worked at rolling a cigarette with elaborate care.

"You got the picture wrong, Dan."

"Then I'm damn' glad of it."

"What can I offer her, Dan?" He leaned forward. "She'll be mistress of Star. Can you offer as much?"

"No," Dan admitted. "I draw your pay and I haven't got an acre of range to my name."

"See!" Starrett exclaimed and smiled. "She will get an ambitious man, one who's going to make a big mark in this Territory. Star will be the biggest spread in all this country, Dan."

"How?"

It brought Starrett up short, frowning. He made an irritable gesture and stood up, ignoring the question. He began to unbutton his shirt and prepare for bed.

"Dan, I don't mind you trying to get Paula. But be reasonable. Do you expect her to turn her back on all I can give her? That don't make sense. Why don't you try to forget her?"

"Would you?" Dan asked.

Starrett paused, shirt half off, and considered this, lips pursed. He spoke slowly. "If I was in your boots and you in mine, I would. That's honest, Dan. Why, man, there's others better suited to become a foreman's wife . . . like Vivian McLear or, even, Ernine Frazin. If they won't do, there's other towns."

Dan stood up. "Like I said, you've changed . . . for the worse."

Starrett opened his mouth to make some hot retort but changed his mind. The two men crawled into the bed, backs to one another, each carefully seeing to it that he stayed well on his own side.

Dan lay staring at the gray oblong of the window. Starrett's near presence was a strain in itself. Both men kept the whole center of the bed between them, each hugging the rail. Starrett moved and Dan felt the slight rock of it.

Dan himself lay stiff and unmoving but his thoughts raced in an erratic circle, getting him nowhere. He wondered, in dull anger, why so many problems had to press in all at once. First, he was faced with the choice of backing Starrett's inevitable gunplay against HC or of leaving Star. He had thought that Paula would help shape his decision but now he realized that she only complicated it.

On top of this had come Jack Bruhn and his gang, making all of them virtual prisoners, complicating even more the knotty problems that Dan faced. How could a man make any valid, reasonable decisions under this new pressure? Bruhn held all the aces and the face cards and yet, in some way, he must be forced out before any real damage was done. The outlaws were peaceful now, Dan admitted to himself. But what would they do if Jack Bruhn's restraint was removed? Dan knew that the big renegade was all that stood between the town and serious trouble. Bruhn gone, would Hiatt molest Ernine, or Pace Odlum attack Paula? It was a definite possibility.

Then his thoughts turned to Paula and to what Starrett had said, a bitter truth that Dan could not avoid, nor did he want to. If he didn't back Starrett against Crane, then he left Star and rode chuckline to some puncher's job in the valley. Even if he stayed on as foreman and the trouble with Crane blew over, what was a foreman's job compared to a spread like Star? Nothing . . . any way you looked at it Starrett had overwhelming odds in his favor. Starrett rolled over on his back.

"Awake, Dan?"

"Yes."

"You've been worrying about Crane and me."

"I don't like gun wages."

Starrett was silent a long moment. "Maybe there won't be any need to worry. Of course, it will make no difference about Paula, but you wouldn't have to worry about range war."

"What's changed you?"

"Me? . . . nothing. I still aim to have that range. But Crane's held here in town just like all the rest of us. His man has been shot up and he's felt Darrow's fist. He's mad, bound to be."

"Don't blame him. I am, too. But what about it?"

"It just come to me, Dan. Maybe there's another way of bringing Crane to terms . . . or getting that range."

Dan stared off toward the window, puzzling at this thing. Suddenly it struck him and he sat upright with a jerk and twisted toward Starrett, seeing the vague shape of the man beneath the covers.

"What's on your mind, Blaise?"

Starrett moved slightly. "A new way of taking care of Crane."

"You mean Jack Bruhn and his gang. You'd hire murderers."

There was only a stony silence, neither denial nor confirmation, but Dan knew beyond doubt that this was exactly what Starrett meant. He spoke earnestly.

"Blaise, listen. You can't do a thing like that. It would haunt you all your life, and nothing's worth that. Think what it would do to Star. You want to build up the ranch on someone's blood."

Starrett moved again and Dan waited, hopeful and tense. Starrett's voice was dry, level. "Dan, I can make up my own mind. And there's no reason for you to worry about Star, either."

"Why shouldn't I—" Dan started but Starrett cut in with swift finality.

"You just went off the payroll, Dan. You don't work for Star anymore."

EIGHT

Jack Bruhn stood at the window of the stage station and looked at the town. He could see the general store, the livery stable and a small and neat house on one of the three roads that joined the main highway just beyond the station. All of them had that blank, dead look that buildings acquire just as the sun lifts above the horizon.

He could hear the stir of the men behind him, a loud yawn, a bang of a skillet as Vause started breakfast on the big, pot-bellied stove at the far end of the room. Tex cursed sleepily as he rolled out of the blankets he had stretched on the floor.

"That's the hardest damn' place I ever spread my blankets. A rock would be twice as soft."

"Ah," Juarez said with a chuckle, "but it is safe, *amigo*. That is something to think of."

"Sure, safe enough." There was a silence and then a boot scraped along the floor. "But the whole town's safe. No need to camp out in this barn."

"Where, then?" Juarez demanded. Tex laughed softly.

"Why there's a new widow in town . . . not bad looking. She might need consoling."

Jack stiffened and nearly swung around to order Tex to leave the woman alone. But he checked himself with an effort of will. Jack was not quite ready for a showdown yet. Still this thing worried him. The situation in this town was different, uncertain and explosive. Molest a woman and you never knew what might happen.

Jack looked out the window again, his thoughts moving in a slow, troubled circle. He glanced southward, across the bridge. Everywhere he looked each square foot of earth was bottomless mud. No man in his right sense would attempt to ride across this desolate range. Safe enough, Jack thought, but it was the only thing that gave him pleasure.

He turned from the window and walked over to the stove. The coffeepot burbled. Vause looked up as Jack approached. He dropped several slices of bacon in the pan and the grease sizzled frantically.

"Gonna take a long time to fix this," Vause said. "Ain't much room to work."

"It'll do," Jack shrugged. He looked over the men in the room, most of them dressed by now, some still seated on their crumpled blankets.

He saw each one more clearly this morning. Tex, rolling a cigarette, looked peaceful enough, but Jack had known for a long time that Tex had plans for leading this bunch. Trouble was, you never knew when Tex would act. A wrong word, an order that might anger him, could set that unpredictable personality ablaze and Tex would make his play.

Jack's harsh eyes moved to Juarez Smith. This morning he looked like a treacherous jackal, even though he smiled at some joke Tex had made. His coarse black hair was tousled and his swarthy skin looked oily in the early morning light, the blue eyes puffy and red-veined.

Juarez would side with Tex, Jack decided. He was Tex's shadow and echo: as Tex thought so did Juarez, as Tex acted, Juarez backed him. So count him against you when the showdown comes.

When would it come? Here, in this town? Bruhn's thick chest lifted in a sigh. He kind of wished it would . . . get it over and end this endless drag of uncertainty and tension. His eyes strayed to his own pallet and just beyond, where the full saddlebags lay against the wall. Fifty thousand dollars there, and more than one gun fight had started for less. Jack had the idea that Tex would actually make his play when they came to dividing it.

Pace Odlum arose from his blankets and strolled to the door, looked out on the street. Jack watched him, noting the graceful, almost feminine movements, the slender figure that a man might believe he could smash with a blow. A strange one, Jack thought.

He had first seen Pace down in the San Juan country and had dismissed him as a stripling, misreading the handsome face, the red-lipped smile and the soft voice. Then he had seen Pace react to the gibings of two swaggering punchers. They had died, swiftly and violently, and Jack could still see the exultant, savage gleam in those pale eyes, the lips pulled back from the perfect teeth in a cherubic smile as he stood, smoking Colt still in his hand.

Somehow you were always glad that Pace Odlum held no anger against you. He joyed in killing, reveled in blood and it was something far and beyond what Jack had seen in other killers. It made you shiver sometimes.

But where would Pace stand if Tex called a showdown? Jack didn't know. There had been nothing in the man's actions, voice or expression to tell him. He might side with Jack, or he could just as easily use that deadly gun against Jack.

"Still warm," Pace said, opened the door wider and took a deep breath. He came back into the room and Jack's eyes followed him. Then Gene Hiatt arose and Jack's attention swung to him.

Another kid, another stripling, Jack thought. I can depend on Gene where I'll have to sound Pace out before any trouble breaks. Count one for me, Juarez for Tex, and Pace either way. But Gene Hiatt didn't swing much weight in Jack's mind.

Sure, he had come to the band wanted by a sheriff. But this life didn't fit him . . . it might in time, if the kid stuck with it. Jack had the feeling Gene was sorry for his bargain and some day they would wake up and find the kid had skipped.

"All right," Vause called. "It's cooked . . . you eat it."

Charley Vause, Jack thought, fair with a gun but better when he knew he had the whole gang behind him. Vause would probably follow Jack's lead. One more for me, then count Denver. Egan would back Tex and Juarez, thinking they had the advantage.

Jack helped himself to food, a mug of coffee and walked back to his blankets. As he sat cross-legged, eating, his hard eyes moved restlessly from man to man, weighing, judging, accepting, rejecting until it seemed that his thoughts went in a crazy circle.

Tex finished the last bite of bacon, the last swallow of coffee. He arose, hitched at his gunbelt and grinned at Juarez. "Well, I reckon I'll see the town."

Jack looked up under his brows. "It's knee-deep in mud out there. Won't be worth it."

Tex turned, still smiling, but it didn't reach his eyes. "I think it is, Jack. Any objections?"

The harsh angles of Jack's face grew prominent and

there was a ripple of muscle along his jaw. Tex waited and Jack shrugged, speared a bit of bacon with his fork.

"Suit yourself. We could use you to check the rest of the houses for guns."

Tex said carelessly, "Tell you what, I'll check the widow's house again real good."

He waited but Jack only shrugged and drank deep from the coffee mug. He didn't miss the swift look that passed between Tex and Juarez. They're waiting, Jack thought, for any shadow of an excuse. Tex finally swaggered to the door. He paused, still not sure but what Jack would object, then went outside. The door swung shut behind him.

Jack sent a sidelong look toward the rest of the men. Pace watched him, pale eyes void of expression, the thin, handsome face as expressionless as an Indian's. Then Pace looked away. There was a knock on the door a few moments later and every man's head jerked up in alarm. With a smooth, flowing motion, Pace came to his feet and his gun appeared in his hand. Jack stood up as Pace walked to the door and opened it.

"Excuse me," Vic Frazin said. Jack grunted.

"Let him in, Pace."

"All of 'em?"

"Just my two sons," Vic said hastily. He stepped aside and Jack recognized Bob Frazin, the older boy. The other was about fourteen, a stocky, awkward kid who looked around in excitement and open admiration. Vic placed his hand on the lad's shoulder, give Jack an ingratiating smile.

"This is Art—my youngest. Helps me at the store and he'll grow up to be a fine merchant someday." Vic smiled around at the rest of the men. "I hope you all slept well."

Jack could not hide his annoyance at this fawning. "What do you want? Be quick about it."

"Sure, sure," Vic said hastily. Art edged toward Charley Vause, his eyes resting a long time on the walnut grip of the holstered Colt. His round face mirrored an awed wonder.

"You're really an outlaw, mister?"

Charley blinked, glanced at Jack, then gave the kid a twisted grin. "Sure, didn't you know?"

"Paw said you was and he said—"

"Art!" Vic said sharply, "mind your manners." He returned to Jack. "I wondered if we could have the keys to the store. Won't be many come, of course, but they do need the things we have to sell. No harm in it, is there?"

Jack fished the keys from his pocket. He gave them to Vic and then looked over at Hiatt.

"Go with 'em, Gene. Give the store another check. You might hang around to see that they don't pull a trick."

The Frazins, boots thick with clinging mud, turned to the door. Hiatt hastily swept up his hat and followed them. When they were gone, Jack returned to his pallet, wondering vaguely why Hiatt had seemed so unusually pleased with the assignment.

Gene walked outside with the two men and the boy. The sun was bright, the day clear except for some low clouds on the northwestern horizon. Water reflected the light from myriad ripples. Gene narrowed his eyes against the glare and stepped off the porch into the mud.

Vic and Bob slogged ahead, but the boy stayed close to Gene, having a hard time with the going but trying to give all of his admiring attention to Gene. Mud sucked at their boots and it was hard work walking even a few feet. Vic visibly puffed and Gene felt the strain in his own leg muscles.

"What's it like to be an outlaw, mister?" the boy asked suddenly.

It shocked Gene and he felt the impact of the question. He lost his stride, stumbled and caught himself. Art's guileless dark eyes still admired him.

"It's . . . well, you wouldn't like it," Gene said in a strained voice.

"Oh, I don't know. Lots of excitement, I bet. Lots of riding." He looked about, disdaining what he saw. "You'd see a lot more than this town and the valley. Jiminy! I bet there's lots of things to see, ain't there, mister?"

"Yes," Gene choked. "Only some you won't like."

The boy looked off into the distance, eyes bemused. Gene looked down the single street with its few buildings. So this is all you see, he thought bitterly. Look again, kid. You're seeing stability, assurance, a normal life free from fear of the law or a bullet. You're seeing a chance to grow up and become a man who can walk with his eyes forward and his shoulders back. It's not much now but it will grow and you can grow with it. I can't.

He had the sudden wild impulse to ride out of here, out of the gang. Maybe he could work his way to California, take a different name, start a new life. But the locked door of the livery stable broke the impulse into a thousand dismal pieces. You stay, Gene Hiatt. Funny how he had never really considered himself an outlaw until the kid had used the word.

Two women waited under the store canopy, heavy coats making both look shapeless. One was around fifty, a grim-jawed woman with gray hair that held no softness. Yet her deep brown eyes were strangely gentle and Gene instantly saw a likeness between her and the girl who stood beside her. His heart lifted at the sight of Ernine, as it had each time he had seen her. Vic came up on the porch and tried vainly to stomp the gumbo off his boots.

"I got the key, Mom," he said and glanced at Gene.

"Is this one of . . . them?" Mrs. Frazin asked and Gene flushed at the contempt in her voice.

"Yes, come to make sure everything is all right."

"For us . . . or for them?" the woman snapped.

Vic didn't answer. Gene caught the girl's eyes upon him. Her glance slid away and a slight touch of color came to the olive cheeks. It was the first time Gene had ever seen anything but aloof dignity in this girl and it surprised him. He wondered for a wild moment if this was the beginning of an interest in him, but the boy's shrill statement shattered the thought.

"Maw, I'm going to be an outlaw."

Mrs. Frazin's hand caught the boy alongside the ear. She glared at Gene, her eyes were icy hard. The sharp, unexpected blow made Art cry out and then look at his mother in injured surprise.

"What was that for, Maw?"

"That was for wanting to be a sneak, a thief and a dirty, cowardly killer."

"Mom!" Vic hastily turned from the door. He looked apprehensively at Gene. The woman continued to glare and Gene felt his face grow fiery red. Vic started to apologize but Gene's gesture cut him short.

"She's right," he said, voice muffled. "I guess you could call us that." His attention swung to the boy. "There's not a worse kind of life than this, kid. When we're gone, forget us, or you'll be sorry the rest of your days."

Art stared. Mrs. Frazin took a deep breath, turned on her heel and stalked into the store, Vic following her. Ernine gave Gene a long, underbrow look, a touch of warmth in her eyes. But it was only fleeting and she walked into the store as though he didn't exist.

Gene followed them and, as Vic started a fire in the big stove, he checked possible hiding places for guns that might have been overlooked. Gene found nothing and he felt glad to escape the place. As he went out the door, he caught Art's secretive, admiring look and the youngster's dark eyes said that he knew an outlaw's life was full of excitement. Gene almost stopped to talk to the boy again, but Mrs. Frazin's contemptuous sniff sent him on his way.

He stepped out on the porch and closed the door behind him. He felt desolate and alone, isolated from all decent people. Again he looked toward the stage station, caught a fleeting glimpse of Denver. Too much against it, he thought. No, the outlaw brand would always be upon him. He turned back toward the stage station, a hopeless despair riding him.

Vivian McLear had been up since just after sunrise, prepared her breakfast and then had started the day's work, finishing the dress for Mrs. Majors. Bright sunlight streamed in the window of the little house on Squaw Creek Road, isolated from the rest of the village.

Her needle moved with swift flashes along the hem of the silken material and it was one of those mornings when she was close to happy again. They came much more frequently of late. As her thoughts turned to Dan Murdock the needle moved more slowly and her face softened. She saw him as he was yesterday, a tall man, quiet, somewhat awkward in the way that is always pleasing to a woman.

She realized she had no more thread. She opened the sewing basket but could not find the same color among all the spools it contained. With impatience, she searched among a larger supply of spools in a cabinet drawer. She straightened, knowing that she

would have to go to the store. She walked to the
window and studied the mud outside, resigned herself
to a sticky plastering, for the dress had to be done.

She arrived at the store, wearing boots, an old dress
and an ancient coat. The gumbo made her small feet
look three times their size. She had glimpsed some
strange men at the stage station but had felt only a
minor curiosity. Travelers often put up at the station
because the village had no hotel.

But something grim and frightened in Vic Frazin's
face and manner and the way Bob nervously watched
the window told her something was wrong. She went
to the thread counter and Ernine came to wait on her.
Mrs. Frazin's voice boomed from behind the roll top
desk.

"Miss McLear, you surely ain't sewing today!"

Vivian turned, puzzled. "Why, yes. Is there something
special?"

Mrs. Frazin came striding down the aisle, seeming
to dominate the store. "Something special, indeed!
Didn't you hear those gunshots last night?"

"Of course, but someone's always celebrating at the
Wyoming Bar."

"Celebrating!" Mrs. Frazin halted a step away.
Ernine placed two spools of thread on the counter and
Vivian gave her a coin.

"Mother is talking about the bandits."

Vivian showed her surprise. "We were robbed?"

"Worse'n that," Mrs. Frazin snapped. "They've took
over the whole town and there ain't nothing any of us
can do. They wounded Lewis and killed Tommy Rikes."

Vivian looked disbelievingly at Ernine, saw
confirmation in the girl's face.

"Tommy! It can't be! Where's Ava?"

"She collapsed and they took her home."

"I'll go over right away." She turned but Vic stopped

her. "Maybe you'd better be careful. Can't tell what these outlaws'll do."

Vivian hesitated. It was not a fear such as the others knew, but something else. She shrugged it off, smiled at Vic.

"I can take care of myself. Besides, it's broad daylight. Ava will need help."

She walked out on the porch, leaving Vic worriedly shaking his head. In her haste she did not see Dan Murdock and she practically walked into him. He caught her, drew back, grinning. But she saw the worry and anger that still lurked in his eyes.

"Makes us even," he said with a chuckle. She flashed him a smile and then sobered.

"I heard about Tommy Rikes, Dan. I'm going to see if Ava needs anything."

Instantly his eyes swept the street, empty now. "Alone?"

"No one will hurt me."

"I'll not take a chance."

She tried to protest but he would not listen. They fought the mud to the street directly across from the livery stable. A bearded man came out, stood in the doorway, stretched and grinned a mocking good morning to them. Vivian gave him a swift glance and tried to hurry on.

"What gang is it?" she asked as they turned the corner.

"Jack Bruhn's outfit. One of them's over at Doc Langer's, hard hit. Might not live. But the rest have sure thrown a tight noose around the town."

She seemed relieved for some reason and it encouraged Dan to talk. She nodded now and then, or smiled. Dan found that he could talk to her like he used to talk to Starrett in the old days. And he spoke of Starrett now and the worries about Star. He did not mention Starrett's new idea, for actually the man had made no open move. But Dan did talk of the outlaws and his voice became tight with anger.

He finished and Vivian sighed. "But nobody can do anything now, Dan. Like you say, we have to wait for our chance." She put her hand on his arm. "And, Dan, do be careful."

Something in her tone made him throw a quick, searching look at her. He was surprised at what he read in her face. Suddenly Dan remembered what Starrett had said. Maybe Vivian was his kind. A man could look far to equal her . . . if he had not seen Paula Preston first. That was the trouble, he thought bitterly.

They reached the Rikes' house, across the muddy street from the Preston's. They walked up on the porch and Dan knocked lightly on the door, not sure of their reception if Ava was still in a state of collapse. He heard footsteps and then the door was thrown open.

Tex Darrow stood framed. He scowled at Dan and his hard, black eyes skipped to Vivian. Surprise flashed over his face. He grinned widely as Vivian gasped.

"Tex!"

Dan wheeled around. Her face had grown pale and she had lifted her hand to her mouth, her fingers pressing against her lips. She was like a person who suddenly looked upon disaster and knew there was no escape. Tex stepped out on the porch, his hand extended to Vivian, a cynical pleasure in his expression.

"A surprise, Belle! It's a long way . . . and a long time . . . from Wichita."

NINE

Vivian looked down at Tex's hand and then up into his face. Some of her color had returned and now her lips had set, giving her a hard look that Dan had never seen before. Her eyes met Tex's in a direct challenge.

"It is a long way—and time. I've forgotten Wichita and all concerned with it."

"A hard thing to do," Tex said and rubbed the back of his fingers along his jaw, considering her, one brow lifted. "Forgetting ain't a one-person thing, Belle."

"You waste your time," she said sharply. "How is Ava?"

"The lady? Good enough, I reckon."

"I came to see her."

"Step right in. She's a mite drunk."

"Your doing, Tex?"

"Belle, I never poured a slug of whiskey down nobody's throat. I brought the bottle, but she did the drinking."

Vivian stepped around Tex to enter. Dan started to follow but Tex moved in front of him and now his black eyes were hard and mean.

"You ain't got an invite, friend. Get on about your business."

Dan looked at Vivian, afraid to leave her. He sensed that in some way Tex Darrow had become an unexpected threat to the girl. Tex's lips moved in a grimace and his right hand lifted slowly toward his gun.

"Git along, dogie. You've strayed."

Vivian turned, just within the doorway. "It's all right, Dan. I want no trouble on my account." Her scornful eyes cut at the outlaw. "Tex will be no bother. He never was."

It was dismissal and Dan saw the mounting anger in the curl of Tex's thin lips. He turned and strode inside. The door slammed and Dan was left standing alone on the porch, feeling both foolish and angry.

He stood a moment, glaring at the closed door. Then he slowly descended the steps to the mud. As he slogged back toward the main street, he tried to make sense of the meeting between Vivian and Tex. He began to wonder if there might not, after all, be some foundation to the whispered gossip of the women of the town and the valley.

Smoke and fire, he thought, and then grew angry at himself. There was nothing wrong with Vivian . . . had never been. Maybe her name had once been Belle, and in Wichita she had met Tex Darrow some time in the far dim past. You back a friend for what he is now, not for what he might have been.

He slogged his way back to the main street and stood directly opposite the livery stable. There was no sign of the two outlaws, but the door was closed and Dan knew beyond doubt it was tightly locked.

He glanced toward the Wyoming Bar. At that moment the door opened and the outlaw, Vause, stepped out on the porch. He threw a swift, searching look northward up the road, then turned and saw Dan. He hesitated a second, then looked beyond the bridge at the morass that once was road and range. He turned back and the door closed.

Dan was surprised that the bar was open. Tommy lay dead in the back room of Larry's barbershop next door and Ava was home. The outlaws themselves had opened it and anger again roiled in Dan's chest. What was this but looting, despite Bruhn's promise?

His anger drove him forward across the street and

into the saloon. He stood just inside the door. Vause was circling the bar, where Pace Odlum and Juarez Smith stood, their muddy boots on the brass rail. Jack Bruhn sat at a far table, dealing solitaire, his big hands looking as though they would smother the cards.

Denver, at the far end of the bar, saw him first. The bearded outlaw cuffed his hat back and grinned through his whiskers. "Now if there ain't a citizen of this damn' town come to have a drink with us. Step right up and help yourself."

Dan ignored him. Vause lifted the glass toward Dan in a mock salute before he tossed it, his head swinging back, his neck convulsing to the impact of the liquor.

Dan went behind the bar. Pace Odlum and Juarez Smith idly watched, glasses before them. Dan bent to look under the bar, found a small bowl with a crack in its side. He placed it on the bar.

Pace looked at it, then up at Dan, openly puzzled. Juarez wiped a dark hand across his slack lips but said nothing. Dan paid no attention to either, but selected a bottle from the back bar, poured his drink. Then he fished in his pocket, pulled out a coin. He held it poised over the bowl, then dropped it. The sound was loud and cheery in the silent room.

Dan picked up his drink and swallowed it. Denver eyed him from under the floppy brim of his battered hat and Dan could not read the expression on the whiskered face. Juarez straightened, blue eyes ugly, not quite certain that he had caught Dan's meaning. Pace remained unmoving, expression inscrutable. Very slowly his red lips broke into a twisted grin.

"The drinks are on the house, I'd say."

"On the house?" Dan asked, "or on a dead man or a widow wondering what's going to become of her? Either way, I can't cheat 'em."

There was a dead silence in the big room. Jack Bruhn watched from the far table, started to reach for his drink and drew back his hand. Denver lost his grin and he soberly studied his drink. Vause looked like a kid caught with his hand in the cooky jar. Juarez didn't move, and Dan could see he was on the edge of anger.

Pace Odlum did not change expression, except that the smile slowly faded. His pale eyes bored into Dan, twin icy probes. Dan met them, accusing and challenging rather than angry. The others obviously waited for Pace to make the decision. Suddenly Dan felt fear. It was a subtle thing at first but it grew and coiled upward as he looked into the pale and inscrutable eyes. He could read nothing of what went on behind them, realized that this deadly stripling might do any unpredictable thing.

Pace slowly pushed his shot glass back with the tip of his slim fingers. He straightened, each move deliberate. Dan's fingers tightened slightly on the edge of the bar and he wondered desperately if he had even the ghost of a chance of dodging a bullet he was sure would come.

"That's the way you see it?" Pace asked softly. Dan could not help the involuntary swallow but he kept his voice even.

"I see it that way."

Pace's right hand moved to the edge of the bar and Dan watched it. Juarez stirred, smacked his hand on the wood, the sound startling.

"*Dios!* This fool—" Pace's swift gesture checked the half-breed.

"He tells us what to do," Pace finished softly. His hand moved to his pocket, not his gun. He fished out a gold coin and dropped it in the bowl. "He's right. Ante up, you hellions. Be honest men for once in your lives."

He looked at his companions. They stood surprised a moment and then each of them pulled out coins and dropped them in the bowl. Jack Bruhn stirred and arose, came heavily to the bar and made his contribution. He stood a moment, hard gray eyes on Dan, and seemed about to speak. Then he turned and went back to the table. Dan picked up the bowl to put the money in the cash drawer. Pace shook his head.

"Leave it there, friend in plain sight . . . so no one will forget." He smiled guilelessly and his voice grew soft "I promise you no one will take anything out of it."

Dan believed him. He hastily poured another shot and downed it as Pace's lips widened in a smile. One brow lifted.

"I scare you, don't I?" he asked, pleasure in his silken voice.

Dan's head jerked up as he started to make a swift denial. But he said nothing. This kid did scare him, but damned if he would admit it. He finally shrugged.

"You'll never know."

"But I do," Pace purred and lifted his glass in a mock salute. "To your guts. It'll be fun to kill you someday."

He tossed the drink and signaled Juarez to follow him to a table where they started a card game. The door opened and Hal Crane came in. He stood just within the room and glanced quickly at each of the outlaws. None of them spoke, only looked briefly at him and then away.

Crane slowly rubbed one hand along his trousers. He saw Dan behind the bar and he nodded curtly and came forward. Denver looked up, then back at his glass.

"Help yourself, Hal," Dan said. He nodded toward the bowl of coins. "And pay the piper there."

Crane looked surprised. "Now who'd expect that when it's free for the taking?"

"New rule," Dan said and swiftly changed the subject. "Where'd you stay the night?"

"The Frazins." Crane poured his drink, paid the bowl. "They're scared to death and talk your head off. Had to share the bunk with the kid. To hear him talk, the damn' town didn't live until these gents walked in."

Dan shrugged. "Outlaws are pretty big men when you're that age."

"I guess so," Crane said sourly. He looked, up when the door opened and Claggett stuck his head in the room. He looked around, saw Crane and signaled to him. Crane swallowed his drink and joined Claggett. They were outside but a moment and then returned, walking directly to the bar. Crane told Claggett what to do about drinks and looked sharply at Dan. He glanced up at the mirror, grunted.

"I guess all of us will be here a spell."

It had a meaning that escaped Dan and he could not read Crane's tight face. He suddenly felt tired and a bit useless. Crane had plainly dismissed him and Dan could understand that only circumstance had broken Crane's reserve toward the foreman of a ranch that challenged his own. So Dan found a deck of cards, walked to a table in a far corner of the room and started a game of solitaire.

He played slowly, sometimes forgetting the game completely as his thoughts swung off to his own pressing problems. They had narrowed considerably since Starrett had fired him. He need not worry about Star Ranch any more . . . but that would take practice. He need not make any plans about himself and Paula, for Starrett had definitely taken care of that.

He suddenly gathered up the cards and slapped the deck down on the table. He arose, impatient to be moving, and strode outside. He paused on the edge of the porch, feeling as though he'd like to slam his fist against someone or something. He looked restlessly along the street, centered on the lumberyard office.

Paula stood at the door and in a second she opened it and disappeared inside. Dan glanced along the street and saw no sign of Starrett. He stepped down in the mud and slogged his way across the street.

Paula was alone in the office, bent before the stove starting a fire. She swung about in swift alarm when Dan entered, green eyes wide, her hands lifting in an instinctive gesture of defense. The fear left her and she smiled, relieved.

"It's you, Dan."

"I scared you," he said contritely. She laughed and dropped a wadded paper into the black maw of the stove.

"You did," she admitted. "But if I'd known it was you...." Her voice drifted off and she looked over her shoulder at him.

The green eyes had deepened and now they were almost blue, and it seemed to Dan that he dare not breathe or the illusion would be gone. He felt a tightening constriction in his chest. He took an involuntary step toward her and then the eyes had changed back to the clear green color and her smile was gay and friendly . . . nothing more. The illusion had lasted such a brief second that Dan could not be at all sure he had seen correctly. And then he knew that now he dared not find out. Now, so close to her, he knew that he had little to offer.

She straightened and watched him, silent, lips slightly parted. Dan walked to the stove and bent down to the small pile of kindling.

"I'll make it," he said roughly.

Paula looked down at his broad shoulders a moment,

her expression a strange mixture of hope and disappointment. Her face softened in understanding and she smiled, then walked beyond the little barrier that divided the office and took off her hat.

"Everything is peaceful this morning," she said. Dan nodded, spoke casually.

"Where's Blaise?"

Paula replied while she placed her hat on a wooden file. "He went to the store, I believe. Dad's with him by now."

The first small flames lit Dan's lean face. Paula studied him a moment until he lifted his head. Then she looked hastily away.

"Dad went to Doc Langer's first. He thinks there must be some way of forcing these outlaws out of town. He's trying to get help."

Dan stood up, made sure the fire had caught, then closed the stove door with a bang. He looked at her, worried.

"Phil could get in serious trouble if he's not careful."

Paula sighed worriedly. "I know, Dan. But Dad don't see it that way. He says we can't tell what they'll do, who they'll kill next . . . or they might take a notion to loot the whole town and set it afire. So he's trying to get help."

"I'll find him," Dan said grimly. "If any of that bunch learns what he's trying to do, they'll . . ."

He didn't finish but stepped outside and closed the door after him, then remained with his hand still on the knob. Go back in, he told himself, and let her know how you feel. He shook his head. Not yet . . . not until he knew where he stood with Starrett. Right now, find Phil, and persuade the man to be careful.

A wind had started. It touched his face with an icy finger and then passed on. He looked up, surprised that the breeze should be so cold. His eyes lifted to the northwest and he suddenly knew what Crane had meant.

Off toward the horizon the dark clouds began to pile high and there was a strange cast to the color of the sky, a dirty, angry blue. Here the sun still shone brightly but Dan knew it would soon be gone. In those far-off clouds, angry winds hurried to batter the town and the valley.

It was a "blue norther." Those clouds carried blinding, driving snow. Those winds would drop the temperature to the bottom of the tube and savagely attack every living thing. Nothing could live in it, a man could be lost and freeze to death between his house and his woodshed.

Dan's face grew dark. With the coming of the blizzard, this ocean of water would swiftly change to slick, glaring ice. There would be no chance now of anyone leaving Bitter, himself or the outlaws. A horse might have a chance to slug through the mud, given time. But ice . . . no.

Nature, grim and unrelenting in this harsh land, was about to seal Bitter off and leave its people to the mercy of the outlaws . . . men to whom mercy, or honor, meant nothing.

TEN

Dan turned back into the office. Paula looked surprised, her face alight and expectant.

"There's a blizzard coming up," he said. "Best be home before it hits."

Her face lost its heightened color. She nodded, now deliberately aloof. Her voice was level and yet he felt a slight tone of irritation.

"Thank you, Dan. I'll take care of myself."

He looked sharply at her, feeling the rebuff and smarting a little under it. Yet he wanted more than anything else to tell her how he really felt. But it was impossible now. Dan shrugged and stalked outside, forcefully closing the door behind him.

He slogged through the mud, still feeling the strong pull of the girl. Gorton's smithy was closed and the whole town looked deserted, pitifully small and helpless against the sweep of the plain and the loom of the high peaks beyond the buildings.

He entered the store. Vic, Bob and Phil stood at the far end of the center aisle, and they wheeled about on Dan's entrance. There were still shreds of alarm in Vic's eyes when he spoke.

"Oh, it's you, Dan."

"Glad you came," Phil said. "We can use your advice."

Dan joined them, touching his hat brim to Ernine, who hovered near the big stove. Art Frazin sat on a barrel, his legs swinging, excitement in his face. The men stood in the cleared space between the stove and Vic's big desk, and Phil stepped aside to make room for Dan.

"Dan, we've got to do something about this situation."

"But what, Phil?" Vic demanded. "How?" He pointed toward the empty rack. "Every rifle and gun has been taken. And even if we had them, what chance would we have against those killers?"

"That's just it," Phil boomed. "They are killers. We simply have to act to protect ourselves. Why, Vic, there's nothing at all to prevent them from shooting down any one of us just as they did Tommy Rikes." His voice lowered, grimly. "I'm also worried about our womenfolk."

Vic pulled a handkerchief from his pocket and patted his forehead. He looked down the aisle toward the big front windows.

"But there's nothing we can do," he said. "Not a thing."

"I don't believe it," Phil snapped. He turned to Dan. "What do you think about it?"

"I've been worried," Dan said at last. "But I don't get anywhere. Now there's a norther coming, and any chance of riding out for help is gone. Whatever we do, we got to do it ourselves."

"But we can't!" Vic insisted, his voice rising a note. Dan ignored him.

"I know what you mean about the womenfolk. Something like that's already in the cards." Phil sighed and threw his hands wide in a futile gesture.

"So what in hell do we do?"

Dan spoke slowly, thinking the problem out. "I think there's one chance, but it's risky."

"Anything," Phil said shortly. Dan glanced toward the door. "We don't have a gun among us but I guess we could always get ahold of clubs or a knife or two."

Vic stared. He licked his lips. "What are you trying to say?"

"There's four of us. The gang is scattered all over town—"

"And armed," Bob Frazin cut in. Dan nodded.

"And armed. So one of 'em comes in right now, say. Phil and Vic would get him to talking. At the right time, Bob and me would jump him. He wouldn't have a chance to use his Colt. We'd get it. Tie him up and hide him in the storeroom."

"You're crazy!" Vic exclaimed in horror.

Dan said evenly, "Then we'd get another one of 'em alone, only this time we'd have a gun. Then we'd have his . . . two guns now. That's the only way it can be done. But we'd all have to help one another."

Vic looked toward Phil who stared bemused at the big stove, a slight gleam in his eyes showing that he approved of the plan. Vic wrung his hands.

"It won't work . . . it's too risky. If we make a slip with the first one, what will happen to us?"

Dan shrugged. "You heard what Jack Bruhn said. It's something you have to face, Vic . . . all of us do. But it's the only way."

Ernine stirred and Dan's attention swung momentarily to her. She looked troubled, a bit frightened. Art leaned forward, seated now at the edge of the counter. His face glowed with excitement and his eyes sparkled. Dan glanced again at Vic and sighed.

"Maybe we'd better all think this over. We can talk again this afternoon and maybe it will look better by then. Think it over . . . good."

He nodded grimly and strode down the aisle. With a last backward look at the silent men about the stove, he stepped out on the porch. Dan's eyes lifted toward the northwest. The clouds were there, still far away and it seemed that the cold breeze had died somewhat. It might veer off, he thought, but with no real hope since he knew all too well the pattern of the storms that swept the valley.

Then he saw Vivian working her way through the mud between the store and the smithy. Dan threw a swift glance at the saloon and waded out in the mud to meet the girl. He looked sharply at her when he came up and she smiled.

"I'm safe enough, Dan," she said, then added, almost like a command, "come with me."

He was surprised but he asked no questions. He took her arm to help her through the gumbo. Looking down the street toward the lumberyard he saw Paula Preston standing at the door of the office. Vivian saw Paula, too, then glanced sharply at Dan. He didn't notice, his eyes on Paula, who turned sharply and re-entered the office.

"She's lovely, Dan," Vivian said. Dan looked at her, surprised.

"She is," he said finally. They walked a few more steps and then Vivian spoke low.

"I can get home all right, Dan. You needn't come along." He knew what she meant and he grinned wryly. "You read signs wrong."

They said nothing more until they reached her home. It was the first time he had ever been in her house and he looked curiously around. The room was not large, almost a box. A plain rug was on the floor and some framed prints on the wall added spots of color to the brown paper. A lamp with flower-decorated globe sat on a small table near the window and a small stove against the far wall radiated a comfortable heat. Vivian untied her bonnet and indicated a horsehair sofa near the windows.

"Sit down, Dan. I'll be back in a minute."

Dan gingerly sat down on the edge of the sofa. He looked around. The room told him as little of the girl as she did herself, gave no clue to her past or her personality. He dropped his hat on the floor and leaned back with a sigh, glad that the problems of the village were shut off, at least for these few moments.

He heard her stir somewhere back in the house. Then he heard her steps again and she came in, bearing a tray that held a whiskey bottle and shot glass. She placed them on the table by the lamp, poured a drink and turned, extending it to Dan. She caught his open surprise and she smiled, crookedly.

"Whiskey," she said dryly, "and Wichita . . . they go together, don't they . . . all part of my past."

She extended the glass and Dan accepted it. She walked to the window, stared moodily out on the desolate world and spoke without turning her head.

"So you know more about me than most, Dan. Does it shock you?"

He considered it. "Surprise, maybe . . . shock, no. Everyone has a past, Vivian."

"Or Belle . . . which do you like?" There was a bitterness in her voice. Then she turned. "I'm sorry, Dan. There are more important things. I'm worried about Ava."

"She's worse?"

"No . . . just drunk and trying to empty Tex's whiskey. I knew him in the past, Dan. No need to tell you all the details, but I'm worried about Ava."

"What about her?"

"She's liable to do some crazy thing that will ruin her whole life, Dan. Tex Darrow is a lying, double-crossing devil . . . believe me, I know. But he can be charming and, oh, so sympathetic! Ava will fall for that."

Dan shook his head. "It don't make sense. Tex's partner killed Tommy, her own husband. And this soon after Tommy—"

"You don't know Ava, do you?" Vivian came to the sofa and sat down. "Ava and I both lived the same life, in a way. But Tommy Rikes came along and Ava married him. He brought her here, but Ava was running from something just as I was. She didn't love Tommy and she hated Bitter. She took it out on him. She felt trapped here and it was Tommy's fault. Maybe it was, but Ava had something I never had. Tommy was crazy in love with her."

"You could tell it," Dan agreed.

"But Ava didn't care," Vivian said heavily. "Dan, if this thing hadn't come up, Ava would have left Tommy in six months."

"And now Tex," Dan said, pursuing her train of thought.

"Now there's Tex," she agreed. "It's made to order for him. He'll promise to take her out of here, he'll promise her the big towns, the excitement and all the things she's wanted." Vivian's lips curled. "Of course, Ava will have to make her payment ahead of time. Then Tex will ride out when he's tired and leave her. You know what the town would do to Ava then, Dan. Tex knows it, but he don't care. That's his way. I know. And I've been paying for it for years."

She suddenly buried her face in her hands. Dan heard no sound and he sat uncomfortably, not knowing what to do. He stirred uneasily.

"What can I do?" he asked. "What can anyone do? Bruhn's gang holds all the face cards and the joker, Vivian."

Her head came up and she swung to him, eager. "Would you do something, if you had the chance?"

He smiled. "I've been trying to find some way to hit those renegades. I wish I had the chance."

"Wait."

She ran from the room. Her steps faded swiftly and Dan paced to the window, frowning, wondering what Vivian had in mind. He turned when she came into the room. Dan saw the gun in her hand and his jaw dropped.

"Where did you get that?"

"I've had it since . . . the old days. I've kept it well hidden. Here, use it."

Dan took the gun. He held it, felt its balance, his eyes alight. He shoved it in his holster, delighted to feel the old familiar weight on his hip again. Then he sobered and slowly handed it back to her.

"Keep it awhile," he said and she stared, not understanding. He shook his head. "No, I'm not afraid to use it, but I don't want any of those renegades to find it on me. I'll come back for it the minute we've made our plans."

"What about Ava?" she demanded.

"How was she when you left?"

"Crying . . . and hitting the bottle."

Dan sighed. "She'll be safe for a while longer."

"I'm not so sure, Dan."

His jaw tightened. "Then she'll have to take her chances, like the rest of us. There's no use grabbing that Colt and trying to face eight outlaws all alone. I need the others. I'll be back as soon as I can. You hide the gun."

He thrust it into her hands, picked up his hat and started toward the door, but Vivian blocked his way. She looked up at him, her eyes clouded and contrite. She put her hand on his chest.

"Dan, what do you think of me now?" She made a small, pitiful gesture. "I mean, knowing that Tex and I . . . well, I guess I'm not . . ." Her voice faded.

He put his hands on her shoulders, but she did not look up. He placed his fingers under her chin and lifted her head. His voice deepened.

"It makes no difference. You know that."

She stepped back. "But it must, Dan. I've been no angel, though hard times can force a person to do strange things. That's no excuse," she added hastily, "but maybe it explains a little. I met Tex in Wichita. I should have known his kind, but he fooled me. Later I drifted into Colorado and then finally came here to Bitter. I thought I could start life new. But . . . the past catches up with you, I reckon. Now you know. What can you think of me?"

He smiled, sensing her distress. "This changes nothing. You're still Vivian McLear, still a woman I'm mighty proud to know. I never condemned anyone in my life for doing what they had to. I don't aim to tell anyone what happened at the Rikes' this morning, or what you've told me. I leave that up to you. Nothing's changed, nothing has to be."

He dropped his hands, smiled and walked to the door. As he turned the knob, she suddenly ran toward him. Her arms went about his neck and she pulled his head down. Her lips met his, pressed close. She stepped back, leaving Dan to stare in amazement at her. She opened the door, smiling softly.

"You've things to do, Dan Murdock. I'll expect you back for the gun."

Dan stepped outside and she closed the door gently behind him. He stood a moment, then stepped out into the mud and started toward the main street, thinking to find Phil Preston.

He still felt the tingle of Vivian's kiss, and the swift pressure of her body was a vivid memory. There had been something in the gesture far, far more than relief that he would keep her secret. It shook him. He remembered Paula's hurt look when she had seen him with Vivian.

Dan shook his head and cursed a little under his breath.

ELEVEN

The breeze returned, stronger now and with an even sharper bite. Dan looked toward the northwest. The dark clouds had piled higher. Dan dismissed this new problem hoping there was a chance of overcoming the outlaws before the blizzard struck.

He turned the corner and found the main street deserted. He slogged by the store and thought he saw Vic Frazin watching, well back from the window. He caught Larry Teter's brief waved greeting from the window of the barbershop and then Dan turned in to the office of the lumberyard.

Paula swung around from the desk. She looked hard at him and her chin lifted ever so slightly before she turned back to the desk. Dan came up to the counter and waited. The silence grew between them. He finally spoke awkwardly, studying his blunt fingers.

"Where's Phil?"

"I don't know," she said shortly. Dan shifted his weight.

"Mad because of—"

"Mad!" she echoed cutting him short and looked up in pretended surprise. "What should I be mad about? You can walk with whom you please."

He grinned and she was all the more angry that she had trapped herself. Dan's smile vanished.

"She'd been visiting Ava, and these renegades are loose. I figured—"

"You did the right thing, Mr. Murdock," she said quickly. "I'm really not interested and it's none of my business."

"But I don't want you to think," he floundered and then became suddenly angry. His words grew gruff and slightly edged.

"At Ava's, Vivian learned something about this gang, and she can help us. I have to find Phil."

"He's around town somewhere," Paula said stiffly.

He pushed himself erect and with a brief nod turned to the door and went out. Paula half rose from her chair and made a swift gesture toward the closing door as though to stop him. But she sat down again and her fingers tightened on the pen until the knuckles turned white. Her eyes moistened but she set her chin and painfully concentrated on her work.

Dan looked down the street toward the bridge and the stage station. Phil might be anywhere, still trying to get support to attack the outlaws. It was a dangerous game and now, with Vivian's offer of the gun, an unnecessary one. Dan decided to try the general store first, so he turned to retrace his steps.

The wind seemed increasingly cold as Dan crossed the store porch and went inside. There were only the Frazins within, and Vic said that he had not seen Phil for some time now. Vic left the implication that he'd prefer Phil to stay hidden for some time and leave folks to solve their own problems.

Dan went outside again. He looked across the way at the livery stable and knew that Phil would not be there. The blacksmith shop had been padlocked when Dan went by, so he could check it off. He wondered why George Gorton had not gone to the smithy this morning and he remembered the man's scowl as he watched Dan talk to Vivian. A strange, dour giant this George Gorton, moody and unpredictable. A hard, conscientious worker one day and owlish drunk the three following. Maybe even now George was at home hitting the whiskey bottle, driven to it by some dark torture of his own.

But this did not find Phil Preston and Dan glanced automatically at the Wyoming Bar. He could watch for Phil there with a minimum of suspicion. He would be with the outlaws themselves and they would see nothing wrong in that. Dan crossed the street.

The moment he stepped inside, Dan's eyes swept the big room and flickered with disappointment. Phil was not here, but it would be an even bet that sooner or later he would appear. At a far table Tex Darrow, Juarez Smith and Egan sat in a deep whispered conference. A bottle sat on the table close to their hands and as Dan looked, Egan poured himself a drink. Tex looked up, caught sight of Dan and his dark eyes held level for a long second. He nodded slightly and listened to something that Juarez said. Dan started toward the long, empty bar but saw Starrett seated alone at a table across the room. Dan poured himself a drink and dropped a coin in the bowl. He picked up his glass and walked to Starrett's table.

"Seen Phil?" he asked in a low tone. Starrett looked up, eyes hard, and his lips barely moved.

"No." He gave his attention to the top of the table.

Dan pushed his hat back. "Mind company, Blaise?"

Starrett slowly looked up, the hard impact of his eyes almost physical. His lips pressed and he shook his head.

"Leave it be, Dan. We had our say last night."

Dan's face grew warm and he felt hot about the eyes. He turned and walked to the bar, his back straight. He placed the full glass on the bar and his fingers gripped the edge of the mahogany. He fought to hold his anger and finally succeeded. He hastily swallowed his drink and the bite of the whiskey served as a counterirritant. He looked in the mirror and saw Starrett's distant image. The man watched the door, expectantly.

Dan eased his balance to one foot and set himself for an indefinite wait. There was no point in being impatient. He watched the reflection of Tex and his friends at their table, and the constant low whisper of their voices filled the room, though he couldn't quite distinguish the words. Once Tex shook his head, Juarez insisted, and Tex shook his head again.

The front door opened and Dan saw Starrett straighten expectantly, pale eyes sharp and alert. Gene Hiatt stepped in. Starrett's shoulders sagged and Dan could see the disappointment in his face. The three outlaws looked up in covert alarm, then settled again to their discussion.

Dan watched Hiatt approach the bar and again he felt the extreme youth of the outlaw. Too bad, Dan thought, a kid like him would hit the renegade trail. Hiatt came to the bar and stood directly before Dan as he poured himself a small drink. He caught Dan's eyes and smiled tentatively.

"Getting colder," Hiatt said. "Be snowing before long."

Dan read a loneliness in the man's eyes; it lurked like shadows far back in their depths. He sensed a fearful appeal for friendship in the voice. It touched Dan, breaking down his dislike. He could not rebuff the search of the eyes that rested a moment on his face, then slid away only to hopefully return again. He spoke reluctantly.

"Looks bad to the north. Winters are hard in the valley."

"You can see it," Hiatt agreed. He poured another drink, placed it on the bar, then circled the end to stand close beside Dan.

"It's kind of like country I know," Hiatt said. "Only we didn't have big mountains like here."

"Further south," Dan nodded, "maybe down toward Kansas?"

Hiatt hesitated and a cloud touched his eyes, was gone again. He seemed glad to talk to someone other than his trail companions.

"Down that way . . . maybe beyond. It makes no difference." He glanced at the mirror. "But I kind of like this country up here. It's big and I guess it's tough."

"No, worse," Dan grunted. Hiatt smiled crookedly.

"But maybe it'll make rich range country . . . grow as the ranches grow."

"If nothing sets us back," Dan said, thinking of Starrett and his ambitious plans. Hiatt smiled. It transformed his face into a boyishness that was surprising.

"Nothing will set you back," Hiatt said. "First thing

you know, this whole valley will be rich as all get out, and the town will grow."

"Bitter?" Dan's brow raised and he chuckled. "Population of twenty-one, clean off the main roads. It'll take some doing to make Bitter anything more'n a crossroad cow town."

"Maybe," Hiatt shook his head. He and Dan talked on, Hiatt asking questions, Dan answering, feeling his dislike for the outlaw lessen. Hiatt brought his talk around to the town itself and then to the people in it. Soon he mentioned Ernine.

Dan looked sharply at him, his suspicions aroused again. But Hiatt didn't notice and he talked on. Dan answered more and more shortly as Hiatt again and again brought the talk around to Ernine. He didn't see Dan's increasing anger. Finally he sighed and looked around the room, back to the ornate mirror again.

"I don't know. You see a girl like her and you start dreaming about things . . . things that maybe won't come true but you still like to think of them, anyhow. She's sure a beautiful girl. Some man would be right proud of her some day."

Dan straightened, jaw hard. "You for instance?"

Hiatt looked around, surprised, saw the murky light in Dan's eyes. He grew confused, contrite, and his voice was muffled.

"I was only thinking—"

"Don't," Dan snapped. "Ernine's too good for any of you crooked killers. She's clear out and beyond you, Hiatt."

Dan strode angrily to a nearby table. He dropped into a chair and saw Hiatt watching him with stricken eyes. Dan felt uncomfortable and cursed at himself for any feeling at all that he might have toward Hiatt. Dan turned about in the chair so that Hiatt was behind him, but he still somehow felt guilty, as though he had let the man down.

The door opened suddenly and Jack Bruhn strode in. The whiskered outlaw, Denver, was at his heels. Tex Darrow straightened so suddenly that Dan knew the group had been discussing Bruhn. Juarez eased back in his chair, swarthy face inscrutable. Egan edged away from the other two as though he feared the implication of association with them.

Bruhn noticed the sudden start of the three men. The gray eyes flicked toward them, away, and Bruhn strode directly to the bar. Denver walked behind it, stroked his beard as he eyed the whiskey bottles. He glanced over his shoulder at Bruhn.

"Any particular poison, Jack?"

Bruhn shrugged. "Suit yourself. Any will do for me."

Denver picked a bottle, poured the drinks. Bruhn took his glass, turned, and his eyes swept the room. There was no change of expression in his rock-hard face when he momentarily met Tex Darrow's dark look and swept on.

Bruhn walked heavily to a table against the far wall and sat down. He placed his glass before him, shoved his hat back from his granite face. Dan caught Darrow's slight signal to Juarez. The breed arose with an air of nonchalance and strode to the bar and started a conversation with Hiatt. Starrett covertly eyed Bruhn, made a few sudden moves as though he intended to get up, and then changed his mind.

As though he could read the man's mind, Dan knew without doubt that Starrett worked up courage to make his proposition to the outlaw leader. But something held him back, some last shred of character that had escaped the corrosive acid of his ambition. Dan felt his own tension grow while Starrett made his silent struggle. Dan's breath grew shallow and he felt as tense as though he himself faced a fateful decision. He knew within his heart that Blaise would not do this thing.

Starrett's fist clenched and beat softly on the table and he looked about the room as though he had never seen it before. Juarez and Denver spoke in low monotones, the only sound. Then Starrett's chair scraped back and he stood up.

Dan himself straightened, eyes glued to the mirror. Starrett stood quite still, his jaw thrust forward and his fist still clenched. His arm swung down to his side and he moved rapidly between the tables to come to a halt before Jack Bruhn.

Dan saw everything magnified as though he watched the final, physical death of a friend. He felt a deep sense of defeat and despair as though Starrett closed a door on all that was of the past, making it worthless.

Bruhn looked up and Starrett came close, bent over him, speaking low and rapidly. Bruhn was surprised, and suspicious. It showed in the long searching look he gave Starrett before he barely nodded and Starrett eagerly sat down.

Dan watched, stunned. He could not fully believe that Starrett had taken this final step. But Starrett leaned forward, eagerly, face alight. Bruhn listened stolidly, eyes now and then cutting to Starrett, but more often looking out across the room. At the other table, Darrow and Egan watched curiously.

Then Dan knew anger. It flooded over him, shook him so that he had to lower his head lest Juarez, Hiatt or Denver see his blazing hatred. He wanted to grab Starrett's coat front and plant his fist in the center of that mouth that now proposed the murder of a neighbor, or at best, an out and out robbery....

There was nothing he could do. If Starrett allied himself with these outlaws, then Bruhn would protect him. Dan watched the mirror with sick eyes and he had to swallow constantly to relieve the dryness in his throat. He poured another drink but the bite of the liquor gagged him and he replaced the glass, still half full. His fist clenched and his palms were sweaty.

Starrett finished talking and Bruhn leaned back in his chair. His thick lips were pursed and he studied Starrett, the gray eyes expressionless. Then he leaned forward and spoke briefly, so low that Dan could not catch the words. Starrett's face fell, but the eagerness immediately returned. He talked fast, one long finger stabbing at the table. Bruhn shook his head and stood up. His voice carried clearly now.

"When I decide, I'll let you know."

He walked away, leaving Starrett sitting alone, biting at his lower lip. Bruhn walked to Darrow's table and sat down. Darrow looked curiously from him to Starrett and back to Bruhn but he said nothing as Bruhn helped himself to a drink from the bottle on the table.

Suddenly Starrett's lips thinned and his pale eyes flashed. With an impatient gesture he arose, then checked himself and walked more sedately to the door. Instantly Dan pushed away from the bar.

By the time Starrett had opened the door and stepped outside, Dan was on his heels. The wind was stronger now, a cold knife that began to slice at the town, but Dan didn't notice. Starrett reached the porch steps but turned when he heard Dan. A single glance at Dan's face made Starrett straighten and grow wary.

"I said you were finished, Dan. That's final."

Dan came up to him. "Finished working for Star, maybe, but not with you." He jerked his head back toward the door. "You're making a deal with Bruhn."

Starrett shrugged. "What's it mean to you, since you don't draw my pay?"

"Plenty, Blaise. Maybe I'd buck Hal Crane in an honest business deal, but damned if I'd hire someone to kill him." Dan's lips curled. "You'd turn mad dogs loose on the town to get your way. You're no better than a killer and outlaw yourself!"

Starrett's nostrils pinched, a little white moon of color showing around the base of his nose. Dan didn't see the blow coming. He had half turned his head to look angrily at the distant mountain peaks. Starrett's fist caught him on the jaw just back of the chin. The force of it snapped his head back and there was a flash of light before his eyes. He felt himself falling.

Then he landed in mud and water that spread along his body and one side of his face. He gulped water and momentarily fought for breath.

TWELVE

The cold water snapped him out of the shock of the blow. He fought for breath, strangling against the water in his lungs. He could do no more than sprawl full length, head hanging, coughing. He was only dimly aware that someone had come down the steps and stood beside him in the muck of the street. Then his eyes cleared and he recognized Starrett's boots.

"That's a sample, Dan," the voice said at a long distance, "of what you'll get if you stick into my business. Stay out of it."

Dan shook his head and his whirling brain steadied. He pushed himself up and Starrett stepped back, confident that the single blow had ended the fight. Dan was plastered with cold, brown mud all along one side. His face was stained with it along one cheek and his hands were filthy.

He looked at Starrett, seeing no regret in the lean,

arrogant face, no remembrance of the long trails they had ridden, the dreams they had shared, the obstacles they had overcome. Dan had been a fool, too open and too trusting. He had come this far with Starrett only to be cast off when the man's ambition and greed had become overwhelming. Fury swept Dan.

He lunged forward without warning and his fist smashed into Starrett's face. The man fell backward, his shoulders slamming into the edge of the high saloon porch. Dan plunged after him but his foot slipped in the mud and he went down to one knee.

Starrett gave him no chance. He charged Dan, who tried to lift himself out of the mud to meet the attack. Starrett bore down and his knee lifted in a short, vicious blow designed to catch Dan in the face while he was still bent over. Dan jerked aside, nearly lost his balance again, but the knee grazed by his shoulder and Starrett, unable to check himself, was swung half around in the muddy footing, arms flailing for balance.

The saloon doors burst open and the outlaws streamed out. Dan had only a glimpse of Darrow's narrow face, alight with excitement, of Bruhn watching impassively, big hands on his hips. Starrett had caught his balance and he wheeled as Dan came to his feet. Dan looked hardly human, his clothes and fists muddy, his face smeared. Now both men advanced cautiously, circling, waiting for an opening.

"Which'll you take, Juarez?" Tex called from the porch.

"The tall, clean one," Juarez laughed.

"Then give me odds," Tex demanded. Denver chuckled.

"Dunno about that. Mud or no, that Murdock gent looks good to me."

Dan only vaguely heard them. Starrett narrowly watched him and Dan waited grimly for an opening.

He saw the faint flicker in Starrett's eyes just before the man stepped in, his fist making a vicious jab for Dan's stomach. Dan caught the blow on his arm, twisted his head aside so that the counterblow whipped harmlessly over his shoulder. For a second Starrett was open and Dan's fist smashed against his mouth.

Starrett stumbled back, his foot slipped and he fell with a body-shaking thud, seated in the mud. Dan waited for him to get up, not pressing the advantage. The wind was sharper now and he felt as though the cold mud was a sheath of ice about his body, numbing his hands. Starrett came swiftly to his feet and now the mud cased his trousers, clung to his hands and the edge of his coat sleeves. He came forward in a crouching lunge, arms extended, taloned hands reaching for Dan, abandoning fair fighting for the barroom tactics of the cattle trails.

His rush carried Dan back to the porch. But Dan's fists lashed in quick piston strokes against Starrett's ribs and the man's rush was checked long enough for Dan to slip to one side and step clear of the porch. Starrett whipped around, amazingly fast for one so large.

His fingers clutched the side of Dan's coat, whipped him close, and the other arm circled Dan's neck. Starrett twisted to one side, intending to throw Dan with the lever of his hip, but Dan sank his fist into Starrett's stomach and as the arms loosened their hold, Dan broke free.

There was now quite a crowd, the outlaws up on the porch, some of them on the steps. Forming a half circle in the street, Dan glimpsed Vic Frazin's putty face, Larry Teter watching narrow-eyed Phil Preston, frowning. Then Dan gave his attention to Starrett, who advanced, circling.

Across the street Paula had been standing at the
window in the lumberyard office when the two men
first came out on the porch. She had watched them,
thinking that both men wanted her, but that she
wanted only one. Then her eyes had snapped wide
when she saw the blow that sent Dan off the porch
and into the mud. Her hand flew up to her mouth as
she saw Starrett come down the steps and stand by
the fallen man.

She couldn't move. Then Dan pulled himself up and
suddenly launched his attack. She watched, aghast,
saw the outlaws stream out of the saloon, saw the
Frazins and her father come hurrying up from the
store.

"No!" she whispered. "Not Dan and Blaise!" She
raced for her coat, and slogged, stumbling, across the
street. She came to her father's side, staring as the
two muddied men circled each other. She took a step
to get between them, but her father's strong grip
checked her.

"Let it be, girl."

"But they can't—"

"Let it be, I said." She could only watch, fearful,
hardly recognizing either man through the coating of
mud. Then she saw Vivian McLear hurry up and Paula
suddenly wished that she had not come. But she had
to break up the fight before he was seriously hurt,
and yet she didn't know how. Her father's hand was
still tight on her arm.

Dan took the initiative. He came whipping in,
checked as Starrett came to meet him, and faded to
one side. Dan's fist whipped along his cheek, catching
him off balance, and his second blow thudded solidly
over Starrett's heart. It hurt and he backed, but Dan
came right in, his arms working like pistons.

He couldn't get in a solid blow that would end the

fight, for Starrett's guard was still quick and good. But the man was tiring and he was hurt. It showed in the twist of the lips beneath the mud mask, the short, gasped breathing, the way the man pedaled backward and tried to circle to avoid the punishing fists. Dan grimly pressed for the victory. He came in close as Starrett's arm dropped.

It was a trick. Starrett suddenly twisted about, his knee coming up in a savage blow that landed true. A shock of pain swept through Dan and it seemed that his stomach came up in his throat. He bent double and Starrett's fist travelled upward in a short piston blow that cracked his knuckles off Dan's chin.

Dan didn't hear it. His consciousness swirled away in a flash of light and pain. He fell, the force of the blow swinging his body to one side. He landed on his back, and the water and mud gouted up around his body. Starrett advanced, face tight and mean beneath the mud. He pulled back his foot to kick the fallen man, then suddenly stumbled toward the steps. He sat down, breathing hard as the outlaws shouted.

Phil Preston's face was dark and scowling. He took a deep breath and walked toward Dan. But Paula darted ahead of him and started to bend down to Dan. Phil checked her.

"I'll take care of it. Best get home."

"But he's hurt!"

"Of course he is, but he's not dead by a long shot. Get home, I tell you."

Paula hesitated and then Vivian suddenly stepped in front of her. She knelt in the mud and lifted Dan's head, started wiping the mud from his face. Phil wheeled around and strode to Starrett. His voice was like a whiplash.

"I never thought you and Dan would ever fight, no matter what the reason. I never figured you to be a man who wins by a foul."

Starrett looked up slowly, his chest still heaving. His pale eyes were angry until he realized that Paula stood just behind Phil, face pale and drawn. His eyes slid away to the muddy figure on the ground, Vivian bent over him.

"Dan was drunk and mean, first time I ever saw him that way," Starrett said. Phil waited, impassive, and Starrett realized the man hardly believed him, that he had cut a poor figure in the eyes of Phil and his daughter.

"He lashed into me, calling me names. What was I to do?" He gave Paula an underbrow look and watched his fingers as he spoke. "He accused me of trying to steal his girl. I wouldn't have a drunk naming her, no matter what the reason." He shrugged. "I guess I started it when I knocked him off the porch."

"You finished it foul," Phil said.

"He deserved what he got," Starrett said bluntly.

He looked at Paula. She flushed and looked away, and then a red shade of anger touched her cheeks. She had never before been the cause of a drunken street brawl and she did not like it.

She turned away, going again to Dan's side. Phil joined her, still frowning, still angered with Starrett and only half believing him. As they came up, Vivian looked impatiently over her shoulder.

"Let's get him inside. This cold mud and water will do him no good."

Paula took a step to help, but again her father blocked her way. He brushed aside Vivian, who hastily arose. Phil glanced toward Larry Teter and Vic Frazin and his voice brooked no argument.

"Give me a hand. Hurry up."

Between the three of them, they picked Dan up and started through the mud to the steps. Starrett arose, moving aside to make room for them. Paula stood uncertainly beside Vivian, watching Dan being carried away. Vivian lifted her skirts and started determinedly after the men.

She loves him, Paula thought, and he likes to be with her. He thinks so little of me that he starts a fight about me in the street. Again outrage and shame flooded over her, but with it was uncertainty. It was not like Dan to do this, but neither was it like Blaise to tell a deliberate lie. She looked at the knot of men who carried Dan across the porch, then at Starrett, muddy but triumphant, his shoulders well back, his teeth flashing a white grin in the brown mask. Suddenly Paula realized that she, the reason for the fight, stood here in the street, where all could see her. The tale would spread over all the valley.

That didn't matter. Dan did. She climbed the first steps of the saloon porch and found her way blocked by the outlaw, Tex Darrow. The man's black eyes bored into hers and the gleam far back in them was frightening.

"Now, ma'am, you don't want to go in there."

"Paula," Starrett said, just behind her, "don't go in." She whipped about to see him looking at Darrow and she got the full implication of his warning. He came toward her, muddied hand extended. "I'll see you home."

Her indecision, her shame and anger, suddenly burst through. She shrank back from his hand. "No. No! Don't touch me!" Almost blindly she descended the steps and stumbled through the muck of the street toward the sanctuary of the lumberyard office. Both Darrow and Starrett looked blankly after her. Darrow finally shrugged and turned back toward the saloon door.

"A pretty filly . . . but damn' flighty. She'll do all

right, once she makes up her mind, I'll bet."

Within the bar, Dan had been stretched out across two of the tables. A racking pain swept over him in waves. There was nothing in existence but pain. It sank steel fingers into his groin and then traced up his body with red hot wires. It was a taste in his mouth, a flaming color in his brain. Gradually he became aware that he had arms, torso, and legs attached to a center of pain. He tried to escape by twisting aside but it was no use.

His eyes opened and at first the light was a haze that came from nowhere and everywhere. Then he saw the swinging lamp above the table, became aware that faces hovered over him. They, too, swam into focus and recognition. Vivian—and he frowned, wondering why she should be here. Phil Preston, worried. Beyond him Denver's bearded face appeared.

A wave of sickness swept over Dan and he felt the cold sweat pop out on his forehead. With it came the memory of the fight. Starrett! He tried to sit up but fell back, dizzy and fainting. Vivian's hand stroked his forehead and cheek.

"It's all right, Dan. It's over. Lie still."

He could do nothing else for a long, long time. Finally he had enough control to open his eyes but he knew he dare not move his body for a time. Phil and Vivian still stood close and behind them grouped the curious outlaws. Phil saw that Dan's full senses had returned. He frowned.

"Quite a fight you had," he said gruffly. Dan said nothing and Phil's frown deepened. "Neither Paula nor I are pleased, Dan, that she should be the cause of a street brawl." Dan quietly looked at him, a frown slowly forming. Then the complete falsity of the statement penetrated and he struggled to sit up. Moving carefully and disregarding their protests, he made it, but clung dizzily to the edge of the table biting his lips against the pain and sickness. Phil shook his head.

"I wouldn't move around much, Dan," he suggested. Dan looked up, pain still glazing his eyes.

"Phil, we didn't fight about Paula. I think too much of her to do a thing like that."

"But drunk—" Phil started. Dan shook his head. "I wasn't drunk. Phil, it was something else."

Then he realized that Tex Darrow, Jack Bruhn, Denver and the others stood watching and listening. He looked down at his muddy hands, the filth on his clothing. He couldn't talk here, not about Paula or the real reason for the fight. His jaw set stubbornly and he eased himself to the floor.

He had to catch himself from the pain that came when his weight was on his feet. Vivian was instantly at his side, her arm supporting him and he stood a moment, fingers sunk deep in her shoulder while Phil supported him on the other side. Phil kicked a chair about.

"Here. Sit down. Lucky Starrett's knee landed a mite high."

"His knee?" Dan asked. "Blaise used his knee?"

Phil nodded and Dan sank gratefully into the chair. Vivian stood just behind Phil and she gravely studied Dan. He felt the search of her eyes as though she tried to find the truth of the matter deep within him. Her face was expressionless until a brief second before she turned away. The way her eyes shadowed and the slight quiver of her lips told Dan that she did not believe him. She knew that Paula was the cause of the fight.

He started to protest and then something held him. He wondered why Vivian cared, and it troubled him. Then weariness and pain flooded over him and he feared he would be sick again. When he looked up, Vivian was gone and he heard the rap of her boots as she hurried toward the door.

She hardly knew what she did, actually. She saw the door through a strange mist and told herself that she was a fool. She had known from the time she fled Wichita that she could never know any real happiness, that there was a mark upon her. But in these days in Bitter, she had gradually felt the past slip into a haze of forgetfulness and now she knew that Dan Murdock had been the reason. But he loved Paula Preston! Her vision cleared when she realized someone stood between her and the door. Tex Darrow stood there, grinning, and there was a wicked knowledge in the sardonic dark eyes.

"What's the matter, Belle?" he asked in a low voice. His grin widened as he looked over her shoulder. "You don't think his kind would pay any attention to your kind?"

It was a slap in the face that took her breath. It snapped her back to reality. But she had no thanks for Tex. He was a symbol of all that had been mean and ugly in her life. Her voice was brittle.

"Why are you always interfering in my life?" she asked. He shrugged.

"*Quién sabe?* Maybe it was meant to be that way. Ever thought of that, Belle?"

She looked at him, a loathing in her eyes that she could not conceal. She saw the slow kindle of anger in his, the little flames that began to flicker far back in their depths. She stepped around him and jerked open the door.

"If it's fate, Tex, there's ways of changing it . . . sudden ways."

She was gone and the door shivered with the force of its closing.

THIRTEEN

It took some time for Dan to feel that he might be able to move again, and then Phil would have left him but Dan insisted that the older man stay. Something in his tone held Phil. He brought Dan a slug of whiskey. The outlaws lost interest and wandered to the bar and the tables. At last Dan painfully pulled himself up and Phil looked relieved.

"Let's go to the store," Dan said. "I need some liniment."

Phil nodded and gave Dan his arm. They moved slowly to the door and received no more than a few curious glances from the outlaws. The moment they stepped out on the porch, the increasingly cold wind cut at Dan like a knife. The mud had caked on his clothing, each step felt as though he walked encased in boards. The soaked clothing felt cold and clammy to his body and it was still with some pain that he managed to descend the steps into the street. Once beyond earshot of the saloon, Dan spoke swiftly.

"I've found a way to get out of our troubles, Phil. I was waiting for you when the fight with Starrett started."

Phil threw him a swift glance. "What is it?"

"Not here—at the store. The Frazins should be in on it, too." He indicated the saloon behind them. "And no need to get those killing jaspers suspicious."

They made the painful journey to the store and entered. Vic Frazin met them, troubled and curious. Bob watched from a counter. Ernine watched with wide eyes, deep and troubled, horrified at Dan's appearance. He smiled crookedly.

"I guess I wouldn't win any prizes right now. Vic, get

some liniment."

Art Frazin came toward Dan, awe in his face. He stared as though he had found a new hero and Dan flushed. He noticed that the boy had started to shape a gun from a piece of wood.

"Golly, Dan! That was a fight!" Art breathed. Dan winced as he eased down onto a box near the stove.

"Nothing to be proud of."

Vic came hurrying with the liniment and Dan eased himself to a more comfortable position, looked at Phil, then at Vic. "I can get a gun," he said.

Color left Vic's face. Bob stirred behind the counter and settled back with a sigh. Phil Preston wheeled about, his face alight with a new hope.

"Where?"

They all leaned toward him, Phil eagerly, Vic and Bob holding their breath waiting for frightening news. Ernine stood quite still by the stove and Dan noticed the troubled shadows that touched her eyes. Art stopped whittling.

"Where, Dan?" Phil insisted.

"At . . . Vivian's."

"Vivian's!" Vic exclaimed. Phil's head lifted and his jaw tightened.

"She offered it to me. I left it at her house until I could see you and we could work out some plan."

Phil shrugged and a note of friendliness had left his voice. "Get it . . . use it."

"Not that easy," Dan shook his head. "It's just one gun and there's eight of them." He looked toward the front door. "If I can depend on all of you, there's one way we could end this mighty quick. We'd be free of the outlaws by nightfall."

"Name it," Phil snapped. Dan looked hard at Bob and Vic.

"How about it? You willing?"

Bob and Vic exchanged swift glances and Vic made an uncertain gesture. "How do we know, Dan? You ain't told us much."

Dan felt his aches and the damp chill of his clothes. He nodded toward the street. "Most of them stay close to the Wyoming, so maybe that's where we'd better make the play."

"With all of that gang there!" Bob exclaimed. Dan nodded.

"I'll go get the gun. Phil, you, Vic and Bob wander over to the Wyoming. I'll get there as quick as I can. I'll have the gun hidden. Each of you get close to one of those renegades. I'll be watching you."

"But, but...." Vic started and his voice faded out.

"When I see you're ready, I'll throw a gun on the whole bunch. It wouldn't work ordinarily, but each of you grab the gun of the man you're watching. That'll give us four guns and we'll have no trouble rounding up the bunch. It ought to be easy after that to take care of the two or three who might be around town."

Vic and Bob did not move. Phil walked to the stove, placed his back to it. His mouth was twisted thoughtfully. He nodded again, decisively.

"It'll work."

Vic's head jerked up. "Only with more luck than anyone can expect. Too much chance of going wrong."

"What?" Dan demanded. Ernine moved slightly and his attention centered on her. The expression on her face puzzled him and he had the fantastic thought that she did not approve. Of course, it was a risk to her father and her brother, but Dan would take the greatest chance.

"If all of us went in, they'd be suspicious," Vic said.

"One at a time," Dan snapped. Vic grimaced impatiently.

"Even then, how do we know we can get close to one

DAY OF THE OUTLAW

of them? They keep moving around."

Dan checked his impatience. "Look, Vic, I pull a gun on all of them. They won't be thinking about you, but about how to get me with a slug. That's your chance. With a gun threatening them, they won't keep you from lifting their Colts. Then there's four of us, covering all of them. It's that easy."

"Sure, but if there's a slip, we'll all get it."

Art's awed whisper sounded loud in the room. "Gollleee!"

"Vic," Dan demanded wearily, "what else can we do?"

"Walk and talk careful and let them stay until this weather clears up. That's the safe way." Vic's eyes lifted to survey the store, all the shelves and corners that carried his property. He took inventory in a single, sweeping glance and determined the dollars and cents he risked in this scheme.

Phil stirred. "It's not the sure way, Vic. You're going on the promise of that big outlaw, Bruhn."

"What else can I go on?"

"Dan's scheme. Vic, when was a killer's word ever worth a damn, a robber's promise worth the breath it takes to make it? They could steal you blind. They could fire the store, kill you and your family, even destroy the whole town."

"They won't," Vic said, but now uncertainty was in his voice. Phil sighed and suddenly turned to Ernine. He took her arm and gently pushed her forward.

"Here's another argument, Vic, your daughter. She's a beautiful woman. You're risking her every moment you let those men stay in town. Maybe your stock isn't worth the risk, but is Ernine?"

"That's not fair," Ernine said swiftly and quietly disengaged her arm. "I can take care of myself like the rest of you."

Dan shivered, feeling the dampness sink into his

bones. He gave Ernine an admiring glance and wished that her father and brother had a bit of her courage. He walked to the stove, grateful of the heat. Ernine looked gravely at him.

"Instead of planning to risk a bullet, Dan Murdock, you should be changing those clothes."

Phil nodded. "She's right, Dan." He held Vic with a direct, challenging look. "Vic, how about it? Going to risk her and make me risk Paula? How about Tommy's widow? And you still don't know when they'll burn your store and your home down around your head. Dan's plan is the only way."

Vic paced from the stove to the counter and back again. Art held his partially carved gun forgotten in his hand, his eyes following his father back and forth. Dan made a futile attempt to clean the mud off his clothing. Finally Vic swung around, arms wide.

"All right. I don't like it. But maybe there's nothing else." He turned to Dan. "When will you be there?"

Phil broke in before Dan could answer. "I'll take him home where he can clean up and get in decent clothes. I think you and me are of a size, Dan."

"Your home?" Dan asked uncertainly. Phil smiled tightly.

"Under the circumstances, I don't think that Paula will mind."

Dan shrugged. He didn't like it, but there seemed to be little else he could do. He made arrangements for Phil to return to the store, once he had started to Vivian's. He would get the gun and, the moment they saw him go into the Wyoming Bar, they would wander over there one at a time, casually. Dan gave them a final warning.

"All you're doing is getting a drink. Don't think of anything else. If you're nervous or act strange, they're going to know it. They're not fools and all their lives they've been watching the little signs. That's why they're not hung or in jail today."

"I'll try," Vic said miserably. Dan's voice cut sharply at him.

"You'll do more than that, Vic. If you don't, we might all be dead in a couple of hours. Let's get those clothes, Phil."

The moment they stepped outside, the cold wind attacked. Dan shivered and glanced to the north and west. The dark clouds hung there as though undecided whether to sweep down on the village or to veer off in a savage attack on the distant Snowtip peaks.

Phil said nothing from the moment they left the store. Both men were silent as they turned down the side street that would take them to the lane where the Prestons lived. Dan cleared his throat and Phil spoke without turning his head.

"You want to explain about Vivian, I reckon, Dan. Better save it until we get home."

"But Paula—"

"She has a right to know, too . . . and direct, not through me."

He said it so there could be no further argument and Dan reluctantly admitted that the man was right. They passed Doc Langer's house and both men looked curiously at the curtained windows, both wondering if the wounded outlaw improved or worsened. They reached the corner and turned left into the lane. Off to their right George Gorton's small shack looked dark and helpless, crouched against the wide spread of the valley and the harsh lift of the Bitter Peaks against the sky.

"We could use George," Phil said with a sigh and added bitterly. "But I figure he's decided right at this time to go on one of his drunks."

"A big man," Dan said. "A strange one."

They said nothing more. They passed the Rikes' house to their right and there was no sign of life. Dan wondered if Ava watched them, or if she still sought a false solace in the bottle. She always wanted to get away, he thought wryly, but Tommy held her. Now she's free, Tommy's gone. It's funny how you always get what you ask for. Maybe tail first, or maybe long after you don't want it any more . . . but you get it. His thoughts were broken when they turned in at the Preston house.

They heard Paula in the kitchen but Phil led the way directly upstairs to his room. He hauled underclothes, shirt and trousers out for Dan, rummaged in his drawer for a pair of thick socks as Dan wearily placed the liniment bottle on the dresser. Phil picked up the big pitcher from the ornate bowl on the marble-top table.

"I'll get hot water right away . . . tell Paula you're here."

He was gone but a short time. Dan had his shirt off and the bruise of Starrett's fist showed clearly on his ribs. Phil placed the pitcher of hot water on the floor.

"Come to the kitchen when you're dressed. We'll have some coffee. You'll need it before you start."

"Does Paula want to see me?"

Phil smiled frostily. "I persuaded her." He walked to the door, and the coldness had left his face. "Dan, maybe I'm judging too harsh and too previous. You always seemed to be a man to ride the river with. I just told Paula that. You've got your chance."

Dan soberly met his searching look. "Thanks. I reckon no one could ask for more. I'll be down."

He moodily stripped out of his dirty clothing. He winced as muscles protested or he touched a tender spot. He wondered what he could say in explanation once he went downstairs. He washed, grateful for the hot water, and some of the ache left his body with the dirt. He started applying the liniment, tenderly rubbing it in. Then it struck him.

He stared out the curtained window toward Doc Langer's. If Paula was upset and angry, if Phil seemed to blame him for being with Vivian, then it was for just one reason. It was hard to believe, but there it was. Paula had to think something of him or she wouldn't be so upset. He felt for a moment as though he had achieved a victory. It might also explain Starrett's touchiness, beyond the disagreement about Hal Crane. Then Dan sobered. This made the talk downstairs all the more important. He slowly finished the liniment and then started dressing. He left the room and started down the stairs feeling like a man going before a judge for a decision that would shape his life for the years to come.

Paula had hot soup and coffee waiting for him on the table. Phil sat by the window, a mug engulfed in his big hands. Paula turned hastily back to the stove when Dan came in and Phil signaled him to be seated. A moment later, Paula sat down.

Dan was grateful for the coffee and pleased that Paula had gone to a little extra trouble in preparing the soup. He said as much and Paula only murmured something, hardly looking at him. But now and then he felt her eyes on him. Phil finally placed his empty cup on the table and leaned back.

"Well, Dan," he said without inflection. Dan took a deep breath.

"First," he said, "about the fight. I don't know where the story started, but Blaise and I did not tangle over anything I said about . . . Paula. She wasn't mentioned."

He saw their surprise and Phil moved uneasily. They didn't quite believe him, although Phil kept this out of his voice, making it dry and matter of fact.

"Blaise says differently, Dan."

He stared at Phil, then to the girl and back to Phil again, honestly amazed. They could see it and now they were disconcerted. Phil leaned his elbows on the table.

"Maybe you'd better tell your side."

Dan toyed with the soup spoon, wishing he could avoid this but knowing that he could not. Nor could he leave any part out and still have them understand. He started talking, low, and then as he went deeper into the story and his old emotions arose again, he talked more freely.

They listened, distant at first, then pulled to him by his sincerity and the shock of what he had to tell them. He mentioned Starrett's ambition and the way he looked to that stretch of HC range, and how at last he had determined to force Crane off of it, and because of this the ultimatum that he had given to Dan to either draw gun wages or quit. Dan glanced up at Paula and read the shock of disbelief in her eyes.

"That don't sound like Blaise," Phil said slowly. His brow rose. "And that's the reason for the fight?"

Dan hesitated and then saw the futility of it. He spoke regretfully and yet with a mounting anger. He told of Starrett's new idea that the bandit gang gave him a chance to force Crane's hand. He told of the conference with Bruhn and then how he had accused Starrett out on the saloon porch.

"I wasn't drunk," he said finally. "I was mad clean down to my boots. We didn't talk of Paula or of any other woman. Starrett shouldn't have told that story."

Phil looked grave and Paula studied her fingers. She looked pleased and yet she also seemed to be troubled. Phil sighed. "Dan, you know what you're saying?"

"The truth, Phil . . . nothing else."

"But . . . man! if this is true, then Blaise will cut bloody hell loose in the town! He'll have Hal Crane killed and maybe that rider, Claggett, too."

He waited for protest or denial but Dan could give him neither. Phil shook his head.

"That's just the same as murder, Dan. That's what you're saying Blaise plans. It's not like him . . . it just isn't Blaise."

Dan realized that they couldn't quite believe him and yet they could not accuse him of lying, either. He was caught between and only events would prove him right or wrong. Yet, if he carried out his plan at the Wyoming Bar, he would have Jack Bruhn to verify what he had just told them. He saw the dilemma and realized that he could say no more right now. He slowly shoved back his chair.

"I'd better be getting on. Time passes."

"To Vivian's?" Phil asked. Paula stirred and Dan gave all his attention to her, though he talked to Phil.

"This morning she heard about Ava and went over there. I went with her, I'd do it for any woman with this bunch of outlaws in town." He almost told them then of what he had learned but checked himself. Paula glanced up at his slight hesitation and Dan went stubbornly on.

"She found out at Ava's where the whole town stood, and she knew something had to be done." Again he looked at Paula. "She asked me to her house and she gave me a gun she had hidden. That's all there is to that."

Dan watched Paula's bowed head. She slowly looked up and searched his face and then Dan knew that he had been right. This girl loved him and he felt his heart leap. But he read a shadow of hurt in her eyes. She knew he had left something out and this was between them. He opened his lips, snapped them shut again. He saw the slight change in her expression.

"It doesn't matter . . . but the gun does. You'd better get it before it's too late."

It was said gravely, as though the gun was of the greatest importance, all the rest fading into the background. But Dan sensed dismissal, something that said she still did not fully know and must think things over. Phil pushed back, his voice relieved.

"She's right, Dan. I'll walk with you to the store. When we see you, we'll head for the bar. You be careful."

"As much as I can. Make sure the Frazins do their part." He looked again at Paula. He thought her lip quivered slightly but couldn't be sure. Phil left the room.

Dan waited, shifted his weight. "Paula," he said tentatively, "I want you to know . . ."

"I know, Dan," she said swiftly. She looked up, her eyes tortured. She came to a decision, for the veil was no longer between them and she stepped close. "Dan, do be careful."

He lifted his hands to her and again Starrett seemed to come between them. Not as a rival now but as the bearer of a bitter truth. Once life settled down to the normal ways, once the town and the valley were free of the threat, what would become of him? He had no answer. He could give her nothing, maybe for a long time, maybe never. It would be best to let things go unsaid. He checked the gesture and smiled, a wry twist of the lips.

"I'll do that, Paula."

She looked at him, first in surprise and then in mounting anger. Her chin lifted and then she turned and, before he could stop her, she left the room. Her steps picked up tempo and in a moment she was running. He took a step after her, stopped. Who could blame her? but what could he do?

He met Phil in the front hall. The older man looked curiously at Dan, but asked no questions. They left the house and retraced their way past Doc Langer's to the store. The cold wind had started to harden the mud and the sheets of water looked still, like dull plates of steel. Phil glanced up at the sky.

"Looks mean, Dan. Might veer off." Phil sighed. "But it's not important now. What we face is just as mean and just as black."

They said nothing more until they came to the store and both of them entered. There were no customers. Vic and Bob waited nervously, but Ernine and the boy, Art, were gone. Vic noticed Dan's unspoken curiosity about them.

"I sent 'em home. It'll be safer if something goes wrong."

"Nothing will go wrong," Dan said with an emphasis he did not feel. He turned to the window and the three men came to stand around him. "Watch for me here . . . just one of you, and don't get too close to the window. We can't do anything suspicious. I'll get the gun and go to the Wyoming. Give me a few minutes and then you come over, Phil. Vic, you and Bob follow after a few minutes."

"We'll time it," Phil said. Dan faced Vic and his son.

"Remember, all you want is a drink. Go to the bar and get it, then get close to one of those renegades. When I see you're set, I'll start the ball rolling. Grab those guns pronto and cover the rest. If you don't move fast, we can upset the whole scheme and then we will have the devil to pay. Understand?"

All of them nodded and Dan wished he could see a little more confidence and sureness in the faces of the Frazins. But they were all he had to work with and time was wasting. He hitched at his trousers and pulled his hat brim low, turned to the door. He paused, took a deep breath and looked hard at the three men.

"Pray for luck."

Phil nodded and Dan stepped outside. He glanced toward the Wyoming Bar, stepped off the porch and, squaring his shoulders, walked to the Squaw Creek Road. Vivian's cottage stood not far ahead.

Just as he turned in the yard, he glanced over his shoulder toward the stage station. It stood aloof and yet threatening, but he saw none of the outlaws near the building. His jaw relaxed a bit and he strode to the porch, knocked on the door. Within a matter of minutes he would have that single, all-precious weapon . . . and then he'd make the big gamble. He heard steps approach and the knob rattled.

The door jerked open and Dan stared, eyes wide, smile frozen on his face. Tex Darrow looked at him, grinning, and yet there was a sinister little gleam in his eyes. His smile widened and he stepped back, making a generous gesture.

"Well, come right in! We've been waiting for you so the party could begin. Step in, Murdock."

Dan knew disaster had struck. Darrow waited, a smiling, dangerous man. Dan shrugged, deciding to play a careful, waiting game. He stepped inside and took off his hat.

Denver Gorce leaned against the far wall, one hand stroking his beard, the other resting close to his holstered gun. Dan saw Vivian seated in a rocker near the stove. Her eyes sparked and her fingers clutched the chair arm as she rocked back and forth with a tempo that revealed her inner turmoil. Dan tried to get some signal that would explain the situation. But she kept her eyes on the floor and her nostrils looked pinched.

Tex Darrow came in behind Dan and then headed

toward the window. He glanced at Denver, who started smiling through his beard, and then Tex laughed.

"Now this is a cozy little meeting."

"What's this all about?" Dan demanded stiffly. Darrow's brow lifted and his grin widened.

"Why, don't you know, Murdock? I thought you and Belle had it all worked out." He crossed the room to the table that held the ornate lamp, and Dan saw the Colt for the first time. Tex picked it up and Dan could not help a sharp, indrawn breath. Tex's dark eyes were cruel and implacable.

"Ain't this what you come for, Murdock?"

FOURTEEN

There was a deep silence pregnant with potential violence. Dan stared at the gun and he felt all hope leave him in a rush. Vivian continued to rock and she spoke in a clipped, harsh tone.

"Someone told them, Dan. They knew I had it. They tore the house apart and found it."

Dan swallowed and his voice sounded heavy. "It's all right, Vivian. It couldn't be helped, I reckon."

"But it can be helped. Someone in this town sold us out. Who? Why?"

Darrow shoved the Colt in his waistband. "Maybe you'll find out . . . if you happen to live. By God, I ought to gun you both down!"

Dan's fingers clenched. Darrow's hand stroked his holster. Vivian never stopped rocking but she looked contemptuously up at the outlaw.

"That's all you ever knew, Tex . . . gunning down. It'll catch up with you, someday."

Tex whipped around, lips pulling back from his teeth. For a dreadful moment, Dan thought the man would draw his Colt on the woman. Dan eased up on the balls of his feet, throwing a quick glance at Denver, wondering if he could beat that outlaw's slug and reach Tex. Then Darrow took a deep breath.

"We'll let it go, Belle . . . this time." He looked at Dan, anger still riding him. "Jack Bruhn wants to see you and he'll decide what'll be done. Me, I'd put a slug in your brisket. Come on."

He walked to the door. Denver waited against the wall, alert now as he watched Dan. Dan took a step to Vivian and placed his hand on her shoulder, his fingers giving her a reassuring pressure.

"We tried, Vivian."

She looked up and smiled crookedly. "But it wasn't good enough. That's always my luck, Dan . . . not quite good enough."

"Quit jawing," Tex snapped. "Start walking or we'll use a gun barrel on your head and carry you."

Dan turned to the door. Tex stepped aside as Dan approached and Denver pushed himself from the far wall. They walked silently to the street and turned to the main road.

It was one of those deep moments of despair, when a man knows he has no way to turn and that all effort is useless. For the time he doesn't even care what happens to him, for that seems unimportant. He can only wonder what has caused the disaster. So Dan's thoughts worried at this problem.

It had to be someone at the store, for only they had known about it. The Frazins might have talked to someone else, say Starrett. That fitted the picture and, for a few moments, Dan accepted it.

The three men turned the corner and started for the Wyoming Bar. Dan could not help a hasty glance at the big store window across the street. He momentarily glimpsed Phil Preston, saw his wide, puzzled eyes, his mouth opened in surprise. Then Phil stepped hastily back. They know the scheme is off, Dan thought, there won't be any showdown at the Wyoming . . . at least the kind we planned. He pictured the relief of Vic and Bob. They no longer need risk their precious necks.

It struck him that maybe they had tipped the outlaws about the gun. It would be like them to play both ends against the middle, to try to keep the respect of the townspeople and at the same time pacify the outlaws, fearful of them as they were of anything that might threaten their business as well as their safety.

Now the three men walked grimly by the livery stable, and the high saloon porch was just ahead. Then Dan saw Ernine's troubled face again as they had discussed their plans to overthrow the outlaws. Perhaps she had been the one. He recalled how Gene Hiatt had looked at her. He remembered Hiatt's talk about her at the bar, and began to wonder if Ernine's worry had not only been for the safety of her father and brother but, just maybe, for Hiatt's safety, too.

Then Darrow kicked open the door before him and Dan had no more time in which to think. He stepped into the big room and his glance circled the place. It would have been almost perfect, he thought. Everyone's here but Vause . . . seven of them they'd have corralled all at once.

Bruhn sat at a table, the rest lined the bar. They turned, looked at Dan with mild curiosity, actually more threatening than open anger. They could kill him just as quietly, he thought. Tex indicated Jack Bruhn and Dan walked to the table, halted a few feet away. Bruhn looked at him, the cold gray eyes expressionless, no movement in the full, harsh lips.

"Did you get it?" he asked.

Tex dropped the weapon on the table. He jerked his

thumb at Dan. "He came for it. We was told the truth, Jack."

There was a slight stir at the bar. Dan saw Pace Odlum lean negligently against the rail, shot glass held in his left hand. Hiatt stood at the far end, head down. Bruhn slowly picked up the Colt. He hefted it a couple of times and then replaced it, looked up at Dan.

"I suppose I ought to kill you," he said evenly. Dan blinked but didn't answer.

Darrow shifted his weight impatiently. "Why wait, Jack?"

Bruhn's massive head turned and his inflexible, boring gaze locked with Darrow's. At last Darrow's slid away and he made an angry gesture.

"Why wait?" he demanded again, but now the sharpness was gone. Bruhn gave the shadowy ghost of a smile.

"You're eager, Tex. Shoot 'em and be done and damned with 'em. That's not always the answer. You'll find out . . . someday."

It sounded strange to hear this big outlaw almost repeat Vivian. Dan glanced hastily at Tex, who stood biting his lip and scowling. Finally the man shrugged.

"Suit yourself, Jack. Me, I'd know what I'd do."

"But you're not me, Tex," Bruhn said softly. "You ain't likely to be, either." He looked at Dan again and his granite jaw set. His voice lifted.

"I'll give you credit for guts, Murdock, even though you have been a fool. Like I said, I should shoot you, but you've done us a favor."

Tex exploded. "Favor! For God's sake, Jack! They'd have killed us or jailed us!"

"That's right," Bruhn nodded. "We only did half a job and this jasper woke us up. We're going over every house in the town. We won't miss a one. We'll tear 'em apart, and when we're through there won't be a damn' chance of a hidden gun turning up again. Murdock woke us up . . . I say that's a favor."

Tex looked nonplussed and he tried to find an answer but couldn't. Bruhn turned to Dan again.

"I return favors, Murdock, though I know you didn't mean any. But this will be the last . . . for you or anyone else in the town. The next time we'll shoot and, by God, you can depend on it." His fist crashed onto the table and there was a dead silence in the room.

Bruhn stood up and his voice became even again. "Get out of my sight, Murdock. Tell your friends how things stand, and tell 'em that the whole damn' town can be wiped out if I say the word. Tell 'em not to take the chance."

He turned to the bar, leaving Dan standing alone. He felt like a culprit who had been summarily dismissed. His hands clenched, opened, and he swung on his heel and strode to the door, ignoring Denver's pointed grin. He crossed the street to the store.

Phil pulled the door open before Dan could reach it, and the Frazins pushed forward as Dan entered. Phil looked as though he was surprised to see Dan alive. Vic glanced toward the saloon, openly worried.

Dan stood a long moment with compressed lips, feeling the backwash of the tension and despair that had held him in the bar. He finally spoke, telling them briefly what had happened and repeating Bruhn's warning. Viv sighed and wiped his hand over his forehead.

"I knew it was risky. I knew something would go wrong. Thank God, we got out of it."

Phil smacked his fist into his open palm. "And we're right back where we started."

"No, worse!" Dan snapped. He looked around the

store but did not see Ernine. He said nothing but strode to the stove and placed his back to it. The three men slowly followed and stood in an irregular half-circle watching him. Dan's face grew bleak.

"They'll watch us like hawks now. They'll be ready for any move we make."

"But who told them?" Phil demanded. Dan stiffened and his searching look moved from one man to the next. The Frazins shifted uncomfortably. Phil met his look with a questioning stare of his own. Dan spoke slowly.

"I'd like to know the answer to that one. Someone here, I think."

Vic and Bob exchanged quick glances and Vic spread his hands, palms out. "Why, Dan, you know we wouldn't do anything like that!"

"Who?" Dan demanded inexorably. Bob tugged at his ear lobe and stared thoughtfully at the floor.

"Pop and me didn't. Ernine wouldn't, I know." He looked up. "Maybe you're on the wrong trail, Dan, trying to pin it to one of us."

"Who else?"

"How do we know Vivian didn't tell someone else beside you about that gun? Maybe she let something slip to Ava, and the word got to 'em that way."

Dan hadn't thought of this angle. Bob could be right. So, as Phil said, they were all back where they started and the outlaws still controlled the town. Suddenly Dan felt bone weary, helpless. He sighed, the sound tearing raggedly out of his chest.

"All right. I reckon there's no use trying to follow a blind trail. We're whipped and we might as well admit it."

Phil shook his head. "Now I am afraid for all of us."

Bob Frazin slowly walked to the front of the store. He looked out the window for long minutes and then called back down the aisle.

"You said they were going to search the houses again, Dan? Well, they're starting."

"Paula!" Phil snapped. Dan nodded grimly.

"I'll go with you."

"Ernine and Mom!" Bob gasped. "Pop, I'm getting home." Vic didn't hesitate. He grabbed his coat from a hook behind the desk and hurried up the aisle after Phil and Dan. For the first time since the store was built, it was locked and deserted during business hours. The four men hurried around the corner, hoping to beat the outlaws to their homes.

As Bruhn had promised, the outlaws' search was thorough. Phil and Dan arrived at the Preston home to find Paula alone. But they saw Vause and Egan unceremoniously enter George Gorton's shack while Tex Darrow came along the street and entered the Rikes' house without so much as a knock. Phil briefly told Paula what had happened. She listened, looked at Dan, and spoke quietly.

"I'm sorry the plan fell through, but I'm glad you're safe." Her eyes rested on Dan for a long moment and then on her father as she added, softly. "Glad for both of you."

Within an hour Vause and Egan came, and they grinned crookedly at Phil as he opened the door. They saw Dan and chuckled.

"Now there's the gent we got to watch. We'd better look real good here. He might have half a dozen Colts hidden away."

Phil spoke stiffly. "You'll find none."

"Now we ain't so sure," Vause grunted. He glanced at his companion. "I'll keep an eye on these birds while you look upstairs."

Dan, Phil and Paula sat stiff and unmoving in the parlor, listening to the sounds Egan made on the floor

above. They heard crashes and thuds that made Paula
wince. Vause watched them closely and there was
nothing they could do. There was another crash and
Paula shifted nervously. Phil spoke angrily.

"Do you have to tear the place apart?"

"Sure," Vause answered, "plumb apart. You ought to
see the shack we just left. When that man wakes up
from his drunk, he'll swear a tornado hit the place."

"Gorton's drunk?" Dan asked.

"Limber-jawed," Vause nodded. "No need to watch
him . . . and he's got another full bottle of whiskey to
work on when he sleeps this one off. Too bad all of you
gents ain't the same way. There'd be no trouble."

Eventually Egan came downstairs. He overturned
the chairs and examined the upholstery, pulling
furniture away from the walls. He worked
methodically, leaving a trail of destruction. There were
crashes out in the kitchen that made Paula's face turn
pale. At last Egan came back into the parlor.

"Nothing," he said shortly. He grinned at Paula.
"Broke some stuff accidental and sure tore up the
house. But you can blame your friend here for that.
Besides, it'll keep you busy and out of trouble for a
while. Come on, Charley. Let's tell Jack this section of
the town is clear."

They left the house as unceremoniously as they
came. After the door closed behind them, Dan, Paula
and Phil remained quite still. Paula's eyes moved
slowly about the parlor, the disarranged furniture,
the contents of the table drawer spilled on the floor.
Finally Dan stood up.

"I'll help you straighten."

It was not an easy task and Dan worked with Paula
until they had to light the lamps. Phil left for about
an hour late in the afternoon, after a brief conference
with Paula that Dan did not overhear. He returned

just before Paula started the evening meal. He shed his coat and warmed his hands over the big wood range.

"Getting colder," he said to Dan, "and the wind's lifting."

"The blizzard," Dan nodded. He hesitated, feeling embarrassed. "Maybe I'd better find some other place to stay."

Paula wheeled around from the stove. "Why?"

"Well . . . there's Blaise."

"I saw Blaise half an hour ago," Phil said evenly. "He's decided to stay with Clay Majors. I didn't argue."

Dan looked hard at him and then at Paula, who turned back to the stove. He knew that they had asked Starrett to leave and that the real decision had been Paula's. He wanted to kiss her but Phil's presence prevented it. Something of his thoughts showed in his expression, for Phil smiled and sat down at the table.

"Better this way, I guess. You'd keep wondering about Blaise if he was here, and he couldn't help but notice it. When will we have supper, Paula?"

The full winter night had come by the time they sat down to the meal. Now and then gusts of wind would hit the house and the whisper of it grew steadily louder. But it was cozy in the kitchen. Dan still ached from the fight but now he hardly noticed it. Phil and Paula had accepted his version of the fight and it was Starrett who had been ejected from the circle of their trust. Still, Dan wondered if Phil had accused Starrett of throwing in with the outlaws. Toward the end of the meal, he asked Phil.

"Almost did," Phil admitted. "But he could deny it. No point of getting in a fight with Blaise myself until I was real sure of it."

"But you do believe it?" Dan asked quietly. Phil

studied his fingernails and spoke slowly.

"Let's put it this way, Dan. I believe you and Blaise didn't fight about Paula, and he lied when he said so. But this thing about Hal Crane is powerful medicine. I still am not sure that Blaise is that kind of man and maybe I won't be until he makes some actual move."

"He will," Dan said regretfully. Phil shrugged.

"You know him better than me . . . or Paula. Anyhow, I'm sure he lied about the fight. Maybe he'd lie about this other thing, too. Best to let it rest."

"I'm glad you believe in me," Dan said simply.

After the meal, Phil built up the fire in the parlor while Dan helped Paula clean the kitchen. It was pleasant to work with her, catch her swift smile at some awkwardness of his, listen to the modulations of her voice. The dishes done, Dan hung the towel on the rack back of the stove and turned to face her.

"I'm through at Star, Paula."

"I know."

He studied her, hopefully searching her face. "As soon as . . . this thing here is over and the weather breaks, I'll have to ride chuckline."

"Will it be so bad, Dan?"

"Oh, I can get a job easy enough, I reckon. Point is, I won't be a foreman . . . just a working puncher. It puts a fence to a man's ambitions and dreams."

Paula's voice was soft. She shook her head. "I think I know what you want to say, Dan. But not now."

It shook him, startled him, and he thought that, despite what she knew, Starrett was still uppermost in her thoughts. She read his mind for she put her hand on his arm.

"I know how I think, Dan. Just make sure yourself. Just remember that I saw the fight. I worried what people would think because men fought over me in the street."

"But it wasn't—"

"I learned that later, Dan. Dan, who was at your side first and who went into the Wyoming Bar with you?"

He looked blank. "Vivian McLear."

"That's just the point, Dan. I ran away. I was ashamed. Now I'm ashamed and doubtful of myself. How can I be sure when I acted as I did? How can you be sure? Think it over, Dan. I will, too."

"But I know—"

"Not now," she cut in. "It's hard to say, but it's best that we wait. I want it that way. Promise? For a while, at least?"

She turned to the door, looked back at him over her shoulder, still smiling, though wistfully. Yet her eyes were level and her jaw was set firmly. Dan knew that this was a time to be silent.

The rest of the evening was strained and grim. The wind mounted steadily in power, its wailing and howling a perfect background for Dan's uncertain thoughts. Phil spoke now and then but he obviously only made conversation. His discouragement showed in every deep line of his face. Paula busied herself with some sewing, though now and then Dan caught her covertly watching him. He was pleased when Phil finally arose and suggested that they all needed rest.

Dan had the same room he had the night before and, strangely, it seemed twice as large and very empty because Starrett was gone. As he undressed, Dan wondered at the swift changes that a single day could bring. In just twenty-four hours the whole course of his life had been changed and the man who had once been his friend was now his enemy.

He blew out the lamp and climbed into the bed. He could not sleep, but lay staring up into the darkness toward the ceiling, listening to the increasing howl of the wind, the occasional creaking of the house. He thought of Paula and the strange things she had said in the kitchen. He partially understood her, that she loved him but doubted her sincerity because of her failure to side with him where all the town could see. Vivian had gone into the bar, giving no thought to what wagging tongues might say. Paula had feared that and, seeing it this way, Dan did wonder. Paula had been honest with herself and with him, had made no excuses. His doubts left him, and he was suddenly content to wait. She had experienced a moment of weakness, but everyone had those moments. And Paula had made no excuses for herself, faced up honestly to her failure. How many would do that?

So Dan finally drifted off to sleep, but it was a troubled one. Several times he partially awoke as winds buffeted the house, seeming to shake it to the foundations. When Dan awoke early the next morning, he saw first the blinding swirl of snow beyond the windows.

He arose and looked out upon a white chaos. The house constantly shook and the snow was a thick and blinding wall, whipped almost laterally by the howling winds of the blizzard. Everything was wiped out and he could not see ten feet beyond the window. A man out in it, eyes whipped and stung by the wind and the snow, would be lucky to see half that distance.

Dan dressed and went downstairs. Phil built up the fire in the big wood range and spoke briefly to Dan. He pointed to the window and Dan looked out. On this side of the house the winds struck squarely and already the snow had piled almost up to the window sill. Dan could not see the wooden shed only a few feet away. Phil spoke heavily.

"Now we're all corraled right here, for sure . . . us and the outlaws. No one's coming in, no one's going out."

Dan spoke over his shoulder. "And no one's going to move around the town, Phil. That means we'll be left alone."

"Until the blizzard's over," Phil grunted. "After that what will happen?" Dan had no answer.

After two steady days of howling winds and blinding snow, Jack Bruhn wondered the same thing. He walked to the window of the stage station and tried to peer through the thick, blowing mists to get some glimpse of the Squaw Creek bridge a few yards away. The world was nothing but white, white that swirled and lanced through the air, that piled against the building, nothing but wind that shrieked and howled around the cornices and shook the window.

There were six men here, caught during the night by the blizzard and unable to leave since. Hiatt and Egan, over at the livery stable, would be equally marooned. Here, they had enough food, and wood for the stove. But the last of the whiskey had disappeared yesterday and already some of the men were irritable because of it.

Jack turned from his futile staring into the swirling mists. Tex Darrow sat on his blankets and played a monotonous game of solitaire while Juarez Smith morosely watched, swarthy face showing his discontent. He licked his lips and Jack knew the man felt the need of liquor. Just beyond him, Pace Odlum lay stretched out, hands beneath his head, looking up at the ceiling. He might be content, he might be ready to explode. Either way, that kid's face told nothing. Denver and Vause sat cross-legged on a blanket and played stud poker for matches.

It looked peaceful enough, but Jack knew better. His gray eyes moved to the full saddlebags against the wall. So far, apparently all felt as he did, that this stop was but temporary and it was not yet time to divide the money. But this confinement had started to get on their nerves. Even Jack felt the need to be astride a horse and riding yonderly. Nothing worse than to be forced to do nothing. And now the whiskey was gone. A man could not even drink, only sleep, eat and play cards. He could feel his nerves start to crawl and could do nothing about it.

Jack returned to his blankets and sat down. He glanced at the windows, seeing only the blinding white of snow beyond, sighed and stretched out. His thoughts moved ponderously and at last he drifted into a half sleep.

Something awakened him. His eyes snapped open and he felt a tension in the room, a tingle of alarm along his nerves. He slowly turned his head to find that Darrow had irritably paced to the window and frowned out on the white world. The man's voice was harsh.

"When in hell will this thing end? I'm tired of sitting here with nothing to do."

"Tell the blizzard, Tex," Denver said with a chuckle and then his smile vanished when Tex whirled around, face tight.

"Now that's damn funny, ain't it?" Tex demanded. Denver eyed him cautiously, then shrugged, and gave his attention to the game. Pace turned his head to watch Tex, and Jack wished he could read the man's expression. Darrow paced to the stove, fiddled there a moment. His eyes cut about the room, rested on the saddlebags.

"There's nothing else to do. We might as well divide the loot."

Jack did not allow his turbulent thoughts to show on his face or in his voice. He asked, lazily, "Now?"

Tex strode to him and halted a foot or so away. His

dark eyes were murky, mean, shifting though they threw a constant challenge.

"Any objections? Any reason why we can't have the *dinero* today as well as tomorrow or next week?"

Juarez swung about. Denver and Egan forgot the poker game and they watched, tense and silent. They were afraid of this and yet Jack could see that they would also like their share of the money. Pace slowly sat up, pulling in his legs and drooping his arms over them. His face told nothing and his pale eyes looked dull. If I could only read their minds, Jack thought desperately, though his square face remained placid. Tex and Juarez want trouble, but what about the others? If I play along, maybe I can tell who to depend on.

"No objections, I guess," he said evenly. He sat up and looked around at the rest, questioning their will, his gray eyes sharp and probing. Stall, he thought, watch 'em and you'll know whether to call this bluff or not.

"Then divide it," Tex snapped. Jack deliberately yawned.

"Fair enough. Some of us ain't here, though."

"They'll get their share," Tex snapped. Juarez slowly came to his feet, his blue eyes alight. Jack sighed and pulled the saddlebags to his blanket.

"First thing, we got to agree on a split."

Tex made an impatient gesture. "Even-steven all around. That's fine with me."

Denver pitched the cards aside and now he, too, had arisen. Jack read the bearded face, the suspicious way he watched Tex, and he thought, one for me. Vause looked uncertain and Pace still was an enigma. Bruhn swiftly judged the situation. Denver could handle Juarez, he could match Tex. It would be over before Vause could make up his mind, but there was still

Pace, of course.

"Even all around," Jack said levelly. "That means nine ways."

"Eight," Tex snapped. "Shorty's in a bad way. Even if he don't die, he won't be ready to ride by the time we leave town. Eight ways, Jack."

As Bruhn had expected, the excuse for the play would be Shorty. He watched Darrow's lean face, aware that Juarez had now edged to one side, but Denver had also half turned with the breed. Vause looked from Tex to Jack and back to Tex again, obviously surprised at the quick developments and very much worried. Pace had not moved. Jack shrugged, his jaw hardening.

"We count Shorty in, Tex. We don't leave this town until Shorty is either dead or riding out with us. Nine ways . . . take it or leave it."

Darrow's black eyes slowly narrowed and his nostrils pinched. He gathered himself for the showdown. Jack's right hand slowly opened so that the big fingers spread and taloned just below his holstered gun.

FIFTEEN

Silence stretched the nerves, tingled along tense muscles, filled the air like a physical substance. Darrow stood half crouched. His right arm remained loose at his side, but Jack knew how swiftly the man could draw and fire. Jack watched for that faint flick in Darrow's eyes that would give him the split-second warning that he needed. Fire ate through a stick of wood in the stove and it fell onto the coals with a snap as loud as a clap of thunder.

Darrow shifted slightly and he threw a sidelong

glance at Pace. Odlum remained stretched out on his blankets, his eyes glittering with excitement, but his arms remained under his head. It disconcerted Tex and he could not determine whether Pace was neutral or might take a hand either way when the bullets started flying. Juarez realized that Denver had maneuvered to threaten him and the breed no longer could back Tex's play against Bruhn.

Tex's eyes cut back to Jack. He couldn't read the odds and Tex was always a man who liked to see them his way. He licked his lips and Jack knew that the showdown had again been deferred. But he did not relax, his hand still taloned. Tex's eyes shifted away.

"It kind of leaves us locking horns, don't it, Jack?" he asked a tight voice. Jack nodded.

"Looks that way."

Tex looked at the saddlebags, then at Juarez, over to Pace. He rubbed his left hand along his trousers as though to wipe off the moisture in the palm. He lifted his shoulders in a shadowy shrug.

"Maybe we're previous, Jack." He looked at the window where the snow still fell. "We sure ain't going anywhere in this. We can divide the money later."

"Nine ways," Jack said, voice level. Tex flushed with anger for a moment, then it vanished.

"Maybe, Jack. No point in arguing now. By the time the blizzard's over, maybe we can tell how Shorty will do."

Jack still didn't move and his harsh voice pressed against the last shreds of Tex's challenge. "Then we don't touch the money, Tex? That's the way you want it?"

Tex turned away, an abrupt and angry movement. His choked voice came from over his shoulder. "Let it ride, Jack, let it ride. We ain't going anywhere."

Juarez slowly straightened and his sigh was deep

and gusty. He looked contemptuously at Denver, then sat cross-legged on his blanket and fished tobacco sack and papers from his shirt pocket.

It was over, Jack knew, as he felt the tension leave. He took his time in putting the saddlebags back against the wall, keeping his face turned from the rest so that they could not see the beads of sweat on his forehead.

This was the first time he had ever broken out in sweat on the edge of a fight, and it worried him. Maybe he was not only getting old but his nerves had slipped a little. He tried to cast that thought aside but the fact remained that he felt almost weak with relief. But there'd come another time and another place, and sooner or later Tex Darrow would make his play for keeps.

Only Pace Odlum had prevented it this time. Darrow had backed down because he could not tell what the pale-eyed young killer would do. Jack knew it. Tex would sound out Pace at the earliest opportunity and, once he was sure....

The storm continued through the rest of the day, but some time deep in the night it passed. When Bruhn opened his eyes the next morning, sunlight streamed its early red rays into the windows. He threw back his blankets and strode to the window, looked out. The reflected light from the glittering snow was blinding and within seconds his eyes were watering. He turned back into the room and walked to the stove, poking up the fire and chucking more wood onto the grates. The noise awakened the others.

"Blizzard's gone," Jack said and they all turned in surprise to look at the window. Denver tugged his fingers through his beard and grinned.

"Don't know whether to eat first or go get me a drink."

"The bar will be damn' cold," Bruhn said dryly. "You'll be lucky if it isn't all frozen."

Denver made a wry grimace. "Eat then, I reckon. But it ain't exciting."

They moved with alacrity about the room as though the last winds of the storm had blown away their irritations and their angers. Even Tex Darrow spoke with a careless air that Jack had not known for a day or two. They hurried through breakfast. As he ate, Jack waited to catch Pace Odlum's eye and he finally succeeded. He made a slight signal and the youngster barely nodded. His thin lips held the ghost of a smile at the corners, a cynical gesture that rubbed Jack the wrong way. But he gave his attention to his plate again and Jack shrugged it off. He needed Pace.

Darrow and Juarez finished first, and Darrow walked to the window and looked out. Juarez spoke in a low tone to him and Tex nodded. The breed immediately went out, almost immediately reopened the door and stuck his head in the room.

"Hey! We don't ride for a while, *amigos*. It is all ice, down under the snow."

"Stuck here some more," Darrow said with an oath. Denver lowered his coffee mug and laughed.

"That won't worry you, Tex. How about the widder?"

Tex grinned. "Sure. Better see how she is after I have a drink. How about it, Pace?"

Odlum calmly lifted his coffee mug. "I need some more of this. Get along to the widow, Tex. I'll be seein' you around."

Tex hesitated, shifted his weight from one foot to the other, but Pace paid no attention to him. Darrow's lips pursed and then he shrugged.

"See you later, then."

Vause and Denver left within five minutes and there was only Jack and Pace. The young outlaw rolled a cigarette, paying no attention to Jack, leaving the first move entirely up to him. It roweled Jack that he should have to come to this kid, but there was nothing else he could do. He felt as though he headed the gang only by Pace's unspoken permission. Jack finished his coffee, leaned forward, elbows resting on his crossed legs.

"What do you think about Shorty?" he asked. Pace shrugged.

"I reckon the doctor knows best."

Jack made an impatient gesture. "I mean about leaving him here if he ain't able to ride with us."

Pace looked up and his cold, pale eyes held a dancing light. The red lips openly smiled, crooked and taunting. "Why, Jack, how should I know? Some say leave him, some say wait."

"But you?" Jack insisted. Pace laughed.

"Me? Why should I have anything to say about it? You're the leader, Jack. You make up your mind and have your say."

Jack eased back, turning the answer over in his mind, and he discovered that he had none. Pace had not made his own position clear. Jack's eyes grew bleak.

"I always figured I could depend on you, Pace."

"Why?" the stripling asked almost as if it was a challenge. Jack blinked and held one hand, palm out.

"Why, I let you come into the gang and we've ridden a heap of miles together, you and me."

"We have," Pace agreed. But an impish look transfixed his expression and one brow arched high as he grinned. "So have people in a stagecoach, Jack. But they split up when they reach the end of the run. Each has paid his fare so there's nothing owing, any way you take it."

Jack's heavy face fell but he tried to hide it with a

quick shrug. "You're saying you don't owe me nothing."

Pace arose and stretched. "Something like that, Jack. I was no drag to the bunch when I threw in with it, and I've carried my load ever since. We're even . . . and I could leave right now, knowing I owed no one of you a damn' thing."

He walked to the door, leaving Jack still seated, staring at the floor. Pace looked out the window and then turned to face Jack again. His voice lifted.

"Like I said, Jack. You decide about Shorty. Don't count me one way or the other. All I want is my share of that bank money whenever the split is made . . . today or next week, here or somewhere else. Now, how about a drink?"

It left Jack exactly where he had been before and he knew the futility of trying to get anything more from Pace. He sighed and pulled himself to his feet. They left the stage station together and, profiting from the others who had beat a path through the drifts, worked their way down the street to the saloon.

The place was bone-chilling cold but Denver and Juarez had already built a fire and the first tentative waves of heat radiated from the stove. Vause was already behind the bar pouring whiskey into the shot glasses. Hiatt and Egan had come from the livery stable and, except for Shorty, the whole gang was in the room. But for how long, Jack wondered heavily.

Until Pace Odlum decides to back either me or Tex, he knew. Right now it was a stalemate and so men drank together here who might later kill one another. Jack stole a sidelong glance at Pace, who leaned negligently on the bar, studying the light through the clear amber whiskey in his glass. This stripling, this killer who looks like a child, rules the bunch, Jack thought. It wasn't pleasant to consider.

Out on Spade Road George Gorton's shack lay buried to the eaves in snow. Within there was a strange half-light that hardly relieved the gloom of the disarrayed interior. Against a far wall, Gorton lay wrapped in blankets and he hazily considered the bare wall a foot from his nose.

He felt the fuzz of whiskey in his mouth, a slimy coating to his tongue. He wondered dazedly what time it was and why the light looked so strange. He was afraid to move for fear that his head would split but already he felt the uneasy craving for another drink. He closed his eyes and wondered what kind of man he had turned out to be, and why some devil within would send him on these prolonged fights with the whiskey bottle. It had always been this way, and probably always would. Some little thing would happen and a savage, killing anger would stir within his mind. Then he would either have to fight or go off by himself and drown the murderous drive in rotgut. He was too much afraid of what he might do if he allowed his anger to control him and so—he would awaken like this days later, weak, chastened, heartily sick of the drunken beast that was George Gorton.

But what this time? He frowned, trying to concentrate and wondering if he could find the whiskey bottle. He couldn't remember now what it was. He rolled over carefully and stared at the snow packed before the windows, seeing the steam of his breath in the cold room.

He arose and, pulling the blanket tight about him, stumbled across the room to the stove, opened the door and peered in at the few spots of red that glowed in the dark bowl. He straightened, swayed, and then, cursing, looked about for newspapers, realizing for the first time that the room had been torn apart. He blamed himself and whiskey.

In a few moments he had the paper and wood in the stove and the flames made a soft roaring sound as the room steadily grew warmer. Now George remembered why he had started on his spree. It was Vivian. He sat on the edge of the bunk, the dirty blanket still about his hunched, gigantic shoulders, and pictured her in all her beauty. He looked at his big hands, the pores ground deep with soot from the smithy, the nails broken and black-bordered. No wonder she would pay no attention to him, a bear of a man, dirty all the time and drunk half of it. No wonder she walked down the street with men like Dan Murdock while George received only her most distant smiles. Dan Murdock . . . George's big hands doubled and he felt the old stir of killing anger. He looked hastily about for the whiskey bottle and saw it across the room, over half full.

To the north of the town, Starrett arose from the table with Clay Majors. Snow against the windows had made a half gloom in the big kitchen, dispelled by the lamp that Mrs. Majors had lit when she started breakfast. Clay Majors had been bluff and hearty as usual and his wife had seen that Starrett was gloomy so she had tried to make a few small jokes. But they had given up even before they sat down to the meal.

Starrett glanced at the snow piled against the window and he wondered how deep it was out on the range. Thank God, there were draws and cutbanks on his range where his beef could shelter. He was glad that it was over and he could now give his full attention to the problems here in town.

Hal Crane . . . that business still hung fire. Now that the blizzard was over, and men could move around the town, he'd try to get some sort of a deal out of Jack Bruhn. This situation was just too

opportune, too good for a man to pass up. He'd be a
fool to take no action when a quiet deal would take
care of a rival and put him in the driver's seat. Who
could blame Blaise Starrett if Hal Crane caught an
outlaw slug in a fight that he had apparently
provoked?

Maybe Dan—damn Dan, anyhow! The fight had
done Blaise no good and he wondered why he had so
quickly told the story about fighting over Paula. It
had been Phil's accusing figure and his glimpse of
Paula herself that had stampeded him and he had
not thought clearly.

They knew better by now. That was why he was
here while Dan Murdock was guest at the Preston's,
with a clear field so far as Paula was concerned. Well,
that would be changed before long. Nothing makes
the world forget faster than being top dog on the heap,
and that would happen just as soon as this HC range
business could be concluded.

He felt a little better when he started to work with
Majors digging their way to the main road. Larry
Teter would be working toward them from his house.
Others in the town would be clearing snow from before
stores and houses. They might not move out on the
range but here in Bitter there would be some freedom
from the drifts.

Then Starrett's shovel blade struck ice. He jabbed
at it and the steel blade rang, bouncing off the solid
sheet. All that water caused by the chinook had melted
and now there was a sheet of ice many inches thick
below the loose snow. Starrett straightened, a new
and more pressing worry clouding his eyes. The ice
meant that his beef could not reach grass. Snow and
a thin crust they could paw aside and have their
forage, but this icy armor would prevent that. He
suddenly wanted to get back to Star Range, but he

knew that it was impossible. He could only depend on his crew to do what they could while he fervently hoped the temperature would rise and the ice sheath be dissipated before too much damage was done.

At the Frazin home, Hal Crane straightened after shoveling a path from the house to the store. Vic and Bob stood breathing hard beside him, leaning on their shovels. Hal thought of his stock and he tentatively kicked at the ice with the toe of his boot. If this didn't go quick, he'd be in trouble . . . and so would every ranch in the valley.

Not far away, Dan Murdock and Phil Preston bent their backs to the shovels, and the path through the drifts gradually extended from the house to the big fence of the lumberyard, along its length to the street. Dan was also aware of the ice and he thought of Star stock out on the range. Then he reminded himself that he no longer had that responsibility and he resolutely dismissed the thought. There were too many other worries.

Phil brought them up when they had finally reached the office and started a fire in the stove. He stood with his hands extended, catching the first faint lift of the heat.

"Dan, isn't there something we can do? Every minute those renegades are in town, I feel like I'm living on top of a powder keg with a lit fuse."

Dan sighed. "What, Phil?"

"I don't know . . . something."

"No guns. They watch us like hawks. If we make a move, they'll be ready for it." Dan looked directly at Phil. "This time they might be mad enough to take it out on the whole town."

"A hell of a note," Phil grunted.

The office became warmer and at last a person could

work comfortably at the desk. Dan helped Phil with a few tasks and then shoveled a path out front to join the one Larry Teter had made to his shop. Now, using these snow trenches, a man could go from one place to another, with the exception of the blacksmith shop, which remained half buried in a white shroud. Gorton must still be hitting the bottle, Dan thought.

He took the shovel back to the lumber office and warmed himself at the stove. There was nothing more he could do here, so, with a word to Phil who worked at the desk, Dan went out again. He followed the path across the street, turned left and the trench took him by the saloon. He heard a burst of laughter but went on by the livery stable, noticing the padlock on the door; then he cut left again, following the trench to the general store. He stepped up on the porch, above the snow at last.

He looked south, seeing the path to the stage station. But beyond that was nothing but white, smooth and unbroken as far as he could see. He turned his head to see the black roof of Vivian's place projecting above the snow, a finger of blue smoke spiraling up from the dull red chimney. She was safe and Dan made a mental promise to shovel a path to her place so that she could reach the stores.

Then he turned and, stamping the packed snow from his boots, went into the store. Gene Hiatt had been leaning across the counter and he hastily pulled himself up and turned toward Dan. Ernine took a step back and for the first time Dan saw that the girl was actually flustered. Dan realized he had interrupted an intimate conversation.

Dan came slowly down the aisle, sensing something here that he did not like. Ernine nervously smoothed the apron she wore over her dress, gave Dan an underbrow glance and then looked hastily away. Hiatt stood as though braced for an attack, like a man who fully expects disaster and yet hopes beyond hope that it will not strike. His eyes begged for understanding even as they met Dan's in an unspoken challenge. Dan looked again at Ernine.

"A couple sacks of tobacco," he said mildly. Her head lifted in surprise and her eyes were suddenly warm and deep. She started to say something, instead changed her mind and hurried away to fill his order.

Dan leaned against the counter. He heard the young outlaw stir and give a soft sigh as defiance left him with the long, expelled breath. Hiatt acted as though he would like to say something but didn't quite dare. He obviously worked his courage up to speak to Dan.

Ernine returned, placing the tobacco on the counter. Dan gravely counted out the coins. He put one sack in his pocket and opened the other, started to make a cigarette. He knew that Ernine and Hiatt exchanged glances but still they said nothing. Dan finished the cigarette and then looked up, deliberately, at each of them. Ernine again flushed slightly and once more a touch of defiance made Hiatt's jaw harden. Dan lit the cigarette and gravely considered the girl for a long moment.

"Thanks," he said at last and then started toward the door. Hiatt's voice stopped him.

"Murdock!" Dan turned as Hiatt came up. The young man studied Dan, made a grimace and tugged at his ear.

"Could I talk to you, Murdock?"

"Sure," Dan waited. Hiatt glanced around the store.

"Not here. Private."

Dan looked over the man's shoulder to Ernine, who now watched them closely, her face a picture of conflicting emotions. He spoke to Hiatt. "Okay. Maybe you'd better. Come on."

"Wait," Hiatt's hand touched Dan's arm. "Tell me where you're going. I'll follow you. I . . . don't want the others to see me."

"I'll be at the Preston place. Follow the snow path along the lumberyard fence to the back door. I'll be waiting."

Hiatt looked relieved, smiled tentatively. "Thanks, Murdock."

Dan looked again at Ernine, back to Hiatt, then shrugged and walked out. He followed the snow trenches along to the livery stable and saloon, across to the lumberyard and then to the Preston home. He stepped into the kitchen and listened, heard no sound. He called Paula's name and there was no answer, and Dan knew that she must be at the office with Phil.

He sat down at the kitchen table and waited for his visitor. So there was something between Ernine and Hiatt. It stunned and frightened Dan more than he cared to admit. He had always thought that someday someone would come along who would crack the cold, defensive wall the lovely girl had built about herself. But who would have thought that it would be an outlaw! Dan made an ugly grimace and tried to evaluate the situation. What would this do to the problem the town already faced? Would Ernine find herself deserted and heartbroken as Ava would with Tex, if Vivian's prophecy came true? More to the point, how could this thing be stopped without stirring up a hornet's nest of trouble, and without hurting Ernine? There was no answer to that. An idea hit him and his eyes narrowed. Maybe this was the way the outlaws had discovered Vivian had a hidden gun. Ernine would not want Hiatt to be hurt and so . . . betrayal made an ugly taste in Dan's mouth.

He was close to anger when Hiatt knocked softly on the door. Dan crossed the room and opened it. Hiatt

stepped in and looked cautiously about as Dan stalked
back to his chair.

"No one here?" Hiatt asked.

"No one," Dan snapped. "I don't know what you want
with me, but you can talk. There's no one to listen."

Hiatt came slowly to the table. He took off his hat
and dropped it on the floor, unbuttoned his coat and
stood uncertainly for a moment before pulling out a
chair and sitting down. He studied his folded hands.
Dan waited, giving him no help. At last Hiatt
shrugged.

"I'm in love with Ernine Frazin, that's the whole
thing, Murdock." Once the words came, he spoke fast
as if afraid to take a breath. "It don't make sense and
I know I don't deserve someone like her. But there it
is, and I can't help it. I'm sure she loves me, too. She
ain't said it in so many words but a man can tell that
sort of thing. I know nothing good can come of it, and
I'd want only the best for her. But I ride the owlhoot
trail and I won't come to any good end, and I couldn't
ever ask any honest, good girl to follow me."

He gulped, looked frightened and fell silent, but his
eyes watched Dan with deep longing and hope.
Suddenly Dan felt sorry for him, sensing again
something basically clean and decent in this man. Yet
Dan could not wholly trust his feeling. Hiatt had
ridden into Bitter with men like Bruhn, Darrow and
Odlum. There had to be something badly wrong and,
much as Dan wanted, he could not frame any
encouragement. He, too, studied his fingers intently
as he spoke.

"You're an outlaw, Hiatt. That's something a man
chooses deliberate. You did."

Hiatt's fist banged on the table. His face was eager
and yet drawn with a futile anger, and his eyes pleaded
all the more for understanding.

"But I didn't choose it. It was forced on me." He saw
Dan's eyebrow lift and he leaned back, began to speak
more calmly. "I guess it's an old story. Paw and I had
a small spread, but it was a good one. Trouble was it
lay right between two big ranches and they both
wanted it, while at the same time they fought among
themselves."

Dan thought instantly of Starrett. Hiatt looked out
the window, his eyes distant, his voice heavy, trembling
now and then as he tried to tell the story
dispassionately.

"There was Paw, me and a couple of hands. Mother
died four years before. We didn't want to give up the
spread and it was hard working against the pressure
of those two big boys. They couldn't buy us, but if they
could start some kind of trouble, maybe they could
force us out. We walked mighty soft for over a year
and managed to stay out of trouble."

He stopped, seemed to gather his balance and his
voice continued at a dead level. "Then they caught
Paw in town one Saturday and first thing he knew
they whippered him into a corner in a saloon so it
looked like he'd started a fight. He didn't have a chance
against the best gunslinger in the whole damn'
country." He added in a whisper, "We buried him beside
Mother two days later."

Dan watched, eyes sharp for any sign that this story
might be false. But there had been sincerity in the
voice that Hiatt strove so hard to keep level, in the
mist that filmed his eyes as he looked out the window,
in the way his fists had clenched until the skin about
the knuckles was pale.

"I tried to keep the place going," Hiatt said at last.
"One of the hands got scared and lit out. Still, I figured
somehow I could stick on. Then I began to miss cows
and I finally caught a couple of Bar O rannies working

over one of my calves. I lost my head and the fireworks started. I took a slug in the shoulder but I killed one of 'em and the other one didn't walk for a long time."

He stopped again and Dan waited. But Hiatt's face was thunderous dark as he relived the past. Dan stirred.

"What then?"

Hiatt jerked slightly and then looked around with a crooked smile. "Why, I found out how easy it was to become an outlaw. You protect your own property but the gent who couldn't walk said I murdered his partner and tried to kill him. I'd come clear over on their range to set a gun trap. Money talked and the sheriff was after my scalp. There wasn't no chance. I'd have gone to the gallows, sure. Between them two big spreads, they controlled everything in the country and they'd teamed up to get me out of the way. Nothing left to do but skip out, quick."

"And this bunch?" Dan asked with a nod toward the window. Hiatt sighed regretfully.

"You can figure how I felt. The ranch gone and I was tagged for murder, had to keep running. The shoulder healed up but by then I had no use for law and order—it hadn't done much for me. I met this bunch in Colorado."

"Joined up," Dan said flatly.

"Why not?" Hiatt demanded and then the belligerence left his voice. "It was a crazy thing, I guess. But I couldn't see much difference between being an actual outlaw and being accused of one. Either way, you're on the run."

Dan nodded slowly. "And now?"

Hiatt leaned across the table, his face eager and pleading. "Look, Murdock, I helped hold up that bank in Colorado. I held the horses, nothing more, but I know that's no excuse. I rode in here with 'em, and I can be branded for what they've done already."

"I'd say so," Dan nodded slowly. Hiatt's hand suddenly grasped Dan's wrist.

"Is there any chance of turning back, Murdock? Could I do something to get rid of the outlaw brand? I'm in love with Ernine, I tell you. I'd give my right arm to be able to go to her, clean, and ask her to marry me. Is there a chance? Any way?"

Dan stared. Suddenly a new hope burst in his chest. Maybe this man, pleading for a new chance, was the very break for which Dan sought.

SIXTEEN

Starrett walked along the street by the barbershop, mounted the steps to the saloon porch and hesitated while still several feet from the door. The impassive panel had suddenly become a symbol. He had often shoved this door open in the past without a thought, but now it was different. The very wood seemed to warn him that he stood poised at a decisive moment. He could go back and life would continue as it had. He would still have Hal Crane's stubborn refusal to overcome.

But once he entered the saloon, Starrett would change everything. He could never turn back. He frowned at the glass with the checkered paper pasted over it. This was certainly the easiest way to solve his problems. It would give him that range he wanted. It would increase his stature as a rancher and that in turn would make him all the better a suitor for Paula Preston. His lips flattened and he impatiently twisted the knob, opened the door, and stepped inside.

The big room was warm and most of the outlaws were here. Starrett was pleased. Now was the time to make the deal and then fade into the background so that he himself could never be touched. Bruhn sat at a table with that pale-faced killer who looked like a kid. Starrett thumbed his hat back and walked to them.

Bruhn looked up, nodded briefly. Pace's pale eyes flicked over Starrett with something akin to contempt. Starrett flushed under it and his voice was harsher than he had intended it to be.

"How about that deal, Bruhn?"

Bruhn looked up again. He was annoyed and it showed for a moment, then vanished. "What deal?"

Starrett pulled out a chair and sat down before Bruhn could protest. "That proposition I made you. There's not much time left to wait. I told you that."

He heard a move beside him and twisted his head to look up. Tex Darrow had come from the bar and he stood close by, looking steadily at Bruhn.

"Jack, you ain't passing up some business without telling us about it?"

"It's penny ante," Bruhn said heavily. Tex glanced at Pace, then shook his head.

"Maybe we'd better hear about it." He sat down beside Starrett. Bruhn slowly drew back and his big face had become granite hard. Pace watched, expressionless. Starrett looked a question at Bruhn, who nodded slightly.

"Say your piece."

"I told you about Hal Crane," Starrett said hesitantly. Darrow cut in, sharp.

"Tell me . . . and Pace."

Starrett again looked to Bruhn but could not read the hooded gray eyes. He shrugged and swiftly outlined the situation between himself and Crane, building up his need for the disputed range and, later, his desire for the whole HC spread. Tex listened, glancing now and then at Bruhn.

"So what do you want done?" he asked when Starrett finished. There was a long pause but Bruhn didn't seem to care now how much was told.

"Well, Crane is caught here in the town. He's the one you hit that first day," Starrett glanced at Tex. "If he was out of the way, then I wouldn't have any problem. You gents are here, and you'll ride out before long."

"But pinned with a murder brand," Bruhn said. Starrett spread his hands.

"Is that new? How about Tommy Rikes? How many of you already have a killing tagged against you somewhere? What's so wrong about another one?"

Pace smiled thinly. "I check and pass. Go on."

"Well, this thing is just right for the job . . . and it don't have to be murder. There's such a thing as starting a fight. You'd know how to do that."

"You could start your own fight," Pace said. Starrett shook his head.

"Not me . . . not and take over that range. I have to be in the clear." He shrugged. "Some don't like me now as it is. I'd thought maybe I could raid HC beef, run them off some dark night over the mountains. It'd hit Crane hard and might force his hand. But now you're here. You could take care of the job easily and quickly. I'd pay you well for it."

The four men were silent. Bruhn looked across the room, face expressionless. Pace studied Starrett, a strange expression in the pale eyes. Darrow watched Bruhn hawklike, and then slowly turned his head to Starrett.

"You sure give us a lot of savvy for a killing."

Again Starrett spread his hands. "Let's not act like woolly lambs. A quarrel's easy to pick, any time and any place. Any one of you could do it. I don't care how it's done or who does it. I just pay five hundred dollars."

Tex leaned back. "You don't rate this Crane very high, do you?"

"It's the best I can do," Starrett said. Tex looked at Bruhn, uncertain now and obviously disappointed at the price Starrett had set. Jack covertly watched him, saw his indecision.

His gray eyes moved slowly to Starrett and he looked at the young rancher without really seeing him. Five hundred wasn't much but, on the other hand, the job wasn't much, either. Darrow, Juarez, Pace, Denver, Egan, Vause or himself could do the job in a matter of five minutes. But there were other things to consider.

He had no compunction about killing a man, and taking care of Crane would be about as easy as shooting the head off a daisy. But this would be just one more killing added to the score against them in the town. The village seemed subdued, but Bruhn knew what men goaded beyond reason might do. This proposed murder might be just the thing that would change the whole picture. It had come dangerously close to changing when Murdock found the gun in that ex-saloon girl's house. Just luck they had caught it in time, and Bruhn knew that luck was a highly ephemeral thing.

He had thought for a moment that Darrow might use this offer as a means of forcing the issue he had evaded once before. But five hundred dollars had disappointed Tex. If it wasn't for the rift in his own gang, he probably would have taken the offer. He cleared his throat and Starrett eagerly watched him.

"I don't know. Like I said before, I'll have to think it over."

Starrett's face fell and Tex acted as though he might protest. But he sank back, saying nothing. Pace watched him, waited and then settled into his chair.

Starrett made an angry grimace.

"Think it over! I tell you, time's wasting."

"We'll be here a spell," Bruhn said heavily. "Nothing changes until we leave."

"But when the roads become passable . . ."

Bruhn cut him short. "Crane won't ride until we tell him he can. That goes for everyone, yourself included. I said I'd think it over."

Pace pushed back his chair and arose. He moved with easy grace to the door and outside. Starrett sat for a few moments, chewing the bitter cud of his disappointment, then, with an angry jerk, he arose and strode outside.

Pace stood at the edge of the porch near the head of the steps. Starrett looked angrily toward the distant mountains, buttoning his coat against the sharp cold. He started down the steps, giving Pace only a passing glance. The outlaw's calm voice choked him.

"Come here, Starrett. Maybe it's not all said yet."

Starrett checked, one foot on the bottom step. He half turned, looked curiously at the slender figure above him, the red lips that held a slight smile, the pale eyes that told him nothing. He slowly remounted the steps.

"What do you mean?"

"You've got the cash?"

Starrett studied him, fearing a trap and yet unable to see one. He finally shrugged.

"Not with me. It's at the Star ranch house. I could ride with you to Star. You'd have it then."

Pace looked down the street, digesting this. "Cash talks loud, Starrett. Beats a bellyful of words four ways from the jack. Too bad."

"But, damn it," Starrett snapped. "It's as good as in your pocket. You ride with me, you get the money at the ranch . . . I'm not out of your sight. How can you lose?"

"There's that," Pace admitted. He added softly, "At that, you might have to get the money."

He smiled crookedly and calmly walked down the steps, leaving Starrett to watch after him, frowning, puzzled, and yet with a new hope. Starrett at last walked swiftly toward the general store and with each step his disappointment lessened.

Pace crossed the street to the lumberyard office. He paused and studied the façade, noting the two narrow windows. He straightened his hat, raking the brim slightly, hitched at his gunbelt and pushed open the door. Phil and Paula were at the desk, Paula seated, Phil standing beside her studying some invoices. They looked up when Pace entered.

"Morning," Pace said pleasantly and came to the counter. He gave Phil a glance and smiled at Paula. She looked hastily down at the ledger. Phil slowly put the invoices on the desk and came to the counter.

"Anything I can do for you?"

"No, just dropped in to pass the time of day. Nothing like getting acquainted with your neighbors." He watched Paula, whose ears reddened, but she didn't look up.

"It's stopped snowing," Phil said carefully. "It will be a nice day and we're hardly neighbors. Besides, we're busy."

Pace slowly turned his head and looked at him, eyes level. His lips pursed momentarily and then he spoke contemptuously.

"That winds it up between you and me, but there's still another neighbor in the room. What do you think of the day, ma'am? I'd say it's not quite so bright or pretty as you are."

Phil gasped but Paula looked up in swift alarm. She spoke quickly.

"Thank you, sir. But we are very busy—"

"Now that's too bad," Pace said regretfully. Phil stepped between him and the girl. His face was suffused with anger and he controlled his voice with great effort.

"Mister, let's get things straight. You and your kind ride in and make us helpless. There's nothing we can do about that. But we want nothing to do with you. That goes for me and my daughter. Why don't you leave us alone?"

"Dad!" Paula jumped up and came to his side, clasping her hands, around his arms. Phil tried to push her behind him but did not succeed. His anger mounted.

"I must ask you to leave, sir. We don't want your company."

Pace slowly straightened and his nostrils pinched. A hot, fierce light came in his pale eyes and he stood poised on the ragged edge of violence. Phil's big hands tightened around Paula's, and her face turned pale. Pace's slender fingers curled slowly into a fist and then slowly straightened again. His glance swung to Paula and he studied her for a long moment. The fierce light died and the red lips moved into a gentle smile.

"Too bad you're so busy, ma'am. I reckon there'll be another time before long."

He touched his hat brim and for the moment he was a handsome man, slender as a rapier and just as deadly. His glance swung to Phil and it became harsh, cold and calculating. He smiled again and walked out of the office. Phil and Paula remained at the counter, staring at the door Pace closed behind him. Neither father nor daughter realized how closely they clung to each other.

Finally Paula shivered and returned to her desk.

She sat down and looked blankly at the open ledger and her lips trembled. Phil leaned heavily against the counter and his fist pounded slowly and softly on the top.

"He'll be back. He's got it in his mind so plain you can see. This thing is going to play out to the bitter end of the string."

"Dad," she said with a slight catch in her voice, "what can we do?"

He shook his head in a dull despair. "I don't know . . . I don't know." A desperate determination came into his voice. "But we have to do something . . . soon."

Outside Pace looked back at the office, wondering a little at himself. It was the first time he had ever let a man talk as Phil had and not killed him out of hand. Pace congratulated himself on his self-control. He had done the right thing if he had any hope of making progress with that green-eyed beauty. A girl wouldn't take to your love-making very well right after you had killed her father. Let it ride, Pace told himself. You'll get along before you leave town—unless Bruhn interferes or decides the bunch should ride on.

The thought swung his mind to other matters and he instantly dismissed Paula as he walked slowly back to the saloon. By the time he entered the place, he had a plan and he wore a secretive smile that he erased immediately. He walked to the bar and helped himself to a drink. Vause glanced at him and Pace asked casually where Tex had gone.

"Now you guess," Vause said with a grin. "He can't keep away from that widder too long."

Pace gave his attention to the drink. He took his time and finally pushed away from the bar. As he started toward the door, Bruhn signaled him over to the table, motioned him to sit down, but Pace shook his head.

"Going out," he explained. "What's on your mind?"

"That deal we was offered," Bruhn said. "I figured Tex was for it. How about you?"

Pace smiled. "Why, Jack, I don't care one way or the other. You're the boss."

He walked away before Bruhn could check him. He stepped out onto the porch and rubbed his hand along his jaw as he thoughtfully looked down the street. He felt pleased, knowing that Bruhn needed him and had twice made a play for his support. And so did Tex. Pace smiled more widely and then walked down the steps.

Paths through the drifts had now been made connecting every house and store. They took Pace on a roundabout course but he finally came to the Rikes' house. He glanced across the street at the silent Preston house and the mental picture of Paula caused his eyes to glow again. But by the time he knocked on the Rikes' door, his face was composed and expressionless.

No one answered and he knocked again, impatiently, louder, The door jerked angrily open and Tex glared at him. Darrow's scowl vanished and the mean eyes widened.

"Pace! What the hell you doing here?"

"Looking for you." Pace peered beyond his shoulder into the hall. "I'm not stopping anything?"

"Just some drinking. Come in."

Tex stepped aside and Pace entered. Tex led the way down the hall and up the stairs with the jaunty air of a proprietor. Pace followed, studying the assured back just ahead of him and feeling more certain than ever that he had full control of the situation. Tex called ahead.

"We got company, Ava."

"Who's it?" The woman's voice sounded blurred,

foggy. "One of us . . . Pace Odlum."

He led the way into a room and Pace followed. The bed had not been made in several days. A table stood by the window holding several empty whiskey bottles and some dirty glasses. One bottle held some amber fluid that glowed golden brown in the light. Ava was sitting in a chair near the table.

Her hair was uncombed and she had pulled a robe over her nightdress. She stared owlishly at Pace, her once magnificent eyes dulled and bleary. Her face was sagged and yet she still had a great animal magnetism showing in the full lips that pouted slightly, in the full curves of her body as she stirred sluggishly and looked at Tex, frowning a little to see him.

"Don't I know him?" she asked, lifting a languid finger toward Pace. Tex dropped his arm familiarly about her shoulder.

"Sure, Honey. He's my friend."

"Then you're welcome, mister. Tex'n me like friends . . . lots of 'em." She leaned toward Pace and her voice dropped to a confidential whisper. "Me'n Tex gonna leave this place. Never liked it, mister, no part of it. Like see lotta people around, lotta excitement. Thought once I didn't, but that was all wrong. So me'n Tex, we're gonna leave . . . gonna have a real place somewhere and have all our friends around all the time. You gonna come, mister? Come see us?"

"Sure," Pace smiled. He looked swiftly at Tex, who grinned crookedly and winked. Ava didn't see it, but frowned at the whiskey bottle, reached for it.

"Poor Tommy," she said and hiccoughed. "Was gonna leave him but he got killed. Didn't treat him right and he loved me. Makes me feel sad, and I don't like feeling sad."

Pace caught Tex's eye again and jerked his head toward the door. Tex nodded, took the whiskey bottle and poured Ava a drink. He whispered something to her, kissed her cheek, but she paid little attention. Tex nodded to Pace and led the way out of the room and downstairs. They entered the tiny parlor and Pace noticed another empty bottle sitting on the floor by a chair.

Tex looked questioningly at him. "Something up?"

"No," Pace said. He sat down on a horsehair sofa, thumbed his hat back. "It's about Jack."

Tex stiffened and some of the humor left his thin face. "What about him?"

"Well," Pace hesitated deliberately. "I don't like the way Jack's handling things."

Tex stared, disbelievingly, and then a new and hopeful light came in his face. But his eyes narrowed with an innate suspicion.

"Let me hear that again."

"It's plain, Tex. I dunno, seems like Jack's slipping. Look the way he lets Shorty Ratner hold us up. He waits around too long and all of us will be looking right at a jail with a hang-noose just beyond. That don't figure. Take this offer of Starrett to take care of Crane. Five hundred ain't much, but it's an easy job. It'd be just that much more to add to the kitty."

Tex listened with growing amazement and delight. He walked to the window and looked out on the street. He covertly glanced at Pace a couple of times, trying to read something in the man's expression. He finally spoke cautiously.

"I've figured Jack was slipping all along . . . getting old. It's time maybe for him to . . . retire."

Pace looked up under his brows, and slowly nodded. "I figure that way, too."

Tex wheeled from the window and strode to him. "Pace, you're saying you want someone else to lead us?"

"Why not?" Pace demanded. "New blood, someone who's not afraid to move like Jack is . . . or so stubborn he'd get us all in a tight fix while we wait for Shorty to breathe his last. I'm tired of it."

Tex hesitated a moment, then plunged. "Pace, would you back me if I took over the gang from Jack . . . made him retire?"

Pace looked steadily at Tex and very slowly his red lips moved in a lovely smile. His voice was level. "Don't you mean kill him?"

Tex started to deny it, then his shoulders slumped and he laughed. "All right. That's the way it'll have to be, anyhow."

Pace arose. "Why, Tex, you do as you think best. It wouldn't worry me one way or the other if Jack was retired . . . or shot. Only thing . . . why put it off?"

Darrow's laughter was almost a crow of triumph. He grabbed Pace's arm in his eagerness.

"Why, man, this is all I need. You'll see action damn' soon."

Suddenly Pace wheeled away, facing the door, frowning. Tex turned, alarmed, his hand dropping to his holster. Ava stood in the doorway, swaying a little. Her right hand held a shot glass of whiskey, her left clutched her robe together at the neck. She pouted at Tex, frowning to bring him in focus.

"Got lonely," she said vaguely. "Didn't like it. Want to see you around, Tex."

Pace chuckled and Tex looked hurriedly at him. A flick of Pace's eyes indicated the woman in the doorway. "Tex, you could always pick 'em. Me, I've got my eye on one, too. But Jack wants to hold tight rein on everything."

"Not for long," Tex snapped. Pace nodded.

"Good! Why, with this town in our hands, we could really make our wait here pay off. It's ready for a picking, but Jack won't cut us loose."

"Then we'll cut Jack loose," Tex laughed. He walked to Ava and took the shot glass from her. He turned to face Odlum and lifted the glass.

"Here's to Jack. May he enter hell soon and all in a sudden."

"Amen," Pace said softly.

SEVENTEEN

Dan tried to hold his elation in check. His face remained masklike and only by a single, sharp glance did he betray his inner excitement. Here was a gift extended to him but he must not too eagerly grasp it. Hiatt was held now by emotion and he might change his mind once this moment had passed. Dan spoke carefully.

"I don't know, Hiatt. You're outlaw, sure, but there might be some way to get rid of the brand."

Hiatt came to the edge of his chair, tipping forward onto the table. "How? That's all I want to know. Think I like this sneaking, running life? Think any woman would want to share it with me?"

Dan spoke cautiously. "You're not wanted for any killing in this Territory. But there is the bank robbery and the stolen money."

"But that was done in Colorado."

"The money's right here," Dan pointed out. "Maybe that could be returned . . . but there's still Tommy Rikes' killing. You didn't fire the shot, but the law can still hold you for it . . . unless you...." Dan's voice drifted off and Hiatt threw himself impatiently back.

"Unless what?"

"You're one of them. The only way we can trust you is to see what you do about it. If you helped us capture that bunch, and then turned the bank money over to . . . say Phil Preston, to see it went back to Colorado, I think the law would be mighty lenient with you,"

"Turn them in?" Hiatt's tone had changed, uncertain now.

"How else can we trust you? . . . or Ernine? After it's over, there's several ranches that could use a rider. They'd make jobs for you. I know Hal Crane would on his HC spread. You'd be clear of this gang, clear of the bank robbery. That trumped-up killing charge back home would mean nothing and, given time, you might even get it cleared up."

"I don't know," Hiatt made aimless tracery on the tablecloth with his thumbnail.

"You got your choice, Hiatt. You can ride along with this bunch, and you know where that trail will end. You won't have a chance, not only with Ernine, but any girl like her—ever. Throw in with us and I can promise that everyone in the whole Valley will back you to the limit." He raised his hand in a warning. "I don't mean you'll get off scot-free. But we'll see the law is lenient and that you have a place to come back to where you can hold up your head when it's over."

Hiatt arose, paced to the stove and back, frowning. He looked appealingly at Dan and away again. He stopped before the table and his voice was despairing.

"Murdock, I've ridden the trail with this bunch. Maybe not for long, but they trust me."

Dan nodded. "I know how you feel, but you still got one of two trails to ride. Does a killer and thief ever trust anyone, or can he be trusted? A dollar gets you a hundred they'll leave you in the lurch someday if it's to their advantage."

"Shorty," Hiatt breathed and then realized Dan looked curiously at him. "Maybe I'll tell you later."

"Look, Hiatt, don't try to make up your mind this

minute. Think it over. Give me an answer by late this afternoon. Is that fair?"

"Enough, I guess."

"Then that's the way it'll be. But give me your answer one way or the other."

Hiatt stood thoughtful, then turned to the door and, without a word, left the house. Dan remained at the table. He knew Hiatt hated even the thought of betrayal, of being a turncoat. But he must if he was to ride free. Only, Hiatt must see it and Dan felt that he had done the wise thing in letting the man decide for himself. Trouble was, the waiting would be nerve-frazzling, to be this close to real help and yet to have to wait.

He already felt the tension off it, the constant rising of hope that he had to beat down. He needed to move about. He checked the stove, stoked wood, checked the damper and then left the house. He nearly turned in at the lumberyard and thought better of it. Phil Preston was already too worried and, if he knew, might ruin everything by trying to force Hiatt's decision.

So Dan walked on to the saloon and did not learn of Pace Odlum's unwanted visit. The outlaws were gathered, as usual, at the bar. Dan's eyes quickly passed over them. Bruhn sat at the table with his inevitable card layout, whiskey bottle and glass. The rest were at the bar with the exception of Hiatt, Pace and Tex.

Dan poured his drink, dropped his coin in the bowl, and set himself to wait. Not five minutes later Pace came in. He walked behind the bar, selected a bottle from the shelf and took it to a table across the room from Bruhn.

Tex Darrow came in. Dan watched him through the bar mirror and something in the man's attitude made him alert. Darrow acted as though nothing was on his mind, and yet there was something of suppressed excitement in the quick cut of the black eyes. He saw Juarez at the far end of the bar and suddenly veered off to join the breed.

He spoke to Juarez, lips barely moving. Dan saw the breed's red-rimmed blue eyes widen and then Tex quickly grabbed the man's arm in a warning. Juarez cut a quick glance toward Bruhn and then assumed a casual air as false as a sleeping rattler's. Dan felt a tingle along his spine. Something was going on under the surface. Tex took a drink, left Juarez and lazily moved to stand beside Egan. There was again a swift, low exchange and then Egan looked both elated and frightened. He instantly tried to make a mask of his face but did not entirely bring it off.

Dan waited, feeling the mounting tension in the room. It was nothing tangible, simply a hunch so strong that he finally turned from the bar and walked outside. He stood at the top of the steps and looked back at the door he had just closed, lips twisted thoughtfully, tongue working the inside of one cheek.

Something important stirred among those outlaws, something that concerned them all. Suddenly Dan wondered where Hiatt was. Perhaps, in some way, the gang learned that the man might turn against them. Dan knew only too well they would strike first and he felt a surge of fear for the man.

He crossed the street to the general store. Ernine and Vic were alone in the building. Vic looked up from a box he had brought from the storeroom, nodded, and continued checking the invoice. Dan walked up to the counter close to Ernine. "Where's Hiatt?"

She looked up, surprised, threw a quick glance at her father. Then she met Dan's question with a challenging look.

"I don't know, Dan. What concern is it of mine?"

Dan spoke in a quick whisper. "He talked to me, you know. Where is he?"

Again she glanced at her father at the back of the store, engrossed in his work. "He went to the livery stable five minutes ago."

Dan nodded and left the store. He came out on the porch and looked across the street at the stable. He saw Hiatt come to one of the dusty office windows and look out on the street, his hands shoved in his pockets. Dan knew relief. Whatever went on at the bar did not involve Hiatt, for there the man stood obviously thinking over Dan's proposition.

Relieved, Dan's gaze idly turned toward the Squaw Creek Road. A single speck broke the white expanse of snow, Vivian McLear working her way toward the village. Dan watched her for long minutes, and he recalled Starrett's statement that a girl like her was for him, not Paula. Now, of course, he didn't believe it.

A movement to his right caught his attention. A bearlike figure crossed the street and stood swaying at the foot of the Wyoming Bar steps. Dan stared in surprise. It was the first he had seen of the big blacksmith since the bandits had come to the town.

George stood spread-legged, staring up at the saloon, his bullet head hunched between his wide shoulders. He clutched a dirty blanket about him, one end trailing in the snow. He wore no hat and his wiry hair stood stiff and wild. Drunk, Dan knew, and some impulse had sent him out of his shack, wandering the streets.

It had happened before, and people stayed out of George's way. He was unpredictable, mean. If he was spoken to, he might pay no attention or, again, he might fell the speaker with a blow of his mighty fist. Dan straightened, remembering the tension among the outlaws. If George wandered in there now, his belligerence might set off a powder keg.

Dan jumped down the steps, thinking he might head George off. But the big blacksmith suddenly mounted the steps of the saloon and weaved across the porch to the door. Dan called his name but George paid no attention. George disappeared inside.

Dan glanced down the street, hoping he could see someone who could help him handle the giant. But there was only Vivian, who worked her way unheeding to the store. Seeing nothing else for it, Dan entered the saloon.

George had trailed his blanket across the big room to the bar. The outlaws had made way for him and they watched the giant fumbling at the cork of a whiskey bottle. Dan saw Egan nudge Juarez and grin. The rest watched amusedly.

Now Dan knew fear for George. The man would be touchy and morose and the outlaws plainly were in the mood to have fun with this swaying, drunken giant. If George started something, his brute strength would mean little. Darrow, Pace, any of them, would shoot the man down without hesitation.

Dan walked swiftly to the bar. He could see George's face reflected in the mirror. The big lips were moist and slack, and the lines of his face had deepened, dulling his expression. His eyes were glazed, barely in focus and his low forehead was deeply creased by a dark frown. Dan eased in beside him but the man paid little attention. Dan picked up the bottle, tapped the cork in it and extended it to the blacksmith.

"Why not take it home and finish it there, George?"

George slowly turned and stared owlishly at Dan. His frown deepened and his voice rumbled from his chest.

"Want to drink here. Leave me alone."

Dan hesitated. He might be able to argue George into leaving, but he gambled on trouble. He looked over his shoulder and saw Darrow watching intently, mean eyes alight. Bruhn saw only the cards spread on the table before him. Dan licked his lips and pressed the bottle on George.

"It's a lot better at home. You know that."

The giant hand petulantly swept the bottle aside. George's head hung low and only his elbows hooked on the bar supported his immense weight. Suddenly George's head lifted. His lips were no longer slack, though his voice was slurred.

"You . . . try to steal her. I seen you."

"George, you're out of your head."

"Seen you," George repeated and he straightened, swung half around. "You'n Vivian. You wanta take her, but I ain't going to let you. Vivian's too pretty . . . girl. Gonna see you don't touch her no more."

He lunged for Dan, big hands outspread, the fingers taloned. He moved fast for so big and drunken a man and Dan barely avoided the bear hug George tried to clamp on him. Now, his anger riding him, the drunkenness seemed to fall away from George, except for the murky light in the bloodshot eyes. He wheeled, big arm swinging and Dan ducked.

This was the thing he feared. He could not face up to George for long and he must end this thing quickly, before the outlaws took a hand. They had quickly jumped back from the bar and now they watched, grinning, forming a half ring about the two men.

Dan caught the glint of the half-empty bottle on the bar. His fists would never stop the giant but a blow with this might lay the man out. Dan threw himself at the bar, hand reaching for the bottle. George's arm flailed and the bottle sailed out of reach to crash on the sawdust floor. His arm continued its wide arc and his fist caught Dan alongside the head.

Dan fell sideways, trying desperately to regain his

balance. He slammed into a table, hung balanced a moment and then the whole thing tipped over, spilling him to the floor and tangling him with a chair.

George made an animal growl and his big hand grasped the edge of the fallen table, flipped it aside. Dan shook his head to stop the spinning. He heard the crash of the table, saw George coming toward him.

He scrambled to get his legs under him and avoid the giant's rush, then realized that he couldn't. Dan desperately grabbed the fallen chair, whipped it about and jabbed up with it, the four legs pointing at George. The chair struck the man in the pit of the stomach and his stride faltered. It was enough for Dan to roll fast to one side and come to his feet.

But now he was trapped, his only retreat around the bar, or along the wall the other way. He tried that but George, eyes narrow and wicked, cut him off. Dan avoided the taloned fingers by a hair, jabbed his fist into the man's face. George only grunted and bore in.

He forced Dan back, but Dan slammed hard blows into the blacksmith's ribs and stomach. They only slowed him and Dan desperately pounded at his face and head. George blinked his eyes and kept coming, not trying to avoid the hammering fists but thick arm reaching for Dan.

They rounded the edge of the bar and Dan was in a cul-de-sac. His breath came raggedly and his arms ached from the constant, futile pounding. He desperately looked at either side and saw no escape. His only chance was a swift, direct attack that might take George off balance just long enough for Dan to slip by him.

Dan's lips flattened and he set himself, suddenly advancing, his fists flailing, each blow landing. They struck on mouth, nose, jaw and eyes. George was blinded and his advance faltered. Dan swung harder.

In another second, Dan would be able to slip by, whip around the edge of the bar and out of the trap. He heard George grunt and wince.

Another half step and Dan would be free. He swung for the rocky chin and the blow connected. His knuckles cracked but George did not go down, only reached blindly, shaking his head, eyes squeezed shut against the rain of blows. His taloned fingers caught Dan's sleeve and instantly Dan was jerked forward.

The man's grip shifted, and the thick arms circled Dan, locked behind his back. Dan tried to break free but couldn't. He tried to land effective blows but George's bullet head was buried against Dan's chest as the big muscles bulged.

Dan felt the pressure increase on his back and around his ribs. He was half lifted from his feet and the pressure was a torture, steadily increasing. His breath was constricted and he could not break loose. He felt his strength flow out and he knew that within a matter of seconds George would kill him.

He clawed his fingers into the bristly hair, trying desperately to find some purchase, force back the head and get a leverage that would break the grip. Pain hazed his eyes and he was hardly aware of the girl who had suddenly appeared beside them, nor did he really hear her voice, though it shrilled through the room, time and again, calling George's name.

Suddenly the killing pressure was gone as George straightened and then roughly cast Dan aside. He fell full length on the sawdust behind the bar and could do nothing but gasp for breath, fighting the intense pain in his ribs and back.

George stood, chest heaving, head hung forward, but his murky eyes now watched Vivian McLear. He swiped the back of his hands across his slack lips. Vivian spoke soothingly.

"What are you doing, George? You've lost your head."

He nodded and stood with big arms hanging slack, still watching her in a strange, dumb adoration. Dan painfully rolled over on his side and pushed himself up with his hands, head hanging as he still fought for breath. Vivian gave her full attention to the blacksmith. She smiled and extended her hand.

"You'd better go home, George. You've had too much. Would you like for me to go with you?"

He blinked, frowned to focus her. Then the bruised lips parted in a wide smile. "Would you? With me?"

"Sure, George. You've never asked me. Here, take my hand."

He stared at the slender hand she extended, afraid to touch it. Then, slowly, he lifted his own and his fingers convulsively tightened around hers. Vivian winced and covered it with a smile.

Dan sat up, his senses returning. Vivian and George walked by him, the blacksmith without so much as a glance, but the girl tried to signal Dan with a single, swift look. The two of them circled the end of the bar and the outlaws moved back to give them room. Vause whistled.

"She stopped it! By God, there's a woman I'd sure like to have around."

George halted in mid-stride and he dropped Vivian's hand. She instantly wheeled toward him but George had already lunged toward the outlaw, so fast that Vause was caught unaware and could not avoid the attack. His hand dropped to his gun, but George's powerful grip tied the man's arms to his side and he was helpless.

Dan tried to get to his feet and stop this new attack. Vivian reached for George's arms, again screaming his name. Tex and Juarez both wheeled about and charged the blacksmith and the helpless outlaw. They tried to break the giant's grip but could not and Vause's face writhed in pain as the pressure slowly bent him back. Then Tex stepped back, his hand blurred.

The shot roared and bounced in the room. George jerked, head snapping back. For a long second he held Vause in the vise of his arms and the muscles spasmodically bunched. Vause screamed in agony, and then George's arms fell away and the giant body toppled sideways to the floor. One leg bent slightly and then fell flaccid.

Vause had also fallen and he gasped on the floor beside the dead man. The echoes of the shot still boomed from the walls and then faded. Dan had frozen, still half crouched and Vivian stood staring at the dead man, her face paling. No one moved and Tex slowly lifted the Colt and blew at the muzzle. Vivian's head jerked up, her eyes ablaze.

"Always the killer," she said coldly. "Always the brave man with the gun, especially when you can shoot from the back. Always your answer, Tex. You could have used the barrel to knock him out, but not Tex Darrow. He likes to see men die."

Tex stiffened and his face suffused. He spat a vile word at her, and his left hand whipped up and across her face, the fingers making a loud smacking sound. Dan came to his feet with an oath and Tex wheeled about.

His lips were thin, the mean eyes narrowed, ablaze with fury. Dan hardly realized what he did. He came lunging forward and then found himself facing Jack Bruhn, who had stepped between the two men. Jack's big hand thrust Dan back and he wheeled to face Tex.

"Put up the gun, Tex. There's been enough killing in this town. Apologize to the lady."

Tex stared at Jack, face still twisted with fury and anger. He slowly straightened, licking his lips, and his glance whipped beyond Jack to Pace Odlum. Pace leaned against the bar, watching, red lips parted, a peculiar glitter in his eyes. He caught Darrow's glance and Pace slowly smiled.

Suddenly Darrow's Colt whipped up and the long tongue of flame leapt from the muzzle toward Bruhn. The slug smashed into the broad chest and Bruhn's body jerked. His eyes snapped wide open in stunned surprise. His lips parted and his hand came halfway up as though to touch his chest.

Then he fell and the floor trembled with the impact of the big body.

EIGHTEEN

Everyone had been frozen with the crash of the shot and Jack Bruhn's sudden death. They stared at the outlaw's body, sprawled beside that of George Gorton's. Tex looked down at Jack as though he couldn't quite believe it.

Dan recovered first and his glance swept the stunned faces. This was war between the outlaws themselves and he realized that he and Vivian stood in a dangerous place. He licked his dry lips and eased toward her.

None of the outlaws paid any attention to him. He touched Vivian's hand and she jerked up her head, eyes dazed. But she understood his signal and, she moved slowly and carefully back toward the door with him.

Tex had completely forgotten Dan and the girl, and none of the others so much as looked their way. They stared down at Jack Bruhn and now Juarez stirred and moved to Darrow's side. Pace still leaned against the bar as Dan opened the door and he and Vivian slipped out.

Suddenly Vivian started to tremble and Dan put his arm around her shoulders to give her new confidence. She caught a grip on herself and looked at him, eyes still showing shock and a touch of fright. But her voice was even, controlled.

"Thanks, Dan, I'll be all right."

"Not yet. Hell can break loose in there. I'll get you home."

They listened but still could hear no sound from inside. Dan turned to lead her away and stopped short. Starrett came striding up the steps and halted. Dan shook his head.

"I wouldn't go in there, Blaise."

"Why not?"

"George Gorton was just killed." Starrett's jaw fell and Dan added, "And Darrow just killed Jack Bruhn. They could start fighting among themselves any minute."

"Jack Bruhn!" Starrett looked stunned. Just then a shot blasted inside the saloon. Dan grasped Vivian's arm.

"It's started. Let's get out of here."

The three of them hurried away, Starrett striding back to the store, Dan hustling Vivian down the street toward the Squaw Creek Road and temporary safety, at least. He listened for more shots from within the saloon, but there were none.

He hurried Vivian down the road, fully expecting to hear the sounds of gun battle in the street behind him. But the village was silent, the false peace was undisturbed. It worried Dan, even more than open warfare. He left Vivian at her door and warned her to stay inside.

"I'm not afraid, Dan. I've known their kind before."

"I know you're not afraid," he replied sharply. "But

many a bystander has caught a stray bullet. I don't know what can happen."

He started to leave but she checked him. "You're not going to be a—bystander, Dan?"

He smiled crookedly. "Yes, to find out what has happened. But I'll duck the bullets."

Returning, Dan walked slowly, ears strained for the sound of violence that never came. He rounded the corner and halted, looking down the main street. It was empty, silent, neither was there any sound from the Wyoming Bar. Dan rubbed his hand along his jaw and considered what he should do. He glanced toward the store and saw Vic Frazin signal to him from the window.

When Dan entered the store, Vic grabbed his arm, frightened. Dan's eyes swept about the store to see Bob and Art standing not far away, Ernine at the side of the window, straining toward the saloon across the street. Starrett was not here. Vic excitedly told the news and Dan nodded.

"Where's Blaise?"

"He went back there," Vic babbled. "I told him not to, but he did."

Dan turned to the window, glanced at Ernine before he looked toward the saloon. She showed anxiety and fear only in her eyes, but they were deep with misery. Hiatt is right, Dan thought angrily, she has fallen in love with him. And what good could come of it? Dan gave his attention to the saloon for a long moment and then determined to go over there. Vic stopped him at the door.

"What will they do now?" he asked.

Dan shrugged. "I don't know. Who can tell about Darrow?"

He escaped from Vic, who wanted to ask more fearful questions, and crossed the street. He slowly mounted the saloon steps, straining to hear some sound from within. He heard only a faint laugh, muffled by the wall.

Dan pushed open the door, alert and tense. He looked toward the place where George and Bruhn had been killed but the bodies had been moved. His gaze swept on around the room, seeing Starrett seated at a table with Pace, talking eagerly while Pace nodded calmly now and then. Dan's lips thinned, knowing that Starrett had lost no time to renew his deal with the outlaws. But why didn't Blaise talk to Darrow, who had surely taken over the leadership?

Dan moved slowly to the bar and the four outlaws who stood there. Vause, now recovered from George's bear hug, stood behind the bar and eyed the rows of bottles. He selected one and passed it to Egan, then took one for himself. Denver nursed a shot glass, a bottle at his hand. He looked up when Dan came to stand beside him, and his eyes were bloodshot.

"You again," he muttered in his beard. "Have a drink. We don't pay for 'em no more, Pace says. We help ourselves to anything we want in this whole damn' town."

Dan felt a shiver along his neck, but he calmly poured himself a drink. He saw Juarez at the far end of the bar and the breed stared dully at the far wall, then scratched his head, frowned. Dan spoke casually.

"Where's Darrow?"

Denver lifted a shaggy brow, stared owlishly at Dan. He pointed to the closed storeroom door behind the bar.

"Tex is in there . . . with Jack and that crazy blacksmith. All three of 'em, waiting for boothill."

"Tex?" the surprise made Dan's voice lift.

"Tex . . . done went where all owlhooters go . . . yonderly and for good." Denver shook his head.

"Damnedest thing you ever saw. Not five minutes after he salted Jack Bruhn, him and Pace tangled. Least, I think they did. Anyhow Pace give Tex a forty-four slug before any of us knew what happened. We got a new leader."

"Pace," Dan whispered and looked up at the bar mirror. He could see Pace and Starrett, and now Starrett smiled as he made his point. Pace nodded and Starrett leaned back, pleased, lifted his shot glass to the slim killer.

He's done it, Dan thought grimly. Maybe Bruhn held off but that killer won't. Hal Crane's life isn't worth a whistle in a blizzard. Dan placed his glass on the bar and walked casually toward the door. He feared that some one of the men might stop him but no one gave him any attention. He opened the door and stepped outside.

"Hey!" The voice was sharp and commanding and Dan's heart sank. He was sure it was Pace but he dared not look back. Instead, he pulled the door closed behind him as though he hadn't heard. He hurried down the steps and across the street to the store, expecting to be halted any second.

He reached the haven of the store and, once inside, felt suddenly weak, as though he had raced at top speed for miles. Vic, at the far end of the aisle, wheeled about and Hal Crane looked up, startled. Apparently the two had been in a deep conversation. Ernine still stood by the window and she looked a hopeful question at Dan. But he didn't notice, his attention being on Crane, thanking his luck that the man had appeared at just this time.

Vic hurried toward him and Crane followed more sedately. Dan brushed Vic aside with a quick word, advanced to meet Crane, took his arm and wheeled him about.

"Hey," Crane exclaimed and tried to check Dan. "You gone loco!"

"In the warehouse," Dan snapped. "Could mean your life." Crane blinked but didn't argue. Dan closed the big door in Vic's amazed face and then led Crane far enough away so that they could not be heard through the thick walls.

"Hal, listen to me. We got to make it quick. Blaise fired me from Star."

"I heard, but—" Dan's impatient gesture checked him. "Blaise plans to get all of HC spread, Hal. He's just made a deal with Pace Odlum to have you killed."

Crane's jaw dropped. "Starrett?"

Dan spoke impatiently, telling Crane the full story of Starrett's attempt to get Bruhn to do the job and Dan's own certainty that Pace had just now agreed to wipe Crane out. Dan glanced toward the closed door.

"You can't get out of town, Hal. But you've got to hide."

"Be damned—"

"You will be," Dan snapped, "and buried. This is no time to be brave." He tugged worriedly at his ear lobe and suddenly lifted his head, eyes alight.

"George's shack! They won't look for you there. It's at the edge of town and, if they do think of it, you can see 'em coming in time to hide."

"Where?" Crane asked dryly.

"That old lean-to against the back," Dan snapped. "It's filled with junk. They won't think of it." He turned to the door. "Better head there quick, Hal."

Crane didn't like the idea. Dan threw open the door and entered the store proper. Vic and Bob stood nearby, looking at him with owlish curiosity. Art stood near the stove, hands shoved in his pockets, boyish eyes alight with excitement. Ernine, still by the window, suddenly called in a low voice.

"Dan! Come here."

In a few swift strides he joined her and she indicated the saloon across the street. Three of the outlaws had come out and they stood in a group on the porch. Dan instantly spotted Pace who seemed to be giving instructions. Juarez and Egan nodded and then the three descended the steps and started across the street. Juarez and Egan swayed a little. Dan wheeled about.

"Vic! You're having visitors. Hal, out the back way. For God's sake don't let them see you!"

Crane gave him a single, startled look. He stood indecisive a second and then strode swiftly to the rear of the store. Dan heard the back door close and he watched the approaching outlaws with more confidence.

Pace led the other two. He opened the door and came in, pale eyes sweeping the room and then resting on Dan and Ernine. Juarez and Egan, looking mean and dangerous, glowered about the room. Pace nodded to Ernine with a crooked grin and then looked sharply at Dan. His voice was dry, flat.

"Don't you stop when someone calls you?"

Dan managed a look of surprise and Pace shrugged. He looked around as Vic hurried up. Bob and Art drifted up the aisle toward them, the lad's face alight with interest. Vic bobbed his head and spoke politely but Pace cut him short.

"Where's Hal Crane? I saw him come in here." Vic looked frightened and glanced at Dan who cut in easily.

"He was here. Left a while ago."

"Where?"

Dan shrugged. "I don't know. What do you want with him?"

Pace smiled and his face looked angelic except for

the eyes. "Why, we want to give him a dose of lead, Murdock. Things have changed considerably since morning."

"Since Bruhn was killed," Dan said dryly.

Pace nodded. "Yes, even since then. Poor Tex tried to argue with a Peacemaker. So, I'm ramrodding the bunch." His voice dropped to a soft whisper.

"I'm a gent who tries to get what he wants. Maybe you don't know that, Murdock, so I'm telling you now."

"I guessed it," Dan said. He shot a glance at Vic. "I suppose you want the whole town."

Pace cocked his head to one side, considering, and his smile grew brighter. "Maybe, I'll decide about the town. It's mine now, you know. But I was mainly thinking about the company of a certain young lady. Thought I'd tell you so you could keep your distance. I've already warned Starrett."

Dan's face turned pale and Pace waited, watching, the smile still touching the red lips. Dan choked down hot words and he felt himself tremble as he stood straight and stiff, hand clenched, fighting for control. Pace regarded him sardonically for a long, long moment and then, regretfully, turned away.

He checked, his attention held by something down the aisle. His hand dropped from the doorknob and he walked to the display of Stetsons, reached for a pearl-gray one, examined it. Vic edged toward him.

"You like it, Mr. Odlum? It's the very best."

Pace put it on, curved the brim. He looked at himself in the mirror, then picked up his old, battered hat and sailed it to the back of the store. Vic smiled.

"Good! I knew you'd know good material and a good buy."

"It fits. I'll take it," Pace said. He started back up the aisle, leaving Vic standing, mouth sagging with surprise. He suddenly wheeled about and hurried after Pace.

"Mr. Odlum! Mr. Odlum! You didn't pay me."

Pace halted, turned slowly, red lips pursed. He studied Vic's worried face, smiled again.

"So I didn't. I guess one slug's enough."

His hand blurred and the Colt blasted. Vic spun half around and fell back against the counter, catching himself. His eyes were round with fright and surprise and he lifted his hand to his side. His lips moved soundlessly and then he slowly turned half around and crumpled in the aisle. Ernine screamed.

"Keep the change," Pace laughed and looked at Juarez and Egan. "Let's go hunting." At the door Pace faced the stunned people,

"I think he'll live—if you get a sawbones in time. That's just to tell you that from now on we pay for all we get in lead . . . if you want to collect."

He touched his hat brim in a mock salute and left, Juarez and Egan following him. Ernine suddenly moaned, crumpled, and Dan caught her. He shouted at Bob.

"Take care of your Dad. Art, get to Doc Langer and bring him here."

The boy, pale-faced, raced toward the rear door. Dan eased Ernine to the floor and worked to bring her around. Bob, horrified and half sick, ripped his father's shirt and exposed the wound. It bled badly but Dan, after a hasty glance, felt that it would not prove to be too serious.

He looked up when steps pounded across the porch, expecting Doc Langer. But Phil, Clay Majors and Larry Teter rushed in. They plowed to a halt just within the door, stunned and horrified to see the girl and the man stretched out on the floor. Just then Ernine moaned and Dan lifted her to a sitting position. Phil Preston's horrified oath ripped through the silence.

"What will they do next?"

Doc Langer's hurried entrance prevented Dan's reply. Art, freckles standing out sickly on his pale, strained face, followed the doctor. Langer briefly checked Ernine first, gave her a sniff of salts and testily told Larry Teter to take her home and see that she was put to bed. He then gave his attention to Vic.

As Dan had hoped, the bullet had ripped through Vic's side low on the hip. It had struck no organs but Doc guessed that it might have grooved the hip joint. There was a chance Vic would always have a stiff leg.

"Wounded men and dead men," Doc growled as he worked.

"That outlaw at my place is about due to cash in. Crane's man will pull through, but now there's Vic. Who else?"

He finished the bandaging and gave Vic smelling salts. Vic's head jerked but Doc kept the vial close to his nose. Vic's head jerked again and then his eyes opened and he looked dazedly up at the doctor. Langer nodded grimly and stood up.

"When Larry gets back, you'd all better give Vic a help home. You stay in bed, Vic. I'll check that wound later tonight." He glared around at the rest, and his voice grew acid-like. "Any more gunshots to clean up?"

Dan shook his head. "Not for you, but there's three in the saloon for Larry to put away." They looked disbelievingly at him and Dan told them what had happened to Gorton, and to Jack Bruhn and Tex Darrow. Pace Odlum now ruled the outlaws.

"Then we're in the middle of hell," Phil said heavily. Dan nodded.

"You've called it, Phil." He told about the hunt for Hal Crane and the reason for it. None but Phil would believe him for a few stunned moments but Preston's confirmation convinced the others. They stood silent, looking at one another, faces ghastly and eyes showing their bone-shaking fright. Clay Majors spoke softly, a whisper that barely reached Dan's ears.

"There'll be nothing left of Bitter—or us—in a day or two."

NINETEEN

Art Frazin, after hurrying back with Doc Langer, stood in the aisle close to his father, watching the doctor examine and bandage the wound. His face had grown steadily more pale, held a greenish hue for a time and then cleared again, back to a strange white that made the freckles stand out like pennies. His lips quivered several times and he made a visible effort to control his tears.

Larry returned, saying that Ernine was now home. He had seen Pace, Juarez and Egan around the Rikes' place and Dan began to worry about both Hal Crane and Paula. Doc Langer, however, sent him in to the storeroom for some long-handled shovels. Using stout denim coats from the shelves, a stretcher was made and Vic was carefully lifted and placed upon it.

Suddenly Art Frazin could hold himself in no longer. He started sniffing and the tears began to flow down his cheeks. He rushed to his father's side but Bob blocked the lad before he could do any possible harm to the wound.

"I did it," Art sobbed, "I did it, and look what it caused. It's all my fault."

Bob's fingers tightened around the slender arm. "You did what?"

Art spoke between sobs. "I . . . sort of figured the outlaws . . . were real men . . . Up to now I liked 'em . . . I listened when you . . . and Pop and Dan talked about the gun."

Bob's face paled and Dan stepped forward to the boy, his hand falling on his shoulder. "What about the gun?" he asked.

"I slipped out . . . told Mr. . . . Mr. Bruhn about it. They knew before you . . . started over there."

"Why, you crazy, pigheaded runt!" Bob said savagely and his hand smacked across the boy's face. Art fell back, arms up across his head, fearing more blows. Dan quickly stepped in between the two brothers, forcing Bob back.

"Take it easy, Bob. He's just a kid."

"But he told—"

"Sure. It robbed us of our chance and this wouldn't have happened today. Art was just a kid putting some hardcases up on a monument where they didn't belong. Now he knows better and he'll never go wrong again. You can't punish him any more than he's doing to himself . . . and will keep on doing, every time he looks at Vic. Leave him alone, Bob. We've got more important problems."

"I ought to—" Bob started but Dan pointed to Vic on the stretcher.

"You ought to get your Dad home and in bed."

Bob glared at his younger brother, then grimly nodded and turned to the stretcher. Dan helped them carry Vic home, a touchy job because of the occasional patches of glare ice. Mrs. Frazin held grimly to her emotions and supervised placing her husband in the bed, then practically shoved the men out of the house.

They returned to the store, Dan throwing several glances toward the Gorton shack. He beat down an impulse to warn Hal, knowing that any suspicious move would bring the killers down on the rancher. He could only return to the store and stand by the window, watching the saloon.

He worried about Paula and threw a covert glance at Phil. He decided not to tell Phil of this new threat. Dan tried to plan ahead but found himself stopped. He should stand ready to side Hal Crane if the man was discovered, but he had no idea how he could be of help, unarmed before the bandits. He should be at the Preston house and he decided to slip out of the store at the first chance without alarming the others. But he knew that here, too, he faced a cold-blooded killer without a chance.

He suddenly straightened when he saw Juarez and Egan come into his vision and cross the street. Dan wondered where Pace had gone but something in the attitude of the two bandits held his attention. Juarez waited on the walk while Egan hurried to the saloon door, opened it and stuck his head inside. In a moment Starrett came out, listened to Egan and then walked with him to rejoin Juarez.

Dan watched the three talk, Juarez grinning and making a motion toward the street that led to the Gorton shack. With a sinking feeling, Dan realized that they had discovered Hal's hangout. Starrett nodded, laughed and clapped Juarez on the back. He turned back to the saloon while the two outlaws, grinning, retraced their way around the corner and out of Dan's sight.

Dan stood undecided for only a moment. He knew that the outlaws had not yet made their kill and there was still time for him to intervene. But how? He didn't know, but time wasted away moment by moment. He abruptly moved to the door, opened it and stepped out on the porch. He threw a glance at the saloon and, so far as he could tell, determined that no one watched him.

He hurried down the steps and along the path of beaten snow to the corner. He saw Juarez and Egan

were now beyond Doc Langer's house and they had
stopped, conferring with one another. Dan's jaw set
grimly, and he walked toward them.

He was almost to the Frazin house and now he could
see the high fence of the lumberyard. He stopped short
when he saw a slender figure hurry along it, from the
direction of the office. Pace Odlum was on a trail of
his own.

Dan felt the skin crawl along his back as he watched
the little killer take the familiar path around the shed
and directly to the Preston home. He paused before
the kitchen door, then started a circle of the house to
the front.

Dan stood immobile. He stared in horror at the house
where he knew beyond doubt Paula was. He could no
longer see Pace, but he could picture the man knocking
on the door, Paula innocently opening it. Dan's glance
cut to Juarez and Egan, still standing close together
and looking toward the Gorton shack. Dan's panic
and uncertainty mounted. He could not be two places
at once and either choice would bring him face to face
with killers.

He swung sharply left, cutting behind the smithy,
beating his way through drifted snow toward the
lumberyard fence. Hal Crane had a slim chance of
evading Juarez and Egan, but Paula would have none
against the unpredictable killer with the angelic smile.
Dan reached the path that led along the fence, and
quickly reached the shed behind the Preston home.
He eased to the corner and studied the back of the
house.

He could see into the kitchen windows. No one was
there and his glance instantly lifted to the few
windows on the upper floor. They told him nothing
and Dan grimly measured the open space between
the shed and the house, glanced up at the windows

again, knowing he must gamble that he would not be seen.

Dan half expected to hear glass break and the roar of a shot as he raced along the path, eyes grimly held to the back door. But there was no sound, the snow muffled his pounding steps and he reached the house without incident. He caught his breath and carefully grasped the knob, slowly turning it and easing the door open. He slipped inside, a sweeping glance telling him the kitchen was empty.

But he could hear voices, Paula's raised in anger. Then Pace answered, voice so low that Dan could not make out the words. He eased the door closed behind him and looked desperately around for some sort of weapon and his eyes fell on the wood-box beside the range. He walked tiptoe across the room and slowly, carefully eased a long heavy piece of wood out of the box. He grimly turned to the door leading into the dining room.

Now he could hear voices more plainly and there was a lifting note of fear in Paula's tones. Pace spoke persuasively and Dan could picture the slim man, confident and dangerous, facing the frightened girl. Dan eased across the dining room.

Suddenly Pace cursed and Dan heard the swift shuffle of boots. Paula screamed and a chair crashed over. Dan threw caution away, lunged through the door and in to the parlor.

Paula had avoided the man's first rush and had placed the table between herself and Pace. She stood poised, frightened eyes moving about the room, seeking some means of escape. Pace stumbled over a chair and he stood, slim fingers on the table edge, pale eyes narrowed, tensing for a swift move that would trap her.

As Dan rushed into the room, Pace wheeled and

crouched, hand slashing down to his holster. Dan knew he could never beat that blurring gun and he threw the billet of wood, its jagged form hurtling directly at the handsome face.

Pace had only a glimpse of the projectile. He ducked and threw up his arm in an instinctive gesture. It missed his head by a whisper and crashed against the far wall. Paula screamed again. Pace had been delayed just long enough for Dan to reach him, but still the Colt blurred up.

Dan's arm swung down and sideways, catching Pace's wrist and knocking the gun aside just as it exploded, the bullet speeding harmlessly across the room and splintering the baseboard. Dan's right fist smashed at Pace, the glancing blow on the cheekbone knocking the gunman aside.

Dan grimly bored in as Pace, half blinded with pain, tried to bring the gun into play again. Dan's fingers grabbed his wrist and he tried to twist the Colt out and away. He discovered then that Pace might be slender but his muscles were whipcord and spring steel. The red lips peeled back in blazing anger and Pace whipped about, slamming a fist into Dan's stomach and also trying to free his wrist from Dan's grip.

He nearly succeeded, the blow making Dan gasp for breath. But he hung grimly on and used his greater size to bear the lighter man back. They hit a chair and both went down in a thrashing tangle of arms and legs. Pace twisted like a cat even as he fell and Dan's grip slipped from the gun wrist. He grabbed frantically, missed, but his hand knocked the gun aside as it exploded again. Then he had the slender wrist in his hand and his arm and shoulder muscles bunched as his fingers tightened and twisted.

Pace's arm slowly moved back and to one side, Dan

exerting a steady, savage pressure that made the boyish face writhe with pain. Pace's knee came up but Dan managed to catch the blow on his hip and again he started the torturing pressure on the wrist and hand that held the gun. Pace tried to claw at his face, worked his hand under Dan's chin and started to force Dan's head back. Dan was hardly aware that Paula stood near, watching.

Suddenly Pace arched, steel-spring muscles forcing Dan's heavier weight up. With a sudden twist Pace threw Dan to one side, though Dan still held grimly on to the little killer. Now Pace was above him and the pale eyes had a wild glare, like that of a cougar.

Dan had a glimpse of Paula just over the outlaw's shoulder, caught the blurring sweep of her arms. The billet of wood crashed against the back of Pace's head and the man went limp, the Colt dropping from his nerveless fingers.

Dan hastily threw him aside, grabbed the Colt and came to his feet. Pace didn't move, lying with arms outflung, narrow face slack, eyes closed. Paula, still holding the billet of wood, stared down at him, her face pale and eyes wide. Suddenly she dropped the wood and swayed. Dan caught her, but she steadied herself.

"I . . . I killed him?"

Dan glanced at the fallen outlaw. "No, just knocked out for a long time. Too bad you didn't. It would save the cost of a trial and a hangman later on."

Paula swallowed, clung to Dan and then straightened and looked at him with a wan smile. He saw the strain she was under and his heart lifted with a new love because of her courage. He forgot Pace for the moment, the gun in his hand. He stepped to her and held her close, then led her to a chair.

He turned then to Pace. The man had not moved.

Dan roughly handled him as he removed the gunbelt
with its looped cartridges. He made adjustments in it
and strapped it about his own waist, took the Colt
from the table where he had placed it and dropped it
in the holster. Paula watched, the color slowly
returning to her face.

"Dan, what are you going to do?"

"Is there a rope in the house?" he asked. She nodded.
"Feel like getting it while I watch this sleeping wolf?"

She hurried to the kitchen and in a few moments
returned with a coiled clothesline. Dan rolled Pace
over and lashed his hands tightly behind his back,
then passed several coils around his body, lashing the
arms tightly to his sides. He stood up and looked
around, saw the horsehair sofa.

He lifted Pace, whose head lolled, and carried him
across the room, dumped him on the sofa. Dan lifted
the Colt, ejected the empty cases and replaced them
with bullets from the belt. He dropped the Colt back
in the holster to find Paula watching him, a new fright
in her face.

"Dan . . . you're not? . . . not the others?"

He swiftly came to her and she arose to meet him.
He kissed her, then stepped back, hands still on her
slender shoulders. His face was grim and his eyes
grave.

"Luck's turned our way, Paula. Nine of these
renegades rode in. Ratner is at Doc Langer's, Darrow
and Bruhn are dead, here's Pace, the worst of the lot.
That leaves five. Maybe we can count on Gene Hiatt,
maybe not. Anyhow, there's four killers still loose in
the town."

"But Dan—"

He touched the holstered Colt. "Now I've got a gun.
Paula, none of us are safe until this bunch is rounded
up to the last man. Right now they're hunting Hal

Crane to kill him. I have to go after the gunslammers that are left. For the whole town, Paula . . . and for you."

She started to protest but saw the determination in his eyes.

She pressed her lips tightly for a moment and then kissed him, and her voice was under tight control when she spoke.

"All right, Dan. You're right, though it kills me to say it."

He glanced toward Pace, still unconscious on the sofa. "He's tied up tight enough. Watch him. I'll be back as soon as I can. Here's the stick of wood. If he tries any tricks, use it."

He picked his hat up from the floor and jammed it on his head. He crossed to the door and was about to open it when Paula spoke again.

"Dan." He turned. Her eyes searched his face as though trying to impress it deeply in her memory. Her voice dropped to a whisper. "Be careful, Dan. Oh, please be careful! I suppose I've been uncertain and maybe a little weak, but now I know I love you. I want you back . . . safe."

His hand dropped from the knob and he took a step toward her. The sound of a muffled shot checked him and he stiffened, his jaw going hard and his eyes bleak.

"They've got Hal Crane." He added grimly, "I'll be back. You can depend on it."

He wheeled and jerked open the door, swiftly crossed the small porch. At the head of the steps, he stopped, loosened the Colt in the holster. He had a weapon now and that was encouragement. But he faced at least four men who would meet him fair or shoot him in the back. This was the showdown at last.

TWENTY

From the porch, Dan could see the Gorton shack and, at that moment, Juarez and Egan came in sight, Juarez working with his Colt. Dan eased back under the shadow of the porch, eyes narrow and angry. The two of them together were too much for him to buck. He must move now to catch these outlaws one at a time or they would gang up to wipe out the small chance that he had.

He saw a glint as Juarez ejected shells and then the two men disappeared behind Doc Langer's house. Dan walked cautiously out to the street, closely watching the Langer house in case the two killers appeared again.

His stride increased when there was no further sign of them, slowing only when he came to the corner and looked down the street toward the stable. He was just in time to see Juarez and Egan disappear around the corner, heading for the Wyoming Bar. His name was called and he whipped around to see Doc Langer standing in the doorway.

"What is it, Dan?" The voice dripped acid. "Another killing? Not one of them, I hope."

"Afraid not, Doc. I think it's Hal Crane. He was holed up at George's."

"I'll get my bag," Langer snapped and disappeared in the house.

Dan walked to the Gorton shack, saw that the door stood half ajar, and he knew Hal Crane must be dead. He glimpsed someone come from the Rikes' house, half checked himself in alarm until he saw that Ava stood on the porch. Still drunk, he thought bitterly, still thinking that Tex Darrow and his kind were the way of escape. He strode on, pushed the shack door further open, and entered.

There was nothing in the room to mark a struggle, only the ordinary chaotic condition in which George lived. He did not see Hal but the smell of black powder was strong and Dan looked at the narrow, closed door across the room.

He pushed it open on the jumble of old iron, wheels, rusting parts, stacks of ancient papers that George kept here. There were no windows, the only light showing through occasional cracks between the boards that formed the outer walls of the lean-to. Dan's eyes adjusted to the half shadows and he saw the still form lying against the far wall.

In two strides he was beside Hal and gently turned him over. His eyes were closed and the front of his shirt was stained with blood. He breathed shallowly and Dan did not like the pallor of the skin and the dull sheen of the eyes beneath the half-closed lids. He twisted around when he heard hasty steps cross the other room.

Doc Langer stood in the doorway, trying to adjust to the shadows. In another moment he knelt beside Dan, practiced hands cutting the shirt to expose the wound. Dan heard a stir behind him and again turned to see Ava Rikes standing in the doorway. He hastily walked to her, shielding the body.

"What's wrong?" she asked. "Is it George?"

She was not drunk. Her face showed the marks of her fight with the bottle and her eyes were puffy and red. But from somewhere deep within she had gathered a new strength. Dan shook his head.

"It's Hal Crane. He's been shot."

"Them?"

Dan understood who she meant and he nodded. Behind him Doc Langer spoke in a soft fury.

"They nearly notched their guns again, and they still might count coup if Hal's luck gives out. He's got a bare chance of pulling through." His voice lifted. "In the name of God, when will this shooting and killing end!"

"Soon, I hope," Dan said heavily. "They killed George Gorton. Then they quarreled among themselves and Jack Bruhn is dead."

"Tex?" Ava asked quickly. Dan turned to look into her questioning eyes. His expression softened and suddenly he felt a deep sympathy for this woman who had tried so hard to find happiness and had always just missed it.

"How about Tex, Ava?" he asked gently. "Did he mean anything to you?"

He sensed her momentary withdrawal. She sighed and made a strange little gesture that might mean everything—or nothing. Her voice sounded weary.

"I don't know, Dan. Everything's been a blur since Tommy—died. I thought I hated him and then I knew I was wrong. It was the town, the valley that I hated. It's lonely and horrible. Now it's too late."

"I'm afraid so, Ava. What about Tex?"

"He's part of the nightmare, Dan. He promised to take me away from all this. I was dazed, hurt, all mixed up. I had to believe him, and I had to leave this place. Mean anything?" She slowly shook her head. "No, him and his whiskey just eased the pain. I came out of it last night. I'll leave Bitter—but not with Tex or anyone like him."

Dan squeezed her arm. "Good. Pace Odlum killed Tex just after Tex shot Jack Bruhn."

She slowly closed her eyes, opened them again. She looked at Dan for a long time and sighed. "I . . . I'm going home."

He thought to stop her and then changed his mind.

When the outer door closed silently behind her, Dan turned to Doc Langer. He worked with deep concentration on Crane and listened impatiently as Dan talked. He told how Pace had tried to molest Paula Preston and that the slender outlaw was now a prisoner. Dan touched the holstered Colt.

"So, we've got a gun, Doc. But there's Vause, Juarez, Egan and Denver. I think that Gene Hiatt will throw in with us, now."

Doc spoke without looking up. "Get along, Dan, and do what you can. I'll take care of Crane." As Dan arose, Doc looked up and the asperity left his voice. "And, Dan, watch yourself. It'd be a shame if Larry had to fit you for one of his boxes or I had to pull lead out of your carcass."

"Careful?" Dan asked and grinned crookedly. Doc shrugged and gave his attention to his work.

Before he left the shack, Dan buttoned his coat over the holster and belt, concealing the gun. He walked to the store and entered it by the back way. He first saw Phil Preston and Bob Frazin standing by the desk, watching Gene Hiatt and Ernine, who talked intently up by the window. Bob and Phil showed their dislike of the situation and their helplessness. They turned when Dan entered, and so did Hiatt. He said another word to Ernine and came striding down the aisle to stop before Dan.

"Murdock, does your offer still stand?"

"Still stands," Dan answered, careful to keep elation out of his voice. Hiatt took a deep breath, nodded.

"All right. I'm on your side. I'm tired of all this killing and robbing. I wasn't meant for it. If you'll help me make things square afterward, I'll do everything I can for you right now."

Dan extended his hand and Hiatt took it. His face became boyish and clear with his wide smile. Phil and

Bob looked on in gaping surprise and Dan swiftly told them of the deal he had made with Hiatt. Ernine came up, her eyes alight. She almost touched Hiatt, glanced hastily at her brother and refrained. Hiatt spoke sharply.

"Juarez and Egan just went into the Wyoming, and I know Vause is there. Denver's at the stable. But Pace is the first gent we'll have to get."

"Pace is tied up," Dan said and the others gasped. He told what had happened and Phil's face turned a purplish red with anger. He glared at Dan.

"You left Paula with that sidewinder! Are you crazy!"

"Wait, Phil," Dan checked the older man as he started toward the door, "Pace is hogtied. I've got his gun. There's no danger for Paula if we move fast." He looked at Gene. "Hiatt, you make a second gun. If we could get one more for Phil we'd even the odds."

Hiatt nodded. "Denver's alone in the stable. I'll be right back—with another Colt."

He turned on his heel and left, not seeing that Ernine half lifted her hand to stop him. There was a silence in the store, a strained and tense quiet. Phil frowned and paced nervously before the desk. Dan watched the front door, impatient for Hiatt's return. Ernine looked at the floor, working a handkerchief between her fingers. Dan glanced at her as she lifted her eyes.

"He'll be all right," Dan said.

"He has to be," she said in a strained whisper. "He just has to be. I'm in love with him, Dan. He's got to come back and be cleared of these things against him."

Bob wheeled around from the desk, his eyes bugging in horror. "What did you say, Ernine? You're in love with him—that outlaw! Have you lost all your senses? By heaven, I'll—"

"Bob," Dan stepped between the man and his sister. "Don't do something you'll regret. I've talked to Gene and know what happened to him. Ernine knows, too. Hiatt will be a good man once he breaks loose from this crowd and makes things straight. That's what he's doing now."

"But—"

They both swung around when the door opened. Hiatt came in, and Dan saw that he held something bulky beneath his coat. Hiatt came striding down the aisle, his face set. He opened his coat and pulled out a belt and holstered gun, dropped it on the desk.

"There's your gun," he said. Ernine looked at him as though he had returned from the dead, then she turned away, her eyes misting.

"Denver?" Dan asked. Hiatt shrugged.

"Tied up tight and gagged, locked in the feed room." Hiatt looked solemnly around at them. "Now I've shown my brand to them and there's no turning back for me. If you lose, I lose."

Dan picked up the gun and started to hand it to Bob Frazin, but Phil grabbed it, eyes bleak. "I figure this is mine, considering Paula."

Bob made no effort to get the belt and Dan felt that the older man would make the better partner. There were just three outlaws left and three men here, though gun speed lay with the killers. Dan spoke briefly, planning a surprise that would even the odds.

Hiatt left the store and walked directly to the saloon. Dan and Phil left by the back way, walked back to the street, keeping the building between themselves and the saloon. They hurriedly crossed the street, cut around the empty stable corral and came to the Wyoming Bar from the rear.

Dan stopped, looked questioningly at Phil. The older man touched the gun on his hip and nodded. Dan walked to the door, the only opening in the rough, solid wall. He gently turned the knob and slowly pressed his shoulder against the panel. The door swung open, silently. There was a small hallway and another closed door that opened on the saloon proper at the far end of the bar. Another door, also closed, gave access to the storeroom in which Ava had hidden when the outlaws had first come.

Dan edged down the hall, ears strained for any sound. There was none until he stood leaning against the door and then he heard the faint lift of voices within. Hiatt would be trying to hold their attention, Dan knew. He touched Phil and both men drew their guns. Dan slowly cracked the door.

He first saw Hiatt and could plainly hear the man's voice. Juarez, Egan and Vause had their full attention on Gene, who forcefully talked about making Pace divide the bank loot. Egan and Vause looked eager, nodded now and then. Juarez frowned uncertainly. Hiatt continued to talk and his eyes lifted beyond the outlaws to the door. He saw Dan.

"There's one argument Pace will listen to," he said. He drew his Colt without suspicion and flourished it. "This is it."

Dan eased out behind the bar and Phil followed him. Hiatt's gun suddenly leveled as Dan spoke quietly behind the three outlaws.

"Lift 'em, gents."

The three men jerked in stunned surprise and Juarez half turned to look at Dan's gun held on his belt buckle. The smoky eyes widened and then turned mean and angry. But he made no move. Egan and Vause stared blankly at Hiatt. Dan spoke to Phil.

"Dehorn 'em."

Juarez was the most dangerous of the three and Dan watched him closely. But Egan, knowing that capture would mean an eventual hangman's rope, made a desperate and deadly bid. Phil moved to obey

Dan, easing along the bar. For a brief second his gun did not cover Egan and the outlaw's hand blurred to his holster. The quick motion swung Dan's eyes momentarily toward him, and Juarez moved with the speed of a striking snake.

Dan whipped around to face him as Juarez faded to one side, his Colt blurring up in a glint of light. He heard the shattering roar of guns and smoke billowed between him and the swarthy face of the breed. He heard the snarling whistle of Juarez's slug past his head and then his own finger tightened on the trigger and the Colt bucked against his hand. Someone screamed nearby but Dan was hardly aware of it. He fired again at the breed, dimly perceived in the cloud of smoke. Then he could no longer see Juarez and realized the man had dropped behind the bar. He whipped about, lunging toward the end of the bar to circle it but Phil caught him. Dan tried to break loose but Phil held him and finally, through the roaring in his ears, he heard Phil's voice, dimly.

"Dan! Dan! It's over!"

He stared at Phil and realized that the guns had stopped. The smoke drifted in long streamers toward the front door, eddying about Hiatt and Vause, who leaned against the bar, tightly gripping his right arm just above the elbow. Egan had disappeared and Dan's searching eyes met Gene's.

"Juarez?" Dan asked. Hiatt's eyes cut to the floor.

"He took a bullet in his mouth, Dan. It's over. Vause has a broken arm and Phil's slug clipped Egan's skull and he'll sleep long enough for us to hogtie him."

Phil's fingers tightened on Dan's arm and he smiled. "It's over, you understand? We're free of 'em."

Only seconds had passed and yet the action had been so deadly fast that it seemed a long time since Egan had made his desperate bid for freedom. Dan holstered his Colt and circled the bar. Juarez was dead and Egan lay sprawled in the sawdust, a shallow bleeding wound along his skull. Dan felt a wave of relief sweep over him. He looked in quiet triumph at Phil and Hiatt, then at the outlaws.

"Can you take care of them?" he asked. "I'll get Pace and bring him over, then we can collect Denver. They'll have heard the shooting at the store. I'll tell them everything's all right." He looked at Hiatt. "Or maybe you'd rather tell 'em."

Gene blushed, grinned crookedly. "I'm needed here but . . . Ernine should know so tell her right away."

Dan chuckled and left the saloon. He went to the store, to find Bob and his sister already standing out on the porch, torn by anxiety. He told them what had happened and Ernine's dark eyes came alight again. He turned to Bob, telling him to get Larry Teter and Clay Majors and go to the saloon, picking up Denver while they were at it. Bob hurried off and Dan turned to Ernine.

"Gene's not touched. I figured him as just one of that renegade band at first, but I was wrong. He's a good man."

"The best," she said quietly. She looked toward the saloon. "Tell him I'm waiting, Dan. Don't be too long."

Dan smiled. He turned and just then saw Paula running toward him. Her face was strained and white and Dan felt a sudden clutch of fear: He jumped off the porch to meet her and she fell into his arms.

"Pace?" he demanded. She gasped for breath.

"He tricked me, Dan. He came to right after you left. He acted as though he knew he was beaten, even talked about it. He asked me to get tobacco from his shirt pocket so he could have a smoke." She looked up at him, fearful and also ashamed of herself. "I . . . felt sorry, I guess. I bent over him to get it. He moved so fast, Dan! He doubled up and kicked me in the stomach. I fainted. When I woke up, he was gone."

Dan's arms tightened about her. "You're hurt?"

"Not really. Bruised. But, Dan, he's escaped. It's all my fault. What will we do?"

Dan led her back to the store, his face hard and bleak. Pace was unarmed and his first move would be to get a gun. He had probably heard the battle in the saloon and he would stay away from there. As Dan led Paula up on the porch steps he looked toward the stage station, apparently deserted and quiet. He knew that Pace would be there, or at least try to make it. He turned Paula over to Ernine and ran back to the saloon, calling Phil and Gene to the door.

He explained what had happened. Hiatt shook his head and Phil looked grave. They could see the station far down the street, dark and threatening against the snow. Dan pulled his Colt from the holster and reloaded it, jaw set. Phil eyed him.

"What'll we do, Dan?"

"Get him," Dan said shortly. Phil shook his head.

"Not that easy. He's holed up where every gun, rifle and round of ammunition in the town has been stored. We won't have a chance."

"We've still got to get him, Phil. He's a mad dog." Dan considered the station, eyes distant and thoughtful. He began to see a plan. "Phil, you and Gene circle the store and work toward the station from the Spade Road."

"He'll see us," Phil objected and Dan made an impatient gesture.

"I'll keep him busy from the front. Phil, don't you go beyond the road. Keep slugs going in the windows from that side. Gene, you circle wide and work in from the back, down along Winter Creek. Keep him busy from that side."

"What'll you be doing?" Gene demanded. Dan motioned down the street.

"I'll keep him busy until both of you are set. Then you cut loose. I'll rush him."

"He'll stop you cold," Gene snapped.

"Maybe. When you know he's concentrating on me, both of you blast the windows. That'll give me another chance to get in closer." They started to object but Dan cut them short. "It's the only way. If we don't get him by nightfall, God knows what he'll do under cover of darkness. No one will be safe."

They argued further but Dan beat them down. Reluctantly, they finally left him and, the moment he saw them cut back of the store, Dan hitched at his belt and started down the street toward the station. He passed the store, glimpsed Ernine and Paula in the window and waved to them with a confidence he was far from feeling. Then he gave his whole attention to the station.

There was no sign of life, but Dan knew that Pace must be watching him. He walked steadily, but was ready to throw himself to either side at the first indication of trouble. He glanced hastily to his left and, over the expanse of snow, saw Phil and Hiatt working their way to the road. Dan lifted the gun, slammed a bullet through one of the windows. He instantly crouched and threw himself to one side. A double flash of fire answered him and the bullets cut the air where he had just stood. At that moment, Phil's gun boomed and Dan heard the tinkle of glass. He came up on the balls of his feet and realized that someone rushed down on him from the right. He wheeled, lips pulled back from his teeth, his gun leveling. He jerked with surprise when he saw Vivian running toward him, but a few yards away.

"Get back!" he yelled and made frantic signals to

her. She halted, not three yards from him and Dan again yelled at her. "Get to cover. Pace Odlum's cornered." Suddenly Phil and Gene's firing died and Dan knew Pace would be throwing lead this way. He jumped to Vivian and they both fell into the deep snow, no protection from a bullet but at least hidden from the outlaw in the station. Dan glared at her.

"Are you crazy?" he demanded. "Couldn't you hear the shots?"

"I heard them," she said. Her eyes softened and deepened as she looked at him. "I worried about you, Dan. I . . . don't want you hurt."

It struck him like a physical blow that this woman was in love with him. His eyes clouded with distress and Vivian understood, the light slowly dying in her face. She swallowed and then managed a wan smile. Dan swiftly looked away, half lifted himself to call toward the station.

"Pace! Pace, listen to me! There's a woman here. Hold your fire until she can get away."

The slender killer replied instantly, Dan's voice locating his target for him. The slugs plowed into the non-resisting snow, the first one close, whipping by Dan's shoulder, the other two going a little higher. Dan had thrown himself flat and now he turned to look at Vivian. She lay crouched in the snow, curled, head down. Dan saw her quiver and then her body seemed to fall in on itself. With an oath, Dan threw himself toward her. Her head lolled sideways as he grabbed her shoulder and Dan turned her over, holding his breath. That first slug that had come so close to him had caught Vivian just at the base of the throat and ranged downward. She was dead.

Dan didn't think in the red haze of fury that swept over him. Phil and Gene both slammed bullets into the building and Dan came to his feet and charged the station in a crouching run, face contorted, eyes ablaze. He reached the door and his shoulder slammed the portal back. He instantly threw himself down and to one side.

He saw Pace at one of the far windows. The man whirled and his Colt threw flame at Dan. Through the haze of smoke Dan saw the pale eyes alight with a strange, mad glee, the moist lips unnaturally red, twisted in a devil's smile.

Something struck Dan with the force of a battering ram and he seemed no longer to have a side. Everything was in a strange, detached slow motion. He felt his hand lift the Colt, saw the muzzle come up. He saw the long spit of red flame lance from the barrel, lance again. He saw Pace come up on his toes, saw the man's gun belch flame toward the ceiling. Then Pace slowly pivoted on the balls of his feet, seemed to be reaching high for something. As a swirling darkness rushed over Dan, he saw Pace pitch toward the floor. Then there was nothing.

A second later Dan opened his eyes and stared about him in disbelief. This was not the stage station, but he recognized the marble-top table and the big pitcher and bowl. He was back in the Preston bedroom. He heard a stir and a soft hand was on his forehead. He looked up and around. Paula, dark circles under her eyes, looked down at him. She called to someone in the hall and then she bent and kissed Dan.

"Oh, darling! You've come back! I've been so afraid."

Doc Langer appeared and fussed over Dan while Paula and Phil stood fearfully watching. Dan's left side felt as though it was filled with iron and he looked inquiringly over Langer's shoulder at Paula.

"How did I get here?"

"Gene and I brought you," Phil answered. "Paula's been nursing you."

"Nursing?" Dan asked, surprised. "But it's only been a little while—"

"Five days a little while?" Doc Langer asked, straightening. "It was touch and go with you, cowboy, but you hung on long enough for us to pull you through."

"Five days!" Dan tried to sit up but pain and dizziness caused him to slump. Instantly Paula circled the bed but Doc Langer bent over Dan, straightened him. Doc stood up again.

"You need rest, but you won't get it, I suppose, until you know what's happened." He took Paula's shoulder and brought her up beside him. "This young lady needs sleep, too. Paula, give him the news and then both of you sleep the rest of the day. You'll see to it, Phil? Good! Then I'll be on my way."

Phil went out of the room with the doctor, Paula pulled a chair up beside the bed, sat down and took Dan's hand. She kissed him lightly on the forehead and then told him what had happened, her voice weary. Dan listened, watching her, realizing what she must have done for him. Despite her fatigue pallor and the dark circles he could not remember seeing her so lovely.

Pace was dead, she told him, and so was Juarez, though Dan knew that. Denver, Vause and Egan were under heavy guard awaiting the sheriff who would come down from the county seat now that the roads were passable. Shorty Ratner had died just yesterday and that accounted for the bandits.

"Except Gene," Dan said.

Gene Hiatt also waited for the sheriff to turn over the stolen money, and everyone in town would do all they could to help the young man become a good citizen again. Paula's voice dropped a tone but it carried a deep note of pleasure. Ernine Frazin had at last found the man for her. Gene might serve a short term but he had a home here once he returned.

Crane was recovering nicely and Paula hesitated when she mentioned Starrett. He had left town, gone to his ranch, she assumed. Phil came back in the room then and took his place at the end of the bed. He looked gravely at Dan.

"The town's free again," he said, "but we paid a terrible price for it. We all owe you a debt, Dan."

"I did what I could, nothing more."

"You faced up to Pace Odlum and Juarez Smith and downed 'em," Phil said with a grunt. "You talked Gene Hiatt into coming onto our side. You saved Paula's life and did what you could for Hal Crane. I think that's enough." There was an embarrassed silence and then Phil spoke in a more level tone.

"Vivian McLear is buried, Dan . . . one more cruel and useless killing added to all the rest. Ava Rikes has come to her senses and she runs the Wyoming. But she wants to sell it and leave town as soon as possible. Vic Frazin's sitting up and starting to worry about the store again. I guess it's all over—thank God!"

Dan sighed. "What about Blaise?"

Phil made a slight gesture. "I don't know, Dan. The whole town knows what he planned to do. I figure he'll sell Star before very long. There's no one he can face anymore." He looked at his daughter and his face softened. He grinned when he turned to Dan again.

"But you've both had enough talk. I want you back on your feet, Dan, as soon as you can make it. The sooner you start learning the lumber business, the sooner I can figure on taking it easy."

"Lumber business!" Dan's eyes widened.

Phil laughed. "Sure, lumber business. Think my future son-in-law would do anything else?" He added slyly, "That is of course, figuring you'll stay around this country."

Dan looked at Paula and her eyes were a deep, soft green. His fingers tightened around her hand. He looked back at Phil.

"Where else would I be? Only Bitter has a girl named Paula."

THE END

LEE E. WELLS BIBLIOGRAPHY
(1907-1982)

Westerns:

Mystery of the Dark
   Mountains (McKay, 1946)
Tonto (Wright & Brown,
   1949)
Tonto Riley (Rinehart/Pocket,
   1950)
Spanish Range (Rinehart,
   1951)
The Big Die (Rinehart, 1952)
Desert Passage (1953)
Gunshot Empire (Avon, 1953)
The Long Noose
   (Rinehart/Avon, 1953)
Death in the Desert
   (Rinehart/Avon, 1954)
The Peacemaker (Ballantine,
   1954; as by Richard Poole)
Day of the Outlaw
   (Rinehart/Dell, 1955)
West of Devil's Canyon (Gold
   Medal, 1958; as by Richard
   Poole)
The Naked Land (Avon,
   1959)
Brother Outlaw (Ace, 1959)
Tarnished Star (Avon, 1960)
Gun for Sale (Avon, 1960)
Shoot-Out at the Way Station
   (Ace, 1960; as by Lee
   Richards)
Savage Range (Ace, 1961)
Apache Crossing (Avon, 1963)
Brand of Evil (Berkley, 1964)
Treachery Pass (Berkley,
   1964)
Vulture's Gold (Berkley, 1965)

The Devil's Range (Berkley,
   1966)
Ride a Dim Trail (Ace, 1966)
Nine Must Die (Berkley,
   1967)
Pageant (Lancer, 1967)
Danger Valley (Doubleday,
   1968; as by Richard Poole)
Incident At Warbow (Berkley,
   1968)
Gun Vote At Valdoro
   (Doubley/Belmont, 1969; as
   by Richard Poole)
Gunslammer (1970)
The Tall Texan (Berkley,
   1970)
King of Utah (Curtis, 1971)
Stolen Empire (Curtis, 1971)
Lord of the Silver Lode
   (Curtis, 1971)
Strangers South (Doubleday,
   1972; as by Richard Poole)
Guns of Happy Valley
   (Curtis, 1977)

As by Lee Richards:

Hell Strip (Gold Medal, 1957)
Lusty Conquest (Gold Medal,
   1957)
The Mercenary Lover
   (Chariot, 1960)
Love Cult (1962)
The Eager Beavers (Beacon,
   1963)
The Sexecutives (Beacon,
   1963)
The Punks (Beacon, 1964)

Lee Edwin Wells was born on June 1, 1907 in Indianapolis, Indiana. He received a diploma in accounting and went on to become a licensed public accountant in California in the mid-40s. Beginning in 1939, he started selling stories to the pulp magazines under his name and a  number of pseudonyms. Wells then began writing novels in the late 1940s and published over 40 books in his lifetime, most of them westerns. Perhaps his most famous is *Day of the Outlaw*, filmed in 1959 by André de Toth and starring Robert Ryan, Burl Ives, and Tina Louise. He also became an active member of the Mystery Writers of America in Los Angeles, as well as writing for several TV shows including *Highway Patrol*. Wells passed away in San Diego on April 29, 1982.

BLACK GAT BOOKS offers the best in reprint crime fiction from the 1950s-1970s. New titles appear every month, and each book is sized to 4.25" x 7", just like they used to be. Collect them all.

www.StarkHousePress.com

Available from your local bookstore or direct from the publisher

Printed in Great Britain
by Amazon